An Alien Paradise

A Science Fiction Romance

Susanne Marie Knight

AN ALIEN PARADISE, formerly entitled XANADU FOR ALIENS.

Copyright © 2015 by Susanne Marie Knight

Cover Art copyright © 2015 by S. M. Knight and its licensors.

ISBN: 9781521592960

Romance Writing with a Twist

http://romancewritingwithatwist.blogspot.com

http:/www.susanneknight.com

Dedication

To Mr. George Salant--
Thank you for having faith in me!

Reviewer Praise For
AN ALIEN PARADISE
And Susanne Marie Knight

5 Stars! Aliens on Earth? A travel agency for extraterrestrials? A Human male from Tau Ceti 3 falling in love with an Earth female? [AN ALIEN PARADISE] delivers all this and more! Ms. Knight gives us a very plausible scenario of galactic intrigue and a wonderful variety of characters. Fall in love with this fast-paced science fiction romance. This novel is definitely a keeper!--Norwood Reviews.

* "Readers should watch this gifted author--she is a star in the making!"--*ParaNormalRomance Reviews*

* "Ms. Knight is a talented, versatile author!"--*Romance Reviews Today*

* "Ms. Knight has captured the true feelings of England in a wonderful tale of love and mystery."--*All About Murder Reviews*

* "A delightfully creative romance that centers on a mystery that will keep the reader guessing until the very end. A fast paced romantic mystery that is sure to be enjoyed by the readers!"--*The Romance Studio*

* "Susanne Marie Knight offers believability coupled with unpredictability to make for a fast-paced, satisfying read!"--*Sime-Gen*

* "One of the rising stars of Regency romance. A formidable talent!"--*Word on Romance*

* "Ms. Knight could certainly compete with some of today's top writers. The author is a rare gem."--*Gottawrite Reviews*

* "Writers who can successfully finish the "what if" in a logical and fascinating way are few, but Ms. Knight succeeds here. A great book for those who love a good suspense and a romantic twist, and those who enjoy a good romance with a well written paranormal base." -*Coffee Time Romance Reviews*

* "Susanne Knight has granted her audience fantasy and mystery combined with a science fictional blend along with a romantic edge to satisfy most any readers taste."--*TCM Reviews*

Introduction

Although planet Terra--Earth to its current natives--is remote, located in one of the spiral arms of the Milky Way Galaxy, it is considered a prime piece of real estate. Indeed, a jewel among the glittering stars. Because of Terra's intrinsic beauty, many lifeforms across the galaxy have desired to possess this paradise.

Such coveting often leads to sin. And so it came to pass, in the far distant reaches of time, an interstellar war was fought for ownership of the third planet from Sol. These hostilities endangered Terra itself, inflicting horrific damages.

Destruction of this precious blue-green orb could not be permitted, and so Galactic leaders forced a truce... and found a solution.

Terra is now a playground for aliens.

To implement this Terran theme park, a substantial number of its natives were transplanted to another solar system, Tau Ceti, Cetus sector, with a type G sun, the same as Sol. This Terran colony was then trained to be in charge of Terra's stately pleasure dome.

For countess millennia, Tau Cetian Humans have efficiently supervised alien sightseers to Terra. Everything has gone smoothly... until now.

Chapter One

Present Day

Petra Richardson looked up from completed stacks of paperwork on her well-worn desk to stare out at the empty classroom. A briny trickle of perspiration slithered a path down her forehead, temple, and then continued down by her ear. She wiped the wetness away with an already soggy tissue. It was hotter than blazes in here, even with the fans.

Thank goodness the room wasn't filled with thirty sweaty teenaged bodies. The students' last day had been yesterday and happily, today was hers. All she had left to do was to tidy up a few loose ends. Then she could start the long summer vacation.

No more pencils, no more books, no more students' dirty looks!

Petra smiled. She enjoyed teaching--young middle schoolers in particular. But now the term was over. It was time to set aside the daily grind. She couldn't wait to hit the beach for much needed fun and frolic. This summer she and Bob Finch, her new boyfriend, had rented a cottage for a couple of weeks at nearby Fire Island, just off of Long Island.

Petra sat back in her squeaky chair, adjusted the hair clip on her makeshift chignon, and dreamed of cool ocean breezes. Oh, she couldn't wait for lazy, crazy, hazy summer days, soaking up Great South Bay's sun, sand, and salt water.

Come mid-August, she'd have to concentrate on creating lesson plans for her science classes in the new school year. But why think about it now? Lesson plans were at least six long weeks away.

A knock sounded on the open door. Nellie Schultz, admin assistant from the principal's office, entered the room fanning her plump face with a bright red #10 envelope. "Sheesh! It's hotter than you know what in here."

Petra left her chair and stood in front of a fan to dry off. "I know. Not everyone is lucky enough to have air conditioning."

Nellie giggled. She knew she had it good. "True. But you only have to suffer through today." She handed over the letter size envelope. "Here, this red hot letter is for you, Petra. It came special delivery."

Special delivery? Petra took the envelope. On the front was her name, Petra Richardson, written in bold black calligraphy. Also in black was "personal and confidential" stamped under her name. That was it. No address for her, no address for sender. And no stamps. Curious.

Nellie waited, obviously hoping Petra would share the contents.

No bloody way. Nellie Schultz had been born to blab. Even as she stood in front of the classroom, she was leaning forward as if eager to catch the slightest whiff of news.

Petra walked back over to her wooden desk. "Thanks, Nellie. I appreciate the special delivery. If I don't see you before I leave, have a great summer, okay?"

"Okay. Sure. You too." With shoulders slumped, Nellie left the room.

Now alone, Petra slit open the envelope and removed one sheet of fine, vellum stationery. An ornate red border decorated the ivory paper, and in the top center was a logo for Taurus City Travel Agency. She'd never heard of that business, so what did they want from her? Curious and curiouser.

Leaning her bottom against the desk, she glanced at the contents. It read:

Dear Ms. Richardson:

Greetings! We at the Taurus City Travel Agency have a unique, once-in-a-lifetime offer for you. You have been highly recommended by one of our chief executives. He met you some years ago and was very impressed with your maturity and your knowledge of astronomy. Your background in education, your teaching at this middle school, and your volunteering at a childcare organization make you perfect for a position we are in need of filling: personal tutor.

The service to be provided is teaching our Chairman's exceptionally bright five-year-old son, Traynor. We are particularly interested in Traynor learning about international cultures--manners and customs.

What we are offering is this: an all expense paid stay at our main headquarters on San Cristóbal Island, in the Galápagos Islands Archipelago, 972 km west of Ecuador. This includes round trip airfare, lodging, meals, and incidentals. If you are *agreeable, the period of your service will be from 30 June until 27 August. A sum total of $20,000 will be deposited directly to your bank account upon your acceptance of our offer.*

You must have numerous questions. To facilitate this transaction, our Human Resource Administrative Assistant, Felicia Alvarez, is available now in your principal's office to answer any concerns you may have. She also will be pleased to accompany you on your journey.

We look forward to your accepting this position and to meeting you soon.

The letter was signed Josephus Hammer, Human Resource Director.

What in the world...?

Petra read the letter again, this time more slowly. As she did, she gathered her questions.

Point one: who was the chief executive mentioned? "Some years ago" wasn't specific enough. She'd been teaching for only three years. In that time, she had never attended a professional conference, and she certainly didn't remember meeting anyone, male or female, from the Taurus City Travel Agency. Or even hearing that name before.

Point two: this chief executive was impressed with her maturity and knowledge of astronomy. She was twenty-six. Naturally, she hoped she was mature, but what a bizarre thing to comment on. And as for astronomy, she really didn't have much training in the subject. True, her field of expertise was in science, but she covered a wide range of topics.

She tapped her finger on her chin. She did preside over the school's small astronomy club, for two years now. But who would be impressed by that?

Point three: how did the travel agency hear about her volunteer work at the YMCA's afterschool program? She'd just started helping out this past year.

Point four: she *wasn't* a personal tutor. Nor had she ever worked with children as young as five, no matter how exceptionally bright. And, more to the point, she had only minimal training in cultural anthropology and sociology, which was basically what the travel agency wanted. So why was Josephus Hammer making her this too-good-to-be-true offer?

An all expense paid stay on the Galápagos Islands? Home to where naturalist Charles Darwin did his research for *On the Origin of Species?*

Petra dabbed at her face again with her much-used tissue. Going to the islands would be a dream come true. A chance of a lifetime. A science teacher's delight.

But...

She had other plans for her summer, plans that included her new boyfriend. She would not be *agreeable* to the terms of service from June 30... by the way, only two days from today, until August 27. Not even for the very tempting sum of twenty thousand dollars.

If the offer was legitimate. A very big if. A really doubtful if.

Tucking the letter into her skirt pocket, Petra grabbed her handbag. She had to share this unbelievable news with Bob. They would have such a good laugh over it. It was almost noon anyway; they could lunch together. Bob, a physical education teacher here at the school, had the most dazzling green eyes and hunky physique to match. Just thinking about him made her heart beat faster.

Petra smiled. She'd visit the restroom first so she could refresh her wilted appearance and reapply her lipstick.

* * * *

Bob was right where she'd expected him to be: in the air-conditioned P.E. office. But instead of sitting behind his desk, he stood by the wall-length mirror and practiced bicep curls with both of his strong arms. The thickly corded muscles of his neck tightened in unison while he rhythmically flexed his upper arm muscles into high, hard bumps.

Mmmm. She loved how Bob looked in his clothes... and also out of them.

He briefly glanced at her, then returned his attention to his right biceps. "Hey, babe. Good to see ya. Have a seat. We'll talk."

Sitting a short ways from the mirror, she automatically smoothed down the bump in the back of her hair that had been caused by her chignon. Her hair now long and sleek--just the way Bob liked it--she smiled at him. "I'm so excited, Bob! End of school and now our vac--"

"What gives with the red envelope? Nellie stopped by, told me about the special delivery, and said you were mysterious about openin' it."

"Good news travels fast, doesn't it? Especially with Nellie doing the spreading." Petra pulled out the sheet of vellum. "Well, it's the weirdest thing. It's some kind of offer to be a private tutor for the summer to a child on--get this--the Galápagos Islands."

He lifted a bushy eyebrow. "Really? Cool. I think ya should go."

She blinked, then blinked again. Was she hearing right? "Uh, Bob, we have plans, remember? Just you and me and a lovely stretch of sandy beach for two solid weeks."

He carefully brushed back his overly long hair. "Oh, I didn't tell ya, babe. Fire Island is off. Me and the guys are headin' out--campin' and fishin' trip upstate. A week, maybe two on Lake Erie." Finished with his primping, he turned around to look at her. "Best damn walleye and bass in the whole northeast, I'm thinkin'."

She couldn't speak. Couldn't move. Did Bob actually mean he was canceling their vacation?

A lump formed in her throat. "Y-You're not... you *are* serious? We're not going...?"

Get a grip, Petra. You're not going to be taken advantage of. No bloody way.

In the mirror, her dark eyes glittered back at her like hard coals. "What about the deposit on the cottage?"

"Don't worry 'bout anythin', babe. My cousin said he'll be glad to take the--"

Petra stood. "I want my money back. Two thousand dollars, and I want it now." She held out her hand, palm up.

He ignored her hand to stretch out both of his. He shrugged. "But, babe, that's a lot of dough. I don't have two thou cold cash lyin' around."

She happened to know for a fact that he did. He kept a stash of money in a steel strongbox, lower left hand drawer of his desk. Locked, of course. For emergencies, he'd explained a month ago when he'd paid his share of the cottage deposit. Well, this here was a darn bloody emergency.

She pointed at his desk drawer. "Just give me the money and you can enjoy your vacation any way you please, and I'll do the same.

"Aw, angel. This'll only be for two weeks. We can reschedule--"

"You can reschedule, Bob." And with someone else, she silently added.

"Now, just give me my money."

She took an intimidating step in front of him. Sure, she was only five six to his five nine and at least one hundred pounds lighter, but she knew how to get at his vulnerable spots. The funny thing was, he knew it, too.

Whatever he said as he unlocked the strongbox got lost in the vortex of her mind. She recognized that she was in the first stages of shock. Cold fingers, numbed brain, sluggish motions. But none of that was important. Her relationship with Bob Fitch was irretrievably over--and right now, it didn't matter if he was aware of that or not.

Taking the wad of hundred dollar bills, she stuffed them into her handbag, mumbled something, and then slammed the door shut on him and his air-conditioned office.

The heat in the corridor felt good, pure, non-deceitful. Everything that Bob wasn't.

Don't think about it. Don't think about anything until you get home.

Good advice. Taking the stairs two at a time, she reached the third floor where her classroom waited for her. All she needed to do was file a few folders, chuck some papers, and then she'd be done.

Done.

She looked around at the putrid color of enamel paint covering the hallways. She'd read somewhere that junior high school could be considered a version of Hell on Earth. She agreed. Not as a teacher but as a former inmate of these very same two-tone green walls.

This school in the New York City borough of the Bronx was technically a middle school--grades six through eight--but it had been once a junior high, before junior highs had fallen out of favor. Her first few months as a new recruit, a new seventh grader, had been hellish. To walk through these corridors had meant she took her life into her hands. She never knew if she would pass through unscathed. Or get beaten up. It had been a role of the dice.

Thankfully, way back when, after Christmas break, the eighth and ninth grade students had tired of dishing out torture. For her, at any rate. After that, she'd come to tolerate this school. She'd even experienced her first crush here, although that was so far back in time, how could she possibly remember who the guy had been?

Eventually, later, as a teacher, she'd grown to love this weathered old building.

Ten minutes later, she shut the door on the memories of this past term's classes... and any lingering thoughts about her aborted romance. Her hair back up in a makeshift bun, her eyes now dry, her lips stilled from trembling, she stoically took the stairs down to the principal's office. She had to drop off some information, and then she could be gone for the summer.

With her hand on the brass doorknob, she braced herself against the chilled temperature inside and, if Nellie was around, any of her nosy questions.

She opened the door. Instead of Nellie's pumpkin face, a slender, mocha-complexioned young woman sat in the reception area, reading something on an electronic tablet.

"Excuse me," Petra said upon entering. "I just have to drop off--"

"Hello!" The woman set her tablet aside and jumped up to her feet. She held out her hand for a shake. "You must be Petra Richardson, right? I'm Felicia Alvarez with the Taurus City Travel Agency."

Omigosh! Petra bit her lower lip. She'd forgotten about the letter and Felicia waiting for her. "Yes, hi." She shook hands. "I'm so sorry I've kept you waiting."

Felicia, a stunner with tightly curled, shoulder-length black hair, had a wide forehead and an even wider friendly smile. Her grip was firm and confident. "No, no, not at all, Petra, if I may call you that. I can't tell you how very happy I am that you've decided to see me."

She darted her gaze to the papers in Petra's other hand. "Why don't you take care of your paperwork, and then we'll go someplace where we can talk, okay?"

"Sure." As Petra wrote instructions for Nellie, she mulled over what she was going to do. Why shouldn't she learn more about Felicia's bizarre offer? Not that she was going to accept, but talking about it would certainly take her mind off Bob.

They left the office, and then the school. Felicia wore a flattering red-orange sundress, and even outside, looked as cool as she had in the air conditioning. Petra, on the other hand, felt rivers of sweat puddling down into her bra.

"You pick a spot, okay?" Felicia chirped. "Maybe someplace where I can get one of those famous egg creams. I've been dying to try one."

"I know just the place." Petra huffed and puffed as she walked up the hill toward the main intersection. The nearby ice cream parlor was cool, dark, and specialized in private nooks where people could talk without being disturbed.

Once they sat in the parlor's red plastic seated booth, ordered and received their egg creams--chocolate for Felicia and vanilla for Petra-- they settled down to business.

"So, Felicia, I take it I should thank you for the special delivery?"

Felicia giggled. "Yeah, well, we figured me delivering it would be faster than relying on the postal service."

"Especially since the offer is supposed to start in two days." Petra took a sip of the foamy sweet drink. Mmmm, delicious.

"Short notice, I know." Felicia also sipped on her drink. A smile of pure bliss lit her face. "Manna from the gods!"

Petra glanced around the area. Only the counter seats were occupied, so they had complete privacy. She got right to the point. "Tell me about the Taurus City Travel Agency and this personal tutor position."

"It's a great place. I just love working there. The scenery is to die for." Felicia laughed again. "I've been working there a year now, and let me tell you, it's the best career move I've ever made. Now, as to the position, our Chairman, Mr. Lacertus, a darling man, I love him! Anyway, he just sent his son, Traynor, to us for the summer so he could receive a good, well-rounded education."

Petra frowned. Lacertus--that was a strange name. Latin, if she wasn't mistaken. It meant something like strength or muscle or vigor.

"Where does Mr. Lacertus come from?"

"I don't know. Someplace off island. He rarely visits. I don't see him much."

That sounded genuine. And now for the twenty thousand dollar question. "Why does your company want me for the job?"

"You were highly recommended. One of our executives remembers you from a prior meeting."

That came straight out of the letter. Surely the woman knew more about it. "Who is this man and when did he meet me?"

Felicia shrugged. "I don't know. That was all my boss, Joe Hammer told me. I think it was at a school function, but that's all I know."

Boy, that was as clear as mud.

Petra finished her drink, then set it aside. "So, bottom line, I'm not a personal tutor, Felicia, no matter how highly I've been recommended. And while I do a brief overview for my classes about cultural anthropology and sociology, I don't consider myself proficient in those disciplines."

"Joe insisted that won't be a problem. After all, the boy is only five. Let me tell you, Traynor is a delight."

"That's good to hear, but my answer is no. Thank you for the consideration, but no."

"More money?"

Petra shook her head.

"Fewer days?"

"Nope. I'm just not interested."

Felicia's dark eyebrows knitted together. "Okay. Wait a minute. Let me get my boss on the phone." She pulled a cell phone from her large handbag. "There's a four hour time difference, so it's only nine in the morning there, but he should be in his office."

Petra let the woman do her thing, but this whole business was way out of her comfort zone. After all, why would she want to subject herself to such a questionable situation? She'd be alone, far from home, completely vulnerable. Were these people on the up-and-up? Could she trust them? Why subject herself to such a huge unknown?

Felicia covered the phone with her hand. "Do you mind if Joe says a few words?"

Petra shrugged. She supposed it couldn't hurt. "Sure." She took the cell phone. "Hello?"

"Greetings, Ms. Richardson. Josephus Hammer here. It is my distinct pleasure to speak with you and to woo you to our fair island."

His voice was crisp, formal, almost British, and yet not quite.

"That's kind of you, Mr. Hammer, but as I told your assistant, I'm not interested in this position." There. She was polite but firm. She wouldn't be bulldozed into anything she didn't want to do. She had refused to be taken advantage of by Bob, and there was no bloody way Josephus Hammer could force her to agree to the job.

"Would you be interested in learning which of our executives recommended you, Ms. Richardson?"

For some reason, Petra was taken aback. "Yes. As a matter of fact, I would like to know who it was."

Naturally she couldn't see the man at the other end of the connection, but she had a very strong feeling that he smiled. "According to my records, Ms. Richardson, it was at a school event, the school at which you are presently teaching. It was eleven years ago."

She gasped. Eleven years ago, she was only fifteen. That certainly explained the comment about her maturity. But... "How can that be possible?"

"I assure you, it is. Eleven years ago at a meeting of the school's astronomy club."

Her eyes must've been bugging out. Wow. She'd never been a regular attendee, but yes, she had been a member of the astronomy club in her ninth year of Junior High. How in the world had anyone known that fact or even remembered it?

Joe Hammer must've been one astute person because he seemed to anticipate the lengthy time in between her responses. He waited for her to reply.

"Yes, that's right," she murmured. "I was a member of that club eleven years ago."

"Indeed."

She now pictured him nodding.

"Our current Chief Executive Officer," he continued, "had the pleasure of attending one of your meetings. As I had said, you made quite an impression on him."

Her mind was a blank. Who could this mysterious man be? She cleared her throat. "Ah, I'm afraid I don't recall him. Is he Mr. Lacertus, your chairman?"

"Mr. Lacertus, yes, chairman, no. Kelvin is the Chairman's brother."

The name burst inside her head with the roar of a twenty gun salute. A flood of memories long denied now released their potent images.

Kelvin? Omigosh, divinely gorgeous, intelligent, teasing Kelvin?

Unruly dark brown hair, skin tanned to perfection, with a bold roaming gaze that seared down into one's soul, Kelvin had asked permission of the teacher to attend one meeting of the astronomy club. As part of his Grand Tour, he had stated. Although he was young--he had looked to be about twenty-years-old--he exuded confidence and authority.

After he had been introduced to the members, she, being literal as was her usual inclination even then, had raised her hand to protest that the Grand Tour wasn't done in the States, but only continental Europe.

Kelvin had given her an amused smile, and then had the nerve to sit behind her. He then leaned in close to her ear. "My Grand Tour is of Earth, my dear Petra."

His masculine scent, his soft breath upon her ear, the laughter in his voice all turned her adolescent body into mush. But the fact that he knew her name, when he shouldn't have--no one had mentioned it in the classroom--had completely blown her away.

"Ms. Richardson," Joe Hammer prompted.

"Oh, ah, yes, I'm still here." Her voice sounded shrill. She cleared her throat again.

"Will you reconsider your answer, Ms. Richardson? Everyone here at the Taurus City Travel Agency is quite eager to meet you."

All this time, Felicia sat quietly across from her, an urgent, pleading look on her friendly face.

Petra bit her lip. She opened her mouth but nothing came out. Then, from somewhere deep inside, the words escaped. "Yes. Yes, I agree."

She sat back, astonished. Why had she said that?

As Joe Hammer issued his properly phrased dialogue of gratitude, along with the statement that the twenty thousand dollars would be deposited into her bank account, Felicia clapped her hands together and jumped up and down in the booth.

"You won't regret this, Petra. Honest you won't." Felicia actually beamed.

Petra doubted that. She regretted her decision already. Now numb, she mechanically said her goodbyes, and then handed the phone over to his assistant.

Her rational mind told her she could still refuse the position. After all, nothing was set in stone. She could have the money transferred back, and that would be that.

But her emotional side countered back. The mystery of Kelvin, Kelvin Lacertus, was too strong a draw. He'd really made an impression on her very young self. She'd even believed herself to be madly in love with him--a love at first sight type of situation. Puppy love, obviously, but very potent.

Unbelievably, she must have made an impression on him as well.

Hmmn. Well, why shouldn't she take advantage of this all expense paid vacation to the tropical paradise of the Galápagos Islands? She certainly had nothing going on now with Bob. Her summer schedule was free and clear. And teaching a five-year-old, how hard could that be?

Petra glanced at her wristwatch. She had to get her *keister* in motion-- and fast! There was a boatload of things to do to prepare for her trip in two days' time.

* * * *

Kelvin Lacertus favored a casual look. In his open-necked polo shirt and faded blue jeans, he was comfortable and he didn't stand out. Besides, here in the Galápagos, suits and ties just didn't blend in. And that was exactly what Kelvin strove to do, blend in among the natives.

Cleaning off the top of his hardwood desk, he then glanced outside at the magnificent scenery surrounding his balconied office. He also strove for perfection at his job. As CEO of the Taurus City Travel Agency, he was ultimately responsible for every customer's satisfaction. Guaranteed. During his watch at the Agency--almost two years now--all had gone well.

However, if there was only one rule of the universe, it would be: everything changes. And so, in nine point three minutes, he was due in the visitors' section to settle a customer grievance.

One tourist, new to these shores, had suffered an unfortunate experience with a Nile crocodile, or more specifically, *Crocodylus niloticus.* It mattered not that warning upon warning had been heaped upon the tourist. Indeed, the very same list of warnings was recited to every tourist who visited these shores.

This particular warning was a straightforward decree: *Do not touch the indigenous animal life.* Easy to understand, uncomplicated, and simple to follow. Even if the natives ignore this rule, it was a mandatory requirement that tourists abide by this instruction.

In this specific case, the tourist had touched, and now was missing a body part.

Kelvin tapped on his portable tablet and pulled up information his Medical Director, Cornwell Young, had proposed as a solution to the tourist's dilemma. As he scanned the information, a knock sounded at the door.

"Enter," he stated, without looking up.

The solid stride of the steps identified the caller as Josephus Hammer, his Human Relations Director.

"Do you have a minute, sir?" the older man asked.

"Joe, so formal. I do have a few minutes. Seven point nine, to be exact. Walk with me to the visitors' section."

Joe, sparse and lanky, had his steel grey hair cut close to the scalp. His lean face featured a multitude of lines revealing his maturity. Clean-shaven, he had a ready grin whenever he was in the mood to laugh. Unfortunately he didn't laugh very often. Dressed in khaki trousers and a blazer, Joe's attempt at casual attire was his black tee shirt.

Nodding, Joe accompanied Kelvin out of the office. "I want to apprise you on the status of our mission."

They walked out onto the wraparound balcony, down two flights of stairs, and then over to the titanium/iridium/steel alloy wall separating the two agency buildings. The office structure he'd just left was designed for native interactions. This one, the visitors' section, contained everything pertinent for aliens and off-world Humans.

At the check-in, Kelvin waited for his identity to be verified in the myriad number of ways recommended by his Security Chief, Sergio Iguana. Handprint, eye scan, DNA testing, and whatever else the security team had come up with. As Kelvin waited, he mulled over Joe's words. Mission. There were a thousand missions that he knew of now hovering about this tiny island on Terra. But Joe was the HR Director, which meant...

"Ah yes, the personal tutor for my nephew. Did the woman agree?" He thought a moment. "Is she still feisty?"

"Petra Richardson? Yes, I would say she is a spirited example of femininity. She initially said she was not interested. Felicia tried her hardest to convince her, offering more money and fewer days as incentives. The young woman steadfastly refused." Joe paused.

"However, Ms. Richardson did come around after I mentioned your name."

"Indeed?" Kelvin stepped aside while Joe went through the same procedure.

For some reason, Joe's words made Kelvin smile. But why should he be pleased at that information? Other than knowing the Terran had agreed to teach Tray, of course. His gut feeling was that she would do an excellent job. And that, of course, was all that was important.

However, he did want to see her again. His younger self had been impressed by her.

A door slid open, allowing them to access the visitors' section. Entering the building, cool island breezes greeted them, along with deferential nods from staffers. Humans from colonies on Capella 8, Bokar, Deneb 4, Shaula 9, and his own place of origin, Tau Ceti 3, operated this hub of constant activity. Thankfully, everyone got along well. They worked together as an effective, congenial group. Which was the way it should be. After all, they were all on the same team.

"My thanks, Joe, to you and your assistant on accomplishing this task. Now that Tray is here--albeit unexpectedly--for his training, it is imperative his instructor is trustworthy and of the highest caliber."

"If I may ask, Kelvin, why have you chosen this particular Terran?"

Why indeed? He glanced at his timepiece, and then set a brisk pace for the mediation room. "I revisited my report from all those years ago. The Grand Tour, it was called back then. Truthfully, little Petra was the only native I remembered." Thoughts of that carefree time made him smile. "You should have heard her sputtering like a banshee when I intimated that aliens had already landed."

"Feet firmly planted on *terra firma,* eh?"

"Planted and taken root. And, for some reason I took great pleasure--"

"Perverse pleasure," Joe interrupted with an unaccustomed grin.

"Right. Perverse pleasure in shocking her out of her predictable, staid, isolated world."

Joe held out his hand, stopping Kelvin's progress. "I do not need to remind you that Terrans are supposed to remain in ignorance of our existence."

Kelvin bristled. As a Lacertus, he was a direct descendant from the original Human colony transplanted to Tau Ceti 3, Cetus Sector. It was an unbroken line that stretched back across the millennia. His family's sacred duty was ingrained in him, just as it was ingrained within his brother Wilhelm, the Chairman of this stewardship of Terra. And as it would be with Traynor, Wilhelm's son.

For Joe to presume to instruct him, Kelvin Lacertus, on sacred obligations was an affront to Kelvin's heritage. Almost akin to high treason.

After taking a deep breath, Kelvin willed himself to remain calm--in command and in control. "Of course, Josephus. I am aware of galactic protocol. I had indulged in a gentle ribbing, that was all."

"My apologies, sir." Joe reddened slightly, obviously realizing he overstepped his bounds.

Kelvin eyed the mediation room door, well within an easy distance, and then turned back to Joe. "When do we expect little Petra? Or rather, Ms. Richardson now. I admit I look forward to seeing her again." He gave a brief laugh. "As does Tray's nanny. The boy is becoming a handful, or so I'm told."

A twitch developed in Joe's right eye. "Young Traynor has had a rough time of it... with the tragedy of his mother's passing. He is the heir. He will rise above this, and with proper supervision, he will settle down."

Kelvin certain hoped so. Dear Moriah had been on a goodwill mission among the colonies when her spaceship exploded in interstellar space.

Joe continued, "As for Ms. Richardson, she and Felicia leave Saturday morning, and will arrive in Ecuador very late in the day. After a night's rest, they will then depart Quito Sunday at noon. With the boat trip here, I believe we can expect her at three in the afternoon."

"Good. Keep me advised of any changes." Kelvin shook his director's hand, and then proceeded into the mediation room. He had two point two minutes to shift gears. Next up on his busy agenda was placating an irate aquatic being from the planet Nephros 3.

Chapter Two

Sundays on the island were slow. Blissfully so. All visitors, even those vacationing at various locations across the planet, seemed to observe this traditional day of rest, thereby providing a down day for the staff. Most of the staff, at any rate, on this, the first day of July.

Kelvin took a sip of fine Ecuadorian coffee, and then regarded six of his key personnel gathered around the meeting room table. "Thank you all for agreeing to my impromptu meeting this morning. I promise to keep it short. We'll be done well before noon."

"Good," grumbled Cornwell Young, Taurus City's Medical Director and resident curmudgeon. "I've scheduled a boat to go fishing."

His kinky black hair shot with grey, the doctor looked five years older than his forty-nine years. Perhaps his profession caused premature aging. In any event, he was much too young for his grumpy attitude. He'd served on the island the longest--fifteen years now. By choice. A native of Tau Ceti 3 like Kelvin, Cornwell constantly complained about living on a backward outpost in the farthest reaches of the Milky Way. However whenever his three-year commitment concluded, he always re-upped without a protest. Truth be told, he loved it on Terra, but he kept that sentiment hidden, along with the fact that deep, deep down, he had a heart of gold.

"Fishing? You? C'mon, Doc, for what?" questioned Wanda Cropper, Manager of Reservations and Accommodations.

"For sea cucumbers, if you must know, you inquisitive cyborg, and no blasted yak-athon's gonna stop me."

A mottled flush discolored Wanda's pudgy cheeks. She was a robust, blonde woman originally from the farm planet Deneb 4, Cygnus Sector. She'd risen up the ranks from kitchen duty, to reservations staff, to Manager of R and A. Last season's brush with a whiptail stingray of the family *Dasyatididae,* had damaged her left eye to the extent that Cornwell had to replace it with a bionic device that, fortunately, matched her remaining grey eye. It was a perfect fit; she looked the same as before: rough around the edges, brassy, and ready for action.

Although she now experienced superhuman vision, Wanda didn't care to be reminded that she wasn't one hundred percent Human. Both eyes glared across the table at the doctor.

Kelvin held up a placating hand. "Sea cucumbers, class *Holothuriodea* of the phylum *Echinodermata,* have been overharvested for some time, Doctor, and that is a serious concern for the island natives. You are well aware of this situation."

Cornwell made an indifferent shrug. "I'm not trafficking in the blasted echinoderm, nor do I intend to harvest the daily quota, Kelvin." The doctor rubbed his large hands together. "I hear tell that eating those flexible warty bodies enhances... shall we say, certain desirable biological responses? I'm doing research, that's all."

"A white hot aphrodisiac!" Sergio Iguana, the current Chief of Security hooted. "So, Doc, you admit you need help to, er, start a fire, eh?"

Sergio hailed from the super hot yellow-orange binary star system in the Auriga Sector. Capella 8 colonists could never escape their planet's ever-present heat, so they always peppered their speech with "hot" phrases or analogies.

"You lack nineteen of my years, whipling." Cornwell smiled, revealing his brilliantly white teeth. "Talk to me when you're my age."

Before matters deteriorated further, Kelvin called the meeting to order. "As you all know, my nephew is here to begin his training on Terra. His tutor should arrive this afternoon. I'll be off the grid intermittently for a day or two, familiarizing the Terran, Petra Richardson, with her young charge and, of course, with our overt travel business."

Frankly, he was looking forward to spending time with Tray. And with the woman. For some reason Kelvin was restless. On edge. His sister-in-law's death had hit him hard. Maybe he needed a break from duties and responsibilities.

He withheld a disillusioned sigh. Right. That wasn't going to happen anytime soon. Taurus City's diplomatic conference was due to start at the end of the week. Held only once every ten years, it was, without a doubt, the most important event in the galaxy. And its success rested squarely upon his shoulders.

An honor, certainly. However, the timing couldn't have been more unfortunate.

Rubbing at his clean-shaven jaw, he allowed his gaze to wander at the tall palm trees visible through the window. Time off for some fun in the sun would do him good.

Kelvin snapped his attention back inside. "As always, if you need to speak with me," he continued, "go directly through Jade. She always knows how to reach me."

Jade Dunbar, his Executive Assistant, slightly inclined her head and accepted the compliment. Her striking red hair, the color of a glorious Terran sunset, swung away from her pale, lightly freckled face. Jade had the delicate appearance of a hothouse flower, but instead of coming from a background of pampering, she was a native of the harsh environment on Bokar, the second planet in the Alpha Circini star system. Jade was a born survivor.

She was also excellent in bed.

"So, let's have a current status report on our intergalactic guests." Kelvin gestured down the table. "Owen, we'll start with you."

As Operations Director for all of Taurus City, Owen Greenacre from Tau Ceti 3, carried a heavy load. Sergio Iguana's security team fell under Owen's jurisdiction, as did Wanda Cropper's reservations and accommodations, and also the culinary department, headed by Niko Starling.

As Kelvin had no interest in hearing about gastronomic matters, Niko, the Denebian head chef, wasn't present at this meeting.

Owen Greenacre cleared his throat. A suave, debonair gentleman of seventy-two, he was easily the oldest of Kelvin's management team. Or rather oldest in years. Cornwell Young acted the oldest. However, with today's comment about intensifying biological desires, the doctor might have finally been "loosening up," as the natives liked to say.

"As of this morning," Owen began in his smooth, practiced voice, "Xanadu hosts one hundred aliens, an increase of fifteen percent over last year's figures at this time."

"Only aliens refer to Terra as Xanadu, Owen," Jade, ever precise, interrupted.

As Owen sent a regal stare Jade's way, Wanda checked her tablet and then also interrupted. "One hundred and one tourists, sir, to be precise. A Kykanopian just checked in a few minutes ago."

"Remarkable," commented Owen.

"There goes the neighborhood," muttered Cornwell.

Kelvin took a gulp of coffee as he contemplated this news. "Indeed. Someone from Kykanop? The ambassador, perhaps?"

While strongly Humanoid, Kykanopians had the unfortunate effect of instilling a sense of unease among the staff. Most likely because of the method Kykanopians used to eat. They had four suction cups on each finger, and ingested their food and drink by using the suction cups. Watching them eat and clean up gave new meaning to the term "sticky fingers."

Wanda looked at her tablet again. "No, the Kykanopian ambassador will be arriving on Thursday for the conference."

"After acclimation, what is this particular fellow's destination?" Kelvin asked Wanda, but it was the Travel Director, Valli Proximus, who replied.

"Machu Picchu, Kelvin. The ruined Incan city high in the Andes Mountains of Peru."

Astonishment buzzed about the table. Kelvin held up his hand to silence everyone. "Are you certain, Valli? The terrain is notoriously rugged, not to mention the uncomfortable altitude and ever-present ravenous mosquitoes."

A look of annoyance flitted across Valli's attractive, yet determined face. "Naturally I am certain. Ellen D. of my Team South America just sent me the notification. She confirms the Kykanopian's desired location."

Kelvin sighed. "Just when I think I am well-versed in alien psychology, the tourists throw me for a loop."

Wanda heartily laughed. "Good example of Terran idiomatic speech, sir."

He smiled at her. "Yes, the natives' language is picturesque, isn't it?"

Cornwell tapped on his antique wrist timepiece. "Time's a-wasting, Kelvin."

The doctor had a point. "Right. Owen, please continue your report."

The Operations Director listed more statistics concerning the one hundred and one aliens, along with the other visitors to Terra: one thousand and twenty three Humans from the colony worlds.

Humans were, of course, far easier to handle than aliens, hence the greater numbers. While Humans needed only a cultural interpreter per group, aliens required one security officer and a cultural interpreter for every three in the cluster.

In addition to security and interpreters, aliens had to be suited up to appear as natives, or in the case of Nephrosians and Yeamonls, as other lifeforms found on the planet. No easy task, to be sure. But the disguises had been perfected for thousands of years. The staff always performed their minor miracles without undo incident.

An interlude on Terra, on Xanadu as the aliens called it, consistently exceeded tourist expectations. This crowning jewel in the cosmos offered a memorable... and expensive vacation for those who wished to frolic in paradise under this exotic pleasure dome.

Since gold was the preferred payment, Taurus City coffers were always hot and gleaming, as Finance Director Todd Boiler, another Capellan on staff, reported.

After Owen finished, all five other staffers took turns reporting the news in their departments, with Cornwell concluding. He regaled everyone with an update on the Nephrosian's artificial limb.

"Blasted blighter had been in a world of hurt, that was for certain. As aquatic lifeforms, the Nephrosians propel themselves through the water with their long, flexible tails. Evidently, this critter's tail had been too curious for its own good. Swishing this way and that, the tail flicked too close to a hungry crocodile." He held out his hands, palms out. "And that was the end of that."

"Lor! The poor little fellow. How did you fix him?" Clearly affected by the story, Wanda dabbed at her good eye. Bionic eyes never teared up.

Cornwell leaned into the table, obviously enjoying the attention. "Luckily, there was a stump left. I just grafted a skinny rubbery hose onto what remained, an appliance modeled after those portable pool cleaners, y'know. Then I sealed it in silicon, and away the blasted beggar went--without a care in the world."

"Sizzling suns! What a scorchingly original idea!" Sergio looked at the doctor with admiration in his ebony eyes. "Sheer genius, Doc."

Cornwell might have blushed, but with his dark complexion, it was hard to tell.

Jade made a small smile. "Word around the compound is that this Nephrosian is becoming very popular with the females of his kind. We might find more males flirting with danger so as to have this chance to be technologically enhanced."

"No." Valli slapped her hand down on the table. "That is not humorous even as a joke. My teams take great care in instilling regulations to these aliens. We cannot be held accountable if they flaunt our warnings without regard."

At her outburst, Kelvin lifted his eyebrow. "We do not hold you responsible for this mishap, I assure you, Valli. Your teams do an excellent job."

"Quite," Owen seconded.

"Top star," Sergio added.

Cornwell got to his feet, ran his dark gaze over his fellow staffers, and then bowed. "Now that we're all in agreement, and the time is almost noon, I'm gonna dash."

Jade and Wanda smirked as the doctor left.

Kelvin also stood. "Meeting adjourned, although evidently, I should have said that a nanosecond sooner. Enjoy your Sunday, people. Remember, tonight is the welcoming party. And again, if anything urgent comes up and you need to speak with me, call Jade."

Small talk followed the meeting. Mostly about the Kykanopian, the upcoming conference, and also about the tragedy that had claimed Moriah Lacertus' life.

"Dear Moriah. Unspeakable. Simply unspeakable," Owen proclaimed. "Say, it's after twelve. Who's up for a spread at my villa? Niko tells me he whipped up something special."

"Hunger consumes me. I'm in." Sergio clapped his powerful hand on Owen's shoulder. They both headed for the door.

Jade slid a sleek lock of hair behind her ear, glanced at Valli, and then Kelvin. "See you later, Kelvin." With a wave, she then gracefully stepped up her pace, joining the men as they walked out of the meeting room.

Wanda stared after them. She looked as if she didn't want to be left behind.

"Go ahead, Wanda. Take some time off," Kelvin prompted.

"Thanks, sir." She sprinted out the door, going after her director, Sergio, and Jade.

Which left Kelvin and Valli still inside.

Kelvin gathered up loose papers and placed them into his briefcase. Usually Valli was the first to leave. That she lingered meant she wanted to talk. Perhaps it was something personal.

"Something bothering you, Valli?"

She brushed her short wavy dark hair back from her forehead. Her eyes, an unusual shade of violet, shone brightly in the noonday sunlight streaming in through the windowpane. "Yes, it's about the Nephrosian situation, Kelvin. I don't want you to think I couldn't handle it. You know I would've attended Thursday's meeting with the injured tourist, only I was off-island making last minute arrangements for the diplomatic conference."

"Of course I know that, Valli." He took her hand and smoothed his fingertips over her soft knuckles.

A shiver overtook her as she smiled up at him.

"The conference is far more important than a disgruntled tourist. Not that the Neprosian remained disgruntled. Cornwell and I had the situation resolved sooner than we'd hoped." He picked up his briefcase. "Besides, I appreciate your efforts to make this conference more impressive than the last one. With nine alien races attending--specifically Nephrosians, Kykanopians, Wn-Ganites, Brhites, Uortizks, Velans, Yeamonls, Phi Pavonisians, and Sirians--we have nine different needs and thought processes to cater to. It's a daunting job, and I appreciate you stepping up to the plate to handle it."

They walked through the door, out into the corridor of the visitors' section. Valli seemed relieved by his reply. "What about this tutor for the Chairman's heir? Are you certain someone from Terra--"

"As you are aware, tradition demands that a Terran native instruct the Lacertus family." He quickened his steps. Remaining inside on such a magnificent sunny day was a crime against nature. "It was one of the cardinal rules handed down at the time of the great conflict."

"Yes, of course. My apologies, Kelvin." Valli lowered her long lashes.

An ocean breeze greeted them as they stepped outside the security wall. He inhaled deeply of the crisp, salty air. "I am convinced my nephew needs to learn from someone untainted by grief. This tutor will be good for him and he will benefit from the experience. You needn't be concerned about the boy. He is a Lacertus."

"Yes." Wind playfully tugged at Valli's dark curls. "Yes, I know he is. Just like his father... and his uncle."

"Indeed. And now, I bid you good day." Kelvin took his leave from Valli to walk alone down to the rocky beach. Setting aside his briefcase, he removed his shorts and shirt, revealing baggy swim trunks. He slipped off his sandals, and then cautiously stepped on the water-smoothed stones, walking toward the nearby inlet. He looked forward to a swim. If he were fortunate, he'd run into a friendly sea lion or two.

Kelvin dropped down onto his haunches to cup a cool handful of seawater. Pouring it down his heated back, he smiled. If he lived to be one hundred, he would never tire of this natural beauty surrounding him.

* * * *

Petra stared out at the curtain of grey fog and drizzle that surrounded the small commuter boat. She shivered. The cool mist seemed to penetrate the cabin interior.

An unwelcome thought haunted her. *Why did I agree to this creepy assignment?*

Felicia reached over from the opposite seat and patted Petra's hand. "Don't worry, okay? It gets better. In another few minutes we'll be able to see the island."

Petra pulled the edges of her rayon knit jacket close against her chest. She hadn't dressed for rainy sixty-degree weather. "But why did we have to leave San Cristóbal? Taurus City's letterhead states that's where the travel agency headquarters is."

"San Cristóbal's the closest island. I guess it's easier to have mail sent to there than to Taurus City. That's what I call the island. It's a gorgeous place. You'll see."

You'll see. Felicia's words echoed in Petra's mind. Right now all she saw were waves from rough seas blown by angry winds and cloaked in stormy fog.

Brrr.

For six weeks this mysterious island would be her home. She had run around like a crazy woman before leaving the Bronx, prepaying her utilities and rent, notifying the post office, and then breaking the news to her parents. Mom had been nervous. Dad had been... unsupportive.

"Just what the hell do you think you're doing, Petra Jane? Traveling at the drop of a hat to the ends of the earth with goddamn bloody strangers? What are they--pirates? White slavers?" Dad had ranted.

To put it mildly, her father could've benefited from an anger management class... or two.

Sighing, she toyed with the silky fabric of her long flowing skirt. No, her parents hadn't wished her a bon voyage.

The small boat gave a lurch and suddenly, the smoky grey fog opened up. Brilliantly blue sky, colorful resort buildings, a red and white lighthouse, and a modest seaport sparkled in front of her. She blinked. It was as if she'd really been at the end of the earth, and then a curtain lifted to show a tropical paradise.

"It's lovely," she breathed.

Felicia clapped her hands. "I told you you'd like it. I absolutely love it here. And wait until you meet our CEO, you love him, too. We all do!" She glanced out the windows and then lowered her gaze with a shy smile. "There's my boss, Joe, at the dock. He's meeting us."

Petra looked, but truthfully, the boat was still too far away from the shoreline. She saw the lighthouse, yachts, and fishing boats in the harbor, but on land, other than buildings and a green mountain in the distance, she didn't see anything resembling people. "You can see him?"

"Golly, I'd know him anywhere. Besides, he's standing by his new catamaran. It's twin-hulled, y'know. Almost thirty feet big. He took me out for a dive once." Felicia giggled.

Oh boy. Somebody had a big crush. Petra smiled. Now that the sun was out, she felt better. Maybe she *had* made the right decision.

"Let's go out on the deck." Felicia jiggled as she stood. She could hardly contain her excitement. "We'll be there in no time at all."

"Sure." Petra followed, and once outside, the tangy sea air helped clear her mind. Soon she spotted a lean man standing on the wharf. He had short dark grey hair, and was wearing dockers and a black tee shirt. He waved at them.

"There he is!" Felicia squealed. "He's meeting us. Isn't he dreamy?"

Josephus Hammer's appearance matched how Petra had envisioned him. Crisp, proper, and... mature. He was probably twenty years older than his assistant. Evidently, the age difference didn't bother Felicia. Her mocha complexion actually glowed as she waved back.

Petra had been head over heels, too, just a very short while ago. Now she was older and much wiser. She'd never make a fool of herself over a man again. That was for certain.

Once the boat docked, the HR Director extended his strong hand, helping Petra up the stone steps onto the pier. "Greetings, Ms. Richardson. It is a pleasure to meet you at last."

So formal! She replied in kind. "Thank you, Mr. Hammer. I'm glad to be here."

"Please, call me Joe." His smile completely changed his solemn demeanor.

She also smiled. His mood was catching. "Certainly, Joe. And I'm Petra."

Felicia brought up the rear, along with Manuel, the boathand with the luggage. "Golly, it's good to stand on firm land. So, here she is, Joe, just as I promised."

The way Felicia stood, fidgeting a little, was like a puppy wagging its tail, waiting to be rewarded by its master.

"Indeed." He nodded in an absentminded way, then turned to Petra. "I trust you had a pleasant trip, Petra."

Ouch. Puppies didn't like to be ignored. Petra hurried to soothe the young woman's feelings. "Oh yes, definitely, Joe. I couldn't have asked for a better companion than Felicia. It's been great. Flying first class all the way... I've never been so pampered."

"Good." As he smiled again, a network of crow's feet extended out from his forest green eyes. "Our CEO will be most pleased."

He loaded Petra's two pieces of luggage into the trunk of a tiny lemon yellow convertible. The car honestly looked as if it had escaped from a bumper car amusement ride, it was *almost* that small. There were only seats for two.

"Felicia, your car is parked down the pier. Manuel will carry your suitcase."

"Sure. Thanks." She brushed kinky, spiraled hair out of her eyes. "So, I'll see you later, Petra, okay? If you have any questions, just give me a buzz."

"I will. And thanks for everything." For some reason, seeing Felicia walk away made Petra feel adrift. Although she'd only been acquainted with the woman for a few days, she'd come to depend on Felicia's cheerful nature. Now she was alone again with the unknown.

Joe opened the car door for her. "We'll drop your things off at your bungalow, give you a quick tour, and then I will take you to meet

Traynor."

Sitting in the scrunched up car, Petra folded her hands in her lap and took a deep breath. Her adventure was off to an auspicious start.

* * * *

Kelvin glanced at his nephew's "new" look, as the boy called it. He couldn't help but sigh. Tray had somehow found a pair of scissors and then had unevenly hacked off the front and sides of his dark mop of hair.

"Tray, what am I going to do with you? You look like one of those chattering magpies on Sirius 3."

The boy giggled. Flapping his arms in imitation of the hairy, fringed birds, he chirped as he "flew" around the wraparound deck of the house.

Kelvin sighed again. That Tray had cut his hair wasn't the problem. His father, Will, had entrusted the boy to Kelvin's care. As the son of the Chairman, Tray had certain responsibilities, even though he was only five. Appearing undignified was not one of them.

Perhaps more to the point was that his tutor was due to arrive momentarily.

Sitting on a deck chair, Kelvin eyed his nephew as the boy completed a "flying" turn about the deck. "We need to cut your hair to make it even, Tray."

"No! No, I'm a Sirian magpie." The boy, a bundle of energy, sped up his dashing about and soon turned the corner, out of sight.

Kelvin sunk his chin in his hand. Here was a devil of a situation. Here he was, responsible for the whole of the Tau Ceti or rather Taurus City enterprise here on Terra, yet he held no sway whatever over a five-year-old boy.

Sobering.

The doorbell ran throughout the house. No time to wallow in inappropriate thoughts.

He corralled his nephew with a few well-chosen words, and then they both walked through the sliding glass doors into the living room to await Ms. Richardson. As soon as sounds were heard at the living room door, however, Tray darted back outside.

That boy is in serious need of discipline.

But that thought completely vanished as Kelvin watched the willowy woman enter the room. He sharply inhaled. The enchanting fifteen-year-old waif he remembered had grown into a beauty that took his breath away. Her dark hair, parted in the middle, hung down in cascading waves just past her shoulders. Still slender, still petite, she wore a camisole top and matching covering tied at her narrow waist, along with a long gauzy skirt. Her sandaled toes peeped out from under the hem.

She walked in as a goddess might, strong and confident in her appearance. As well she should. She was like the Greek goddess Artemis--wild, determined, and pure.

He raked her with his gaze, inhaling her flowery fragrance. There was something special about Terran women. He'd always believed that. But more so with this Terran woman. Something elemental, something primordial. Something that appealed to every sense that a man possessed.

Her eyes, a mixture of butterscotch and honey, widened at seeing him.

She remembered him. Good.

"Kelvin." Joe suddenly appeared by her side. "May I introduce Ms. Petra Richardson?"

Kelvin stepped forward and extended his hand. "Charmed, Ms. Richardson. Although we have met before, yes?"

The slightest blush colored her high cheeks. She shook his hand. "Yes, a very long time ago. I'm flattered that you remember me, sir."

Her shake was firm, her skin warm. Her touch engendered a tickling sensation--one that penetrated down to his innermost regions. He held her gaze. "But of course I do. You were a most engaging child."

Blinking rapidly, she lowered her brows and then took a step back.

By the stars, he had alarmed her? How was that so?

Joe came to the rescue. "Where is Traynor?"

As if the boy had heard the question, he scurried down the deck making guttural bird cries. This time he'd found two branches that had fallen off a palm tree. One in each hand, he flapped them, making a jump every so often as if to take off to the skies.

Kelvin turned toward the row of floor to ceiling windows and settled his hands on his hips. He watched the boy continue his run. "There is your new charge, Ms. Richardson. As you can see, my nephew is a lively child with a vivid imagination. Unfortunately, he just had a run in with a pair of scissors. He lost the battle. This is the result."

She walked over to the sliding glass door and looked out, obviously watching for the boy's next turn around the deck. When he came back around, he waved a palm branch at her.

"He's darling! A typical boy," she exclaimed.

Kelvin exchanged a glance with Joe. Tray wasn't exactly typical.

Tapping her finger against her chin, she tilted her head. "Tell you what. Another pair of scissors can fix the damage. Do you have clippers? Hair-cutting gear? I'd be happy to give Traynor a trim. I often cut my father's hair."

Joe lifted an eyebrow at Kelvin.

Kelvin nodded. "Right. Go ahead and have Georges bring the equipment. I'm curious to see how Ms. Richardson will persuade an active child to sit still for a haircut."

"Will do." Joe stepped over to the open glass door and shook her hand. "I will see you later, Petra. If you need anything, please call. Good luck with this latest assignment."

After she said goodbye to Joe, Kelvin gestured toward the white contemporary couch facing the windows. "Come, let's sit. I'm being an inattentive host. Would you care for some refreshments? Coffee? Iced tea? Something stronger?"

Petra glided over to the couch, sat on the cushions, and then placed her handbag next to her. She smoothed her skirt's material down at her knees. "Thank you, no. I'm fine."

He mixed himself a vodka tonic, splashed in a lime slice, and then sat adjacent to her in one of the white contour chairs. Leaning back, he studied her.

She glanced around the large room, her gaze skimming over the glass coffee table, the many potted fern plants, and the monochrome modernistic paintings. She then settled on a decorative statue of Cupid.

Perhaps the sight of the Roman god of love displeased her for her plump lips thinned. "Mr. Lacertus, I can't, for the life of me, figure this out. Why did you choose me to tutor your nephew?"

He started to speak, but she held up her slim hand. "I'm aware of what

Joe and Felicia said. But it just doesn't wash. I need to know the real reason, if you don't mind."

"The real reason," he repeated. Stalling for time, he took a refreshing sip of his drink. "Well, first, please call me Kelvin."

Her eyes crinkled up and her shoulders hunched forward, ever so slightly. Why was that?

"My name amuses you?"

She flushed. "You do know your name is a measurement of absolute thermodynamic temperature?"

Petra Richardson was of a literal mind; he explicitly remembered that about her. She was also a science teacher, through and through.

"Indeed it is, Petra, if I may. And if I gage the temperature in this room correctly, it is not only sixty eight degrees Fahrenheit, but also can be stated as two hundred and ninety four Kelvin."

She tapped her sandaled foot on the plush, cream-colored carpet. "I'll take your word for it. You very neatly avoided my question."

"So I did. Astute of you to notice." He took another cool sip, and then set his glass down on a side table. "If you truly want to know--"

"I do."

He couldn't tell her the real reason. What the devil could he say?

He decided on the emotional card. "My nephew, Tray, was sent here unexpectedly. His mother, my sister-in-law, died in a tragic accident. Will, my brother, wants his son to be distracted from his grief, so he can deal with the pain in his own way, without having to be constantly surrounded by it."

"Oh, I'm so sorry." Petra leaned forward, an expression of complete sympathy covering her delectable face.

"Thank you. Tray does, of course, miss his mother, however the concept of death is rather complex for a five-year-old. And, as you've seen, he does have some behavior problems that must be corrected."

"Like the hair cutting?"

Kelvin smiled. "Yes, I suppose he was acting out with that. But then again, who can understand what goes on in the minds of children?"

A minute passed... as did Tray continuing his bird-in-flight routine.

Petra took a pillow from the side of the couch, fluffed it, and then replaced it. "You're doing it again. You haven't answered my question."

He grinned. His gut had been correct. This young woman was decidedly on the ball. "Sorry. So, here was the dilemma--what do I do with a pre-school-aged boy in the summertime? Answer--find a person who is good with kids and likes to teach. Most of my acquaintances are connected with the travel agency, so I had to look elsewhere for the tutor. In the end, I dug out the notes I'd made during my Grand Tour." He looked at her. "Do you remember that?"

She tried to hide her smile, but she failed. "Yes, you said you were on your Grand Tour of Earth." A mischievous smile lifted her lips. "Tell me, did you get to cover the whole planet? Even go to the moon, perhaps?"

She was teasing, of course.

"As a matter of fact, I did do both. Luna is a very dusty place, I'll have you know. At least the side facing Earth is." He wasn't joking, but naturally, she thought he was.

Her smile gave way to laughter.

"In any event," he continued, "as I told Joe, you were the only person I remembered from the tour. Even then you had been determined to teach. And you were quite feisty, too. I figured, why not find Petra Richardson and ask her? To my great relief, you accepted. And now here you are."

"I see."

By the set of her lips, she obviously was thinking over what he'd said. Whether she believed him was another matter.

He picked up his vodka tonic, finished it, and then stood. "It's time for you to meet Tray. Besides, he must be tired out from flying around the deck all this time."

"Good. I'd like that."

She made a move to get up, but he held up his hand. "No, you stay put. I'll bring him in."

Outside on the deck, Kelvin jogged in the opposite direction, and came across Tray. "Time to meet Ms. Richardson now."

"No." The boy pouted.

Saying no was a game, one that Kelvin didn't want to play right now.

"Yes," he insisted. Using his arm, he scooped his nephew up around his waist. Holding a bundle of energy that fidgeted and kicked wore at his patience. "Traynor, it is time to settle down. Time for you to act like a Lacertus."

The little boy stilled. "Yes, okay, Uncle Kel. I'll be good."

Kelvin breathed a sigh of relief. He put Tray down, and then held his hand. "Let's go meet Ms. Richardson."

* * * *

Petra usually didn't feel overwhelmed, but oh boy! She wiped nervous sweat from her forehead. Kelvin Lacertus, her first ever crush, was just as finger-licking good as her memory had advertised.

Deeply masculine with piercing grey eyes and deep-cut dimples that extended down to his strong jaw, this man exuded sensuality and delicious male virility. It had taken all her self-control to act as if he was just another man, one who didn't melt her insides like gooey roasted marshmallows.

Her heart rate probably soared off the charts... so much so that she was afraid her heart's frantic beating could be seen through the thin material on her top. Concentrating on her breathing, she willed herself to calm down. To collect her scattered wits. To focus on the boy, and not his wickedly attractive uncle.

She fisted her hands until her nails bit into the soft skin on her palms. Yes, that was better. Now she needed a mantra. Immediately she thought, *Kelvin Lacertus doesn't affect me. He doesn't affect me.*

Good. Glancing around the room again, she frowned slightly. Although beautifully decorated, it was sterile, showing nothing of the owner's personal tastes. Except for that ridiculous Cupid figure. Maybe that was a statement. Maybe this room was built for seduction.

Well, I'm not taking any chances, Mr. Cupid. I'm not going to be hit by your arrows. And that's a promise.

Turning her back on the statue, she folded her arms across her chest.

Kelvin walked into the living room holding his nephew's small hand. "Petra, I'd like you to meet my nephew, Traynor Lacertus."

The little boy let go of Kelvin's hand and then zoomed over to stand in front of her.

His fringed bangs revealed a lot more forehead than his hair should have. Very short spikes stuck out from his uneven sides. Traynor had done a master's job of shearing.

His gaze, as dark as his uncle's, roamed over her from head to toe. "Hello, Ms. Richardson." He stood on his right leg, bent his left leg, and then held onto his ankle with his left hand. "I'm very happy t'meet you."

"I'm very happy to meet you, too, Traynor. And please, call me Petra." She extended her hand.

Traynor put out his right hand, but also hopped on his one leg.

"Traynor," his uncle's voice warned.

The boy stood on both feet, and then shook her hand. "You feel good, Petra," he said, and then giggled.

"So do you." Smiling, she patted the cushion next to her. "Would you like to sit?"

He did, and then dangled and bumped his feet against the edge of the couch.

Kelvin lifted a dark eyebrow. "I rest my case." He turned toward the door. "Here's Georges with the clippers. Let's see what miracles you can work, Petra."

Traynor definitely was a bright boy. Immediately he shook his head from side to side. "No! No cutting. I'm a chattering magpie."

While Kelvin got the rectangular case from his assistant, Petra was left to figure out how she could change the boy's mind. "Chattering magpie? I haven't heard of magpies since those old cartoons, Heckle and Jeckle."

"What's a Heckle and Jeckle?" Traynor blinked his puppy dog eyes at her.

"Two mostly black birds, like crows, who always seem to get into trouble." She thought a moment. "They both always look their best, though. No uneven feathers for them."

Traynor chewed on his lower lip. "I wanna look like Heckle and Jeckle."

"Hmmn." She considered his words. "I guess I could fix your feathers, but you'd have to stay still."

Kelvin returned to the couch with the case. "That would be quite a trick, Petra."

Traynor squirmed on the cushion, validating Kelvin's statement.

Reaching into her handbag, she pulled out a grape-flavored lollipop. Sometimes she had trouble with her ears during flight takeoffs and landings. Sucking on a hard candy usually helped to equalize the pressure.

"I'll give you this if you sit still." It was a bribe, of course, but the way Kelvin looked at her made her feel like she was a genius.

"Okay." Traynor held out his hand.

"Deal." She handed him the lollipop. "Let's go outside on the deck. Maybe we'll see some magpies."

And outside, she wouldn't have to worry about hair cuttings messing up the light carpet.

As Traynor willingly scampered off to the deck to get his hair shorn, Kelvin leaned over, whispering into her ear. "You are simply amazing, Ms. Richardson."

His praise... and his masculine scent of sandalwood, leather, and musk... zipped down her spine, activating her inner core.

Whoa, girl. I definitely do not want to go there.

Pressing her lips together, she walked onto the deck, fanning herself with her hand. Lazy sea breezes lifted her hair, beckoning her to relax.

She'd relax all right, but later--once she was away from Mr. Finger-Licking-Good. She spotted a bar counter with stools. She appropriated one of them. "Okay, Tray, time to set your bottom down."

Traynor noisily complied. She opened the case, removed a hairdressing cape, and then draped it around his meager shoulders.

Kelvin grabbed a pair of sunglasses from somewhere and leaned against the deck railing to watch the action. He crossed his arms in front of his chest, which pulled his polo shirt tight across his muscular frame.

Yummy.

She turned back to concentrate on her task. With the lollipop safely in Traynor's mouth, it was time to begin. She adjusted the clippers to cut the correct length, and then turned them on so he could get used to the buzzing sound. Then she tipped his head slightly forward, and slowly moved the clippers up the back of his head.

Traynor's hair was easy, so fine and silky, unlike her father's. Soon the wooden flooring was decorated with the shorn locks. Turning off the clippers, she then trimmed a few stray hairs with scissors. Satisfied, she stepped back to admire her handiwork.

His young face looked rounder, his eyes bigger. He even looked a bit older.

"What do you think?" she asked Kelvin.

"He looks like a magpie to me." Kelvin's smile wreaked havoc with her overheated body parts.

"Really?" Traynor took a hand mirror from the haircutting case, and held it this way and that. Rolling the lollipop around in his mouth, he then scrunched up his little nose.

Uh oh. That isn't a good sign. Her heart sank.

But then all was A-OK, for Traynor gave her a thumbs up. He scrambled down off the stool, and dashed over to the discarded palm branches. Once again, he took up his running and jumping down the deck.

Kelvin helped her put the hair gear away. Being so close to him was torture--of the most delectable kind. Dark chest hair peeked out from the open neck of his polo shirt. A slight five o'clock shadow darkened his jaw. Soft swirls of hair on his forearms tantalized her.

What would it feel like to run her hands up his arms? Up over his shoulders? Down his muscular back?

She silently repeated her mantra: *Kelvin Lacertus doesn't affect me. He doesn't affect me.* Then she sighed. Too bad she didn't believe it.

"Only on the island a couple of hours and you're already a big hit." He closed the case and then smiled in his own sexy way. "I'd say that calls for a drink."

"Ah, no thanks. If you don't mind, I think I'll go back to the bungalow and crash out. Jet lag seems to be seeping in with a vengeance."

"But of course it is. I do apologize for not taking that into account." He placed his hand above her elbow and led her back into the living room.

Warm, wooly chills vibrated up her arm.

"After you have your rest, we'll have dinner here," he continued.

Dinner? She gulped down nervously. He sure didn't waste any time, did he? Looking around, she eyed the door as a means to escape. It was isolated here at his house. Romantic, true, and with soothing sounds of the ocean as music. But she couldn't--no, she wouldn't--agree to have dinner with him.

She narrowed her gaze. Did he expect she would immediately fall into his arms? What a bloody smooth operator.

Just as she opened her mouth to refuse, he set his sunglasses on top of his head and gave her a wink. "Some of the agency staff will be here, to welcome you. A very informal get-together outside on the grounds at seven o'clock. Food, eats, good conversation, and music. How does that strike you?"

"Oh!" Her face burned brightly, she just knew it did. He didn't intend a seduction at all. Far from it. How could she have jumped to that ridiculous conclusion? Could it have been wistful thinking on her part?

"Oh, ah, sure. That'll be great." Her voice sounded flat, but fortunately he didn't seem to notice.

He snatched up a group of keys, removed one, and then gave it to her. "I'll walk you to your car."

"My car?"

"Yes, the yellow bug outside. It'll be your transportation while you're here."

Still flogging herself for her outrageous assumption, Petra just nodded. "Thanks. I, ah, appreciate everything you're doing to make me comfortable."

"Nonsense." He escorted her out into the corridor. "I want you to feel at home here, Petra. After all, we're on the same team."

What he said *was* true. They were all on the same team. And not every man had a hidden agenda.

Since the party was only in two hours, she didn't dawdle in saying goodbye. Now behind the steering wheel, she turned the engine on, waved to Kelvin, and then drove the short way back to her bungalow.

Chapter Three

As Petra sipped a glass of fruity sangria, she swayed to melodious tropical music issuing from speakers placed all around the grounds. Palm trees rustled in the cool ocean breezes, prickly pear cacti stood as sentinels around the three-foot high lava rock wall encircling Kelvin's estate, and the darkening dusk signaled the end of a very long day.

"It's so lovely here, isn't it? So different from where I grew up." A brawny blonde woman extended her sturdy hand for a shake. "Good to meet you, Petra. I'm Maizie. I work in Travel, under Valli Proximus."

People had been coming up to Petra all evening, introducing themselves and being very friendly. So many people, so many unusual names. Not that Maizie was unusual, but Valli Proximus was. She turned out to be a cold brunette who liked to look down her regal nose at everyone.

"Nice to meet you, Maizie. What do you do in the Travel Department?"

"I head up Team Antarctica." Maizie's pale blue eyes twinkled. "I'm not as busy as the Ellens, but I do get enough tourists to keep me hopping."

Petra took a sip of sangria. "The Ellens?"

The woman smiled broadly. "Maybe you haven't met them yet." She pointed toward the long tables filled with food. "Ellen F. is by the punchbowl with Joe Hammer, and Ellen C. is over there admiring the floral baskets. I don't see the other four. Maybe they had other plans."

Wine caught in Petra's throat. She'd noticed the two women earlier. They stood out because they were identical twins: slender, with precisely cut, short black hair.

"There are four more? Also identical?" Petra couldn't help but gawk. Sextuplets? "But, Maizie, why do they have the same first name?"

"Lor, who can figure it out? That's the way things are done where the Ellens' are from." Maizie shrugged her broad shoulders. "F does Australia tourists and C handles Asia."

How very, very peculiar.

"Whoa. Food's still coming, I see." Maizie rubbed her ample belly. "I

41

need to refill my plate before I head out. It's a long time until breakfast, y'know, and I sure hate being hungry." She then gave a friendly wave. "Nice meeting you, Petra. See you around."

Wow. Petra leaned against the rough trunk of a palm tree, trying to make sense of what she'd just learned. Sextuplets were given the same first name and then differentiated by the letters of the alphabet? Just where in the world did the Ellens come from?

Or even Maizie. The woman reminded Petra of Wanda Cropper, the Reservations and Accommodations Manager. They didn't look alike but both had frizzy blonde hair and a no-nonsense manner. Both were sturdily built. Both used the exclamation "Lor".

Petra set down her wine goblet and massaged the bridge of her nose. Too many bizarre things to think about. Sensory overload was giving her a headache.

Looking for a place to sit by herself for a few minutes, she glanced about the grounds. Her gaze drifted and found Kelvin. He sat under a blue canopy, having an animated conversation with his assistant Jade Dunbar, Chief of Security Sergio Iguana, and Finance Director Todd Boiler.

Iguana and Boiler--strange last names.

Another sweep showed all the guests in deep conversations. Good, she wouldn't be missed.

Petra quickly walked toward the back of the house, past a tennis court, and then over to the lava rock surrounding the perimeter of the property. She sat on a wooden plank bench, and spread out the chiffon material of her long skirt. She'd packed only two dressy long skirts, and in less than a day, she'd worn both of them.

Soft music filtered back to where she sat. Closing her eyes, she smiled as she listened to it and inhaled aromatic fragrances from the surrounding flower bushes.

Then a different scent invaded her nostrils. A deep, musky scent. She heard a noise, too.

Opening her eyes, she spotted a man--a huge man built like a warrior--jump over the low wall. His eyes were golden, and his rusty hair was long, hanging down to his immense shoulders. Much of his face was covered by a bushy beard of the same color. He stayed frozen for a moment, crouched.

Panic overtook her, but then she willed herself to remain calm. After all, if she was in danger, with one scream she could alert all Kelvin's guests and the security chief.

She watched as the man slowly stood. Then, inexplicably, he shimmered.

"Oh!" She couldn't help it; she gasped.

"You." The man pointed an unrelenting finger. "Why are you malingering on that bench?"

The shimmering had steadied, then vanished. No trace of flickering remained.

She blinked rapidly, again trying to compose herself. "Oh, I, ah, was just taking a break from the party." She shrugged. "Too many people for me."

He nodded his great head as if he was ruler of all he surveyed. "On that we are in accord."

They both lapsed into silence. She fiddled with her dangling earring, furiously thinking. She'd feel safer if she kept the conversation going. "Are you here for the get-together?"

"We were not invited."

"Oh. Well, the party is actually for me, so consider yourself invited." She smiled.

He watched her with his golden eyes.

Talk about feeling uneasy! She pushed the material of her skirt back close to her, and then clasped her hands in her lap. "Would you like to sit?"

"Why?"

Terse and to the point.

"Well, it's a beautiful night, the flowers smell nice, and it's so relaxing listening to the music." Even to her ears, she sounded rather childish. "This is my first night on the island."

He lifted one of his bushy eyebrows. "Indeed? Where do you originate from?"

Strange way to phrase it. "From New York. The Bronx." She would've liked to ask him the same question, but something, maybe self-preservation, buttoned her lip.

"From here. Interesting. Your words explain much."

"Do they? Do I look so new to the island then?"

Instead of answering, he took her up on her offer. He sat beside her.

Too close for comfort. She slid to the edge of the bench. What else could she say to keep the ball rolling?

"My name is Petra. Petra Richardson."

Again, he said nothing.

She prompted, "And you are?"

He turned his head and growled at her. "We are called Hunt. As you, we have just recently arrived. Attending the diplomatic conference is our purpose."

The imperial "we". How peculiar. "I hope you find time to enjoy this gorgeous scenery, too, Hunt."

His frown was fierce. "This place is fabled to be a pleasure dome. We do not see the allure."

A pleasure dome. The beginning of British poet Samuel Taylor Coleridge's famous work, "Kubla Khan", suddenly popped into her head.

In Xanadu did Kubla Khan

A stately pleasure dome decree:...

Petra had never heard that phrase used in any other context before. She smiled. "This island *is* sort of like paradise, like Xanadu, isn't it? How very poetic of you, Hunt."

Hunt stared at her, his compelling eyes glowing hypnotically. "We thank you for your kindness, Lady. You are far more considerate than most of the natives inhabiting Xanadu... the island. We are fortunate to meet you."

With that, he held out his hand. For some reason, she was afraid to complete the handshake. Then again, she was afraid *not* to shake his hand.

* * * *

Kelvin left the wicker chair, then arched his back. After sitting so long, that action felt good, so he extended his arms overhead for a stretch.

"I should be calling it a day," he commented to Jade, who still sat in the shade of the canopy even though the sun had long since set.

Sergio had already left. After their impromptu discussion, he had wanted to get to work on implementing Kelvin's new suggestions for additional security measures for the upcoming conference.

Jade gazed up at Kelvin and licked her coral-colored lips. "I would rather call it a night."

Kelvin smoothed his unruly hair back with both hands. One of the hazards of working intimately with someone was the danger of carrying that intimacy into the bedroom. That was when things tended to get awkward.

Truth be told, he liked Jade. Running his gaze over her lustrous hair and svelte feminine contours, he felt his body harden. More than liked. However, women had a tendency to want exclusivity. It was a biological fact of life.

Kelvin practiced the opposite philosophy. The more, the merrier was his view on life.

He glanced around at the remaining partygoers. There were plenty of young nubile females on staff, if he were so inclined to indulge.

He wasn't. Not tonight.

Holding his hand out, he helped Jade to her feet. He had to be considerate and let her down gently. "Great event, Jade. My thanks for arranging all the details. Petra seems to be adapting well."

Speaking of Petra, he'd lost track of time, and of Petra. He scanned the grounds. Where was she?

"Are you looking for the Terran?" Jade flashed her blue eyes his way. "Some time ago I saw her leave the party and slip past the tennis court. Perhaps she had a assignation."

Assignation? Petra just arrived this afternoon. She didn't know anyone on the island.

He nodded curtly. "Thanks. I'll go have a look."

Leaving his assistant behind, Kelvin briskly walked toward the back of the estate. While he walked, he stewed. Why hadn't he ordered someone to watch Petra? Be her bodyguard. Not that there was danger on the island, but she was an innocent. She could easily be taken advantage of.

He spotted her a short distance away on an isolated bench in front of the lava stone wall. She wasn't alone. A man sat by her side.

As Kelvin approached, his nostrils flared, his eyes narrowed, and he fisted his hands. Perhaps she wasn't as innocent as he'd thought.

He took another look. Oh hell. She was with one of the aliens.

Using a tree for cover, he studied the alien. Naturally the alien wore a disguise--a Human skin, the agency liked to call it. The skin was firmly in place, and no shimmering disrupted the visual field.

That was something to be thankful for. So, to which race of beings did this one belong?

He caught of glimpse of golden eyes. Double hell. This was Hunt, ambassador from the planet Uortzk.

Kelvin cursed his bad luck. He found Uortizks even more irritating than Kykanopians.

Uortizks were an old, more advanced race than Humans. And while they were indigenous to the Milky Way galaxy, their present planet was not the planet of origin. Rumor had it that the original Uortizk had been destroyed, possibly by the Uortizks themselves.

Massive, wooly creatures, these lifeforms were known for their underlying hostility toward Humans. Only one Uortizk currently visited Earth. Hunt would be attending the scheduled diplomatic conference as the Uortizk ambassador.

Kelvin inhaled deeply of the fragrant island air, then exhaled his frustration. As CEO, he had to extend the utmost consideration and diplomacy to any and all of the alien ambassadors.

He stepped back onto the grass and completed the distance to the bench. "Petra, here you are. I see you have met our distinguished visitor, Ambassador Hunt."

Kelvin crossed his fingers behind his back. The fact that Hunt wore his Human skin was a good sign. All visitors were aware that they needed to take extreme precautions with the natives. Terrans believed they were alone in the universe. It was Taurus City's intent and sacred trust that Terrans were allowed to remain ignorant.

But how had Hunt known she was not a staffer?

"Greetings, Kelvin Lacertus." Hunt stood and then bowed his large head. "We have had the pleasure of talking with one of your natives."

"My new employee," Kelvin corrected. "Petra will be instructing my nephew, Traynor."

"The Chairman's son. Yes, we have heard of the boy's arrival here."

Petra stood, her long skirt softly flowing about her ankles. "I hope you don't mind, Kelvin. I invited Hunt to the get-together."

"Not at all." Kelvin lied smoothly. "Ambassador Hunt is aware he is always welcome at appropriate agency functions."

As this event was Human only... and on the Human side of the island, Hunt was definitely not welcome. And he was cognizant of that fact, so why had he crashed the party? Perhaps the more urgent question was how had he left the alien section without sounding alarms?

The Uortizk's imitation Human face didn't reveal any answers.

"It grows late," Hunt rumbled. "We shall return to our quarters." He bowed. "Lady, Kelvin Lacertus."

With an agile leap, he bounded over the wall and strode out into the lush surrounding trees.

Petra brimmed full of questions. Kelvin knew the signs; she almost bubbled over with them. But he would have to deny her. Further talk would have to wait.

Kelvin extended his arm for her to take. "Let's walk back to the party."

She started to speak, but he forestalled her. "I have one call to make, and then we'll chat."

He pulled out his cell phone and punched Sergio's number. "Sergio, I'm with Petra." Meaning Kelvin couldn't talk freely. "A head's up. Ambassador Hunt showed up at the party, and is now returning to his quarters. Make sure he gets back safely."

By Sergio's intake of breath, he was just as shocked as Kelvin. Some careless security officer's head would roll tonight, that was certain.

Kelvin pocketed the phone. "Sorry. Business. Now, tell me why you left the festivities to be by yourself. Was one of my staffers rude?"

"Oh no. Not at all. Everyone's been very friendly." She fumbled with the decorative earring hanging from her earlobe as if she was nervous. "I guess it's just been such a long day. I should've made my regrets earlier and gone back to the bungalow. But I'll do that now."

A suspicion formed. Was she planning an assignation as Jade had theorized?

"It's late. I'll drive you, Petra."

"But then you'll have to walk back here."

He patted her hand. "Not to worry. I'll get someone to pick me up." *And keep watch on you.*

Reaching the gathering, Petra then made the rounds saying goodnight to those who remained.

Kelvin watched her for a moment, then stepped aside to redial his security chief. "Send an officer to pick me up at Petra's bungalow in ten minutes. And assign another one to make sure she doesn't leave. First thing tomorrow, Sergio, you'll brief me on just what the hell happened with the alien section's breach in security."

"Yes, sir."

Kelvin slipped the phone back into his pocket. The unaccustomed emotion of anger coursed through his veins. Something unheard of was happening at Taurus City. Something that set his teeth on edge. Something not aboveboard.

His jaw clenched, he waited for Petra to be done. Taking her arm, they walked over to her yellow car.

Chapter Four

Petra's first morning as Tray's tutor zipped by quickly, and so did lunch, which they both ate on the wraparound deck encircling Kelvin's magnificent house. The early hours were spent getting to know her new student's strengths. Now, as the sun shone through an afternoon haze, she prepared to take Tray down to the beach so he could burn off excess energy. Maybe after that, he would be ready for some quiet time.

The beach wasn't far. To her surprise, instead of a wide-open expanse of white sand, it was absolutely littered with large, noisy... and smelly sea lions. Since the animals had staked claim to the beach first, she and Tray carefully made their way around the creatures.

A series of honking greeted them. If Tray was to have quiet time, it certainly wouldn't be at this location.

He let go of her hand and then ran straight down to one of the more vocal seals looking their way. "My friend! My friend!" he called out.

Oh good gosh. Following as fast as she could on the uneven sand, Petra dodged sprawled out sea lions. She'd been advised by Kelvin's assistant Jade Dunbar that the animals were tame, but honestly, who could know that for sure? Seeing the little boy wrap his arms around the seal's long neck caused her heart to rise up in her throat.

She dropped to her bare knees and gently pulled Tray away from the sea lion. "Goodness, Tray. You look like you're choking the poor thing."

"No way." The boy patted the creature's sandy side. "Heckle's friendly. He likes me."

Heckle was friendly all right. She received a wet nose next to her cheek, along with a blast of fishy breath.

"This one's name is Heckle, is it? Then where's Jeckle?" She had to smile. The boy learned fast. Before yesterday, he'd never heard of the name Heckle.

To put some distance between her and the amorous sea lion, she stood, and then brushed sand from her bare knees.

An infectious grin lit up Tray's mischievous face. He twirled around with his arms outstretched, yelling, "All the other ones are Jeckle!"

"Naturally. How could it be otherwise?" She fondly ran her hand over his buzzed off hair, and then reached into her beachbag. "Here's your pail and shovel, Tray. Maybe you can find a fish treat for your pal."

"You bet!" He immediatly set to work, using his shovel to dig in the sand.

While he was occupied, she laid out a towel, sat, and then looked around. The waters of this protected bay were calm, beautifully turquoise, and obviously teeming with life. Every now and then a seagull swooped down to catch a fish.

She shivered. The temperature was in the low seventies, and although she wore shorts, she'd bundled up on top with a hoodie. Tray had stated he had no need of a sweatshirt, but she carried one all the same. Little boys were often positive about things one second, and then, just as positively, changed their minds the next.

Some time passed. She must've spaced out because a chorus of honking sea lions snapped her awake. Two men--one tall, the other stocky--walked along the shoreline splashing the water with their feet.

She did a double take. The tall man seemed to have a blue glow around the edges and the other one had bushy white hair and eyebrows. The color white was so vivid, it almost hurt her eyes to look at him.

Spotting her, they both waved, and then walked over to the beach towel. The tall man no longer had a glow.

She shook her head. She must've been mistaken. The sun probably had reflected the color of the turquoise water onto the man.

"Hello!" the tall one said. "It iss good to meet up with you. Are you a native? Iss the boy your child?"

Petra got to her feet. "No, actually I'm from New York, tutoring Traynor Lacertus."

The shorter man nodded. "The Chairman's son." Wearing crisp, clean linen shorts and shirt, he stood at attention. "I am Dutto, here to visit the wondrous sight known as the Grand Canyon. Such a monumental gash slashing into the innards of Xan... the Earth--I am agog to view it. So many of my compatriots have related to me about this masterpiece."

He paused, and his brilliant hair reflected the light of the sun. "The canyon is in your country, I believe. Am I correct, young woman?"

Although, relatively speaking, she was young, she hadn't been addressed as "young woman" in a very long time. "Yes, you're right, Dutton. The Grand Canyon is located in Arizona, in the northwestern corner of the state. I'm sure you'll love sightseeing there." She extended her hand. "I'm Petra, by the way."

The man's pale eyes widened and bushy eyebrows stood straight out as if he was alarmed. He darted his gaze over at his companion, and then looked back at her. His Adam's apple bobbed. "Delighted... to make your acquaintance," he muttered as he extended his hand for a shake.

His touch was cool. Cool enough to cause a chill to shimmy down her spine.

After contact, they both quickly disconnected.

"Petra iss a lovely name," the other man spoke up. "I am Oblan and I head for the bad caverns. Also in your place of origin, I believe."

She couldn't help smiling. "Yes, in New Mexico--the Carlsbad Caverns. It's nice to meet you, Oblan and Dutto. I hope you both enjoy your vacations."

"We thank you," Oblan said. "We are most eager to proceed. Ellen B. of Team North America hass been most helpful with the arrangements. And now, I believe we should go. Good day to you, Petra."

With that, both men inclined their heads and then returned to the shoreline of the beach.

Petra sat back down. Those men were strange. Very strange. She couldn't quite put her finger on what exactly made her uneasy about them. Was it that Dutto obviously hadn't wanted to shake her hand? Or that his bizarre eyebrows seemed to have a life of their own? Or was it Oblan's way of stressing the "s" in his speech? And what about that blue glow about him when she'd first seen him?

What countries did they come from? And since they were both headed for the southwestern U.S. states, why did they first travel to the Galápagos?

Tray looked up from his digging work and pointed a sandy finger in the direction of the stocky man. "He has chattering magpies where he's from."

"The one with the white hair? Dutto? What country is that, Tray?"

The boy shrugged, and then returned his attention back to the large hole he was digging. Dry sand had given way to oozy, silty mud. His puny arms were so covered with slime, it was a sure bet a bath or shower was in his future.

A few minutes later, she heard him mumble a word. "Serious." That was all he said.

Petra frowned. Was Tray referring to taking his digging seriously? Or was he answering her question?

She asked him what he meant, but he just shook his head and continued to pull out more ooze.

Serious. As far as she knew, there were no countries or cities named Serious. She thought a moment. Maybe he meant Dutto worked for Sirius SM Radio. Or...

A wild notion hit her. Maybe Tray meant the star Sirius. Also known as the Dog Star, Sirius was located in the constellation *Canis Major*. But why did that pop into her head? That was completely out of the realm of possibility.

Shrugging aside Tray's cryptic mumble, Petra lifted her face up to the sun in the hopes of getting a tan.

* * * *

Kelvin pushed his chair away from his desk, and then walked outside onto the office deck. The afternoon sun was low in the sky; it had been a long day. He leaned against the railing and allowed the salty sea breeze to revitalize him. As he took deep breaths, he reviewed what he had accomplished.

All in all, he was pleased. Security chief Sergio Iguana had ferreted out the breach that had allowed Hunt, the Uortizk ambassador, to leave the alien section undetected. One of Sergio's officers, a new recruit from colony planet Bokar, had, to use a Terran colloquialism, screwed up. The officer was now on administrative leave pending a more thorough investigation. Additional training for every officer in the field was also scheduled.

However, no harm, no foul. And although Kelvin had wanted to spend the day with his nephew and the Terran Petra Richardson, the rest of the time had flown by with the usual assortment of activities. Plus an array of out-of-the-ordinary activities as well. Preparation for the conference, scheduled to begin four days from now, kept everyone fully engaged.

He shrugged. He'd make an effort to visit with Tray and his teacher tomorrow. Now he needed to relieve his restlessness with something pleasurable. A game of tennis, perhaps? A brisk swim? A roll in the hay, to use another descriptive Terran phrase?

The intercom buzzed from the box on his desk. Kelvin walked back inside and pressed a button. "Yes?"

"The Velan Tarrnak is most insistent to see you, sir," Jade Dunbar's voice interrupted the silence. "He just returned from a visit to the Himalayas and claims he has valuable information for you. He refuses to speak with anyone else."

Velans came from the Velorum star system, located in the Vela Constellation, Beta Quadrant. Natives were hairless Humanoids with velvety green skin, but what truly set them apart was that their race was strongly psychic. If a Velan wanted to speak, a person would be foolish not to listen.

Kelvin wasn't foolish. "Have Tarrnak come in."

Jade escorted the Velan inside the office, then lifted her russet eyebrow. He knew her well enough to decipher the gesture. She was asking if he wanted her to stay.

He didn't. "You may go now, Jade. Please see that Tarrnak and I aren't interrupted. Thank you."

Although she wasn't pleased, she obeyed. Pressing her honey-colored lips together, she then exited the room and closed the door.

As soon as the click of the door sounded, Tarrnak's Terran façade shimmered away. He stepped out of his Human skin suit and now stood in front of the desk in his natural form. Of medium height, he hunched over as if readying to sprint into a run. He was upset; anyone who was aware of Velan physiology knew the signs. A glowing greenish shroud faintly covered his face while an unpleasant earthy odor emanated from his pores.

"Please, have a seat, Tarrnak." Kelvin pressed another button and the sliding glass door closed. "My office is secure. Have no fear that our discussion will be overheard." He motioned to the nearby chair. "Tell me what distresses you. Did something disagreeable occur on your Himalayan trip?"

The Velan took several gulps before speaking. His velvety skin rippled as the air flowed through his body. "Not the beauty of the mountains that disturbs. Nor the frigid cold and burning white heat of this star shining on the sacred Himalayas." As he shook his bald green head, the shroud dissipated, revealing the intensity of his bright green eyes. "No, 'tis a warning for you, sir, that I bear. For you, for the Lacertus family."

"Indeed?" Kelvin maintained a calm visage but fisted his hands under the desk. "Go on, please."

"The majestic mountains provide space for deep meditation. 'Tis well known among my people. These surroundings, along with the thin atmosphere on this paradise, permitted a message to come through to me. 'Tis about the boy, your nephew. He is in danger. In danger along with his mother."

Kelvin could sit no longer. He paced the large area in front of the bank of windows. For several seconds he composed himself before speaking. "You are unaware of Moriah Lacertus' recent goodwill mission. It ended tragically. An internal flaw in the Hawken engines allowed matter to mix with anti-matter. The ship exploded, killing everyone onboard."

A shudder zapped its way down his spine. "It was an accident."

"My condolences, sir, however, are you certain 'twas an accident?"

Hell. What a thing for Tarrnak to say. The official investigation sited an unstable core in the Hawken engine. Without correction, the volatile core would degenerate... and so it had. It had been Moriah and fifty other brave souls' fate to suffer the consequences. No blame had been attached to the crew. The manufacturer paid a hefty fine, but that was all. Wilhelm, his brother, had accepted the findings of the report.

Kelvin faced the Velan. "What, exactly, was the message you received?"

Tarrnak spread out the palms of his lime green hands. "Only that the boy--Traynor, is it?--is in danger. I regret I did not know his mother had already passed into the beyond."

"You mentioned me as well. And the Lacertus family, which also means my brother."

"Allow me to reflect, sir, so I may recall the exact phrasing."

The Velan closed his eyes and then hummed in a low tone. Evidently that was his way to concentrate. After a moment, when he opened his eyes, it was as if a bright emerald jewel had burst into existence. "Yes, 'tis as you say. Your family succession to the chairmanship of Taurus City is at risk." Tarrnak lowered his gleaming gaze. "'Tis all I know, most hallowed sir. All I know."

"I thank you, Tarrnak." Kelvin returned to his desk. "If you receive any additional messages, please, do not hesitate to contact me."

"Of course, sir." The Velan bowed, and then stepped into his Human skin. All at once, his image fizzled, then steadied. He appeared as a normal Human. He then left the office.

Analyzing this information would have to wait. First and foremost was Traynor's safety. Kelvin contacted Sergio and ordered protection for the boy--two officers to hover near him around the clock.

Next, he put in a request for a call to Tau Ceti 3 to speak with his brother. Because of the vast distances involved, communication wasn't automatic, however, using positron technology, he was assured of speaking with Will by the end of the day.

Kelvin drummed his fingers against the desktop. For the moment, he would not share the Velan's information with anyone. He would, though, speak with Petra so she would not be taken aback by the bodyguards.

He himself had to be on the alert. For some reason, now, after countless millennia of his ancestors overseeing this paradise for aliens, some entity desired an end to the Lacertus reign. As it stood, he trusted no one outside the family. Everyone was suspect.

He paused. What about Petra? Surely she didn't have a hidden agenda.

But what about last night? Her private one-to-one with the Uortizk? Although she hadn't left her bungalow after Kelvin had dropped her off, he was still troubled by the ease with which she had talked to Hunt. Uortizks were notoriously poor conversationalists.

As Kelvin had surmised, he couldn't trust anyone.

* * * *

Petra rang the doorbell on Tray's large white house with him persistently hopping by her side. He hadn't rested at the beach, nor had he stopped his perpetual motion all afternoon. It was a sure bet that when bedtime came, he'd hit the pillow fast asleep.

"I like you, Petra." He gazed up at her with his dark grey eyes. He blinked once, then twice.

Oh dear. The little boy looked as if he was going to burst into tears.

She got down on her knees and enveloped him in a hug. "I like you, too, Tray. We had fun today, didn't we? We'll do it again tomorrow, okay?"

He buried his face at the base of her neck. "'Suppose so," he mumbled.

Allowing him to remain against her for a long minute, she then pulled away and kissed him on the forehead. "I *know* so. I'll see you bright and early at ten?"

"Nine," he countered.

"Nine thirty, then." She laughed. "You drive a hard bargain."

Georges opened the door. He was an impressive man--young, imposing, built like a rock. His somber face immediately split into a grin, then dropped back into seriousness. "Young sir, the nanny, she looks for you."

He then focused his razor sharp gaze on Petra. "You are late, *mademoiselle.*"

She felt chastised. "I know. We were just in the back, though. We couldn't tear ourselves away from the swings. I hope Conni wasn't too upset."

Georges made a continental shrug with his huge shoulders. *"Alors,* I shall pacify that one." He held out his wide hand. "Come inside now, young sir, and I take you to Conni. Your uncle will be back *immédiatement.*"

With his head down, Tray slowly walked through the doorway, dragging his feet. As he reached the staircase, he turned around to look at her.

"See you at nine thirty," she called out.

Georges inclined his shorn head. "Have no fear, *mademoiselle,* the boy will be ready."

The door closed with a click.

Now she was left with the age-old question: what should she have for dinner? Returning to her yellow bug of a car, she pondered her dilemma.

Another vehicle--boldly bright red and a bit larger than her convertible--pulled alongside hers in the parking area. There could be no mistaking its dashing driver: Kelvin Lacertus himself.

Getting out of the driver's seat, he walked around and stood next to her. "Hello, I hoped you'd still be here, Petra. How was your first day? I apologize for not joining you today."

He was dressed business casual--khaki slacks and pullover shirt. She still wore her shorts and hoodie. It was easy to feel at a disadvantage standing next to Mr. Suave-and-Dreamy.

"The first day was great. Tray is such a darling little boy. We had a good time. I'm sure he'll be used to me by the end of the week."

"But of course he will. You're easy to get used to," Kelvin murmured, living up to her nickname for him. "I've an idea. Let's have dinner together and you can tell me all about Tray's endearing ways."

When he smiled, the left side of his mouth lifted a notch higher than the right. Somehow, she got the impression that he was mocking her.

"No, thank you. I--"

"You must eat, Petra." He leaned against his car and folded his arms across his appealing chest. "And I must have a report on my nephew's progress."

He had a point. "Dinner here?" Nervously twirling the hoodie string, she glanced over at the house. Again, she grew uneasy. Maybe she feared she was ripe for seduction.

His smile deepened. "No. In town there's an excellent seafood restaurant called The Shining C. Its grilled lobster will melt in your mouth."

His words, though innocent, made her lick her lips. If only *she* could melt in his mouth.

Petra Richardson, behave!

"Okay, that sounds... good. I'll just freshen up and be back in a half hour."

His dark eyebrow lifted. "The restaurant isn't formal. No place on the island is. But certainly, go ahead and change. However, I'll pick you up."

That probably made more sense, so she agreed. "Fine. I won't be long."

He opened the car door, waited until she was settled, and then closed it. "Thirty minutes, Petra."

As she drove away, she couldn't help feeling a bit like a lobster ensnared in its trap. No matter what the lobster did, it ended up defeated... ended up being eaten.

* * * *

The Shining C was a busy place. Maybe because there were so few restaurants on the island. People congregated around small bamboo tables outside on the patio while others sat inside, under a palm frond trellis, open on the sides to the cool ocean breezes.

Petra chose the inside accommodations. A roof of palm trees swaying overhead, the rhythmic beat of Latin music vibrating on the sea air, and a potent tropical drink in her hand, she sighed her contentment. This was living.

"What a beautiful place. Dining under the stars, yet protected when it rains." It was still dusk, so only a handful of stars could be seen, but as the night progressed, the heavenly display promised to be spectacular.

"I'm glad you like it." Kelvin sat back in his curved chair. "Our head chef, Niko Starling, designed it himself. He aims to please."

Kelvin had changed his shirt to a long sleeved cotton pullover. He looked endearingly casual and confident, as if he were the captain of a small boat, working the sails in his deck shoes.

The cool gusts of sea air made her glad she'd chosen a sweater reaching down to mid-thigh to wear over her jeans. High heels and dangly earrings dressed up the outfit. The afternoon sun had tanned her face, giving her a bronze glow.

Feeling secure in her appearance, she smiled, and lifted her fancy alcoholic drink. "Well, if what the chef concocts is as tasty as this chi chi, then I'm definitely returning to The Shining C."

He smiled back, and then circled his index fingertip over the top of her hand. "I'm certain you'll enjoy the food. Everyone does, no matter where they're from."

Discreetly, she slid her hand away from his, and then hid it on her lap, under the table. This chi chi drink was potent enough without adding in Kelvin's intoxicating pheromones.

Fortunately, the server arrived and they placed their orders. With that out of the way, Kelvin said, "So tell me about my prodigy nephew."

As she related her observations, she sipped her drink and idly glanced around at the other patrons. A few she recognized from last night's dinner party. Owen Greenacre, the mature Operations Director, sat at the far end of the restaurant. He tickled the earlobe of one of the Ellens from the travel department.

Which Ellen was it? There had to be a physical clue to tell the women apart.

Haughty Valli Proximus was also present. She sat perched on a bar stool, passing the time with another one of the identical Ellens. Goodness, did the sisters go through life wearing nametags?

Petra then shifted her gaze to Jade Dunbar, who was engrossed in a conversation with curly-haired Todd Boiler, the deliciously handsome finance director.

Nibbling on her drink's garnish--a chunk of pineapple--Petra frowned. So many of the men she'd met here at Taurus City were deliciously handsome. It was almost as if a disclaimer had been posted on job applications: average-looking specimens need not apply.

"Why are you frowning, Petra? Has your drink suddenly soured?"

"Oh, no. Sorry. I just..." She felt heat rise to her cheeks. She couldn't mention what, exactly, she'd been thinking. "Well, you know, I was wondering about the Ellens. There are six of them, aren't there? How in the world does anyone tell them apart?"

Kelvin's rich chuckle caused many a restaurant patron to glance his way. He finished his drink--a vodka tonic--and then signaled for another. "Forgive me, my dear. I needed that laugh. A rather difficult day today, to be sure. However, your question is a very astute one, and I must confess, to my shame, I have no idea."

He caught a dark man's eye three tables over, and then gestured. The man, also handsome and probably in his fifties, excused himself from his companion--a hulky looking woman with a fierce demeanor, massive muscles, and lots of oddly shaped tattoos--and walked over to Kelvin.

Petra hadn't met the man before.

"Blasted inopportune time to be interrupted, Kelvin," the man huffed. "I was making headway with the Brhite."

"The Brit," Kelvin quickly corrected. "Your pronunciation is atrocious, Doctor. It's a good thing Ms. Richardson isn't an English teacher."

"Ah, yes." The man darted his gaze from Kelvin to her, and then made a formal bow. "The intrepid Ms. Richardson. I'm Cornwall Young, medical practitioner of these Galápagos parts. Very pleased to meet you."

She returned the handshake. "Happy to meet you, too, Doctor."

Kelvin cut in. "We won't keep you, Doc, but Petra has an excellent question concerning the Ellens. How does one tell them apart?"

The doctor rubbed his hand over his heavy five o'clock shadow. "Y'know, that's a trillion dollar question, but I've figured it out, so I'll tell you. It's the smell. Each Ellen has a distinctive scent."

He turned and sniffed in the direction of the bar. "The one with Valli is Ellen F. from Team Australia. She reeks of peppermint. As for the Ellen ol' Owen's trying to hit on, she's Ellen E., Team Europe. I'd describe her as mango flavored."

Petra breathed in both peppermint and tropical fruit. "You're right! That's amazing."

The doctor tapped on his broad nostril. "Not a big deal, child. Good olfactory senses."

Kelvin cleared his throat. "Thank you for your assistance, Doc. Here's our food now. I'm sure you're eager to get back to your British companion."

"Absolutely. I'm gonna git." He waved his hand. "See you around, Petra."

She waited until the doctor returned to his table before speaking. "He's very nice. I like him."

Kelvin set his napkin in his lap. "Cornwell is a valuable member of the team."

Lackluster praise. She shrugged, then took a bite of grilled lobster. The lobster *did* melt in her mouth. Heavenly.

Another sip of chi chi put her in an expansive mood. "I have another question I hope you don't mind answering."

"Indeed?" He speared a piece of broccoli. "Your curiosity astonishes me. What now tickles your fancy?"

"On the beach this afternoon, I met two men, Dutto and Oblan. They didn't give their last names and I didn't ask where they're from. They both plan to travel to the States--Arizona and New Mexico, respectively. So my question is why are they starting their trip here, in the Galápagos?"

Kelvin lifted his eyebrow. "The tall fellow and the cold one, eh? They both, as do many of our clients, have certain special needs that we at Taurus City are equipped to handle. We pride ourselves on providing exactly what our customers require. So, yes, our clients travel here first, get set up, and then continue out on their scheduled itinerary. Does that answer your question?"

It didn't, really, but she let it slide. Special needs, he'd said. What kinds of special needs? She slowly looked around the dining room again, specifically at the people who hadn't attended last night's get-together. Maybe they were clients of the travel agency.

She focused on the doctor's dinner guest--the Brhite, he'd called her, then corrected by Kelvin as the Brit. The woman did look unusually muscular and fierce. Maybe she was a professional weight lifter. She was also incredibly flexible. The angle of her elbow stretched to an almost impossible angle as she scratched her back.

Interesting.

She continued her perusal. The happy couple two tables over looked completely functional. A man and woman finished their meal, made some small talk, and then he gallantly assisted her from her chair. Walking toward the exit, they passed by Petra's table.

"Deliciouss," the man exclaimed to Kelvin as the couple walked by. "Ssimply deliciouss."

Maybe they came from the same place as Oblan. But speech impediments didn't require special facilities.

Darting her gaze to a man dressed in amber, she watched him dip his spoon into soup. He appeared to find the action funny, especially when he lifted the spoon to his mouth.

"How very quaint," she heard him say to his companion, a bald man with a slightly mossy color.

What special needs could either of those gentlemen require? While she believed Kelvin--sort of, anyway--she wasn't quite convinced.

A small smile played about Kelvin's lips. "I see you are scrutinizing some of our clients. Trying to discern their needs, are you? Take a look over there." He nodded toward the outside patio where four very tall people sat.

Two men and two women were very slender as if they had no muscle mass whatsoever. When the server brought them a round of drinks, they all pinched their lips together, obviously displeased... but with what? The server?

"As you see, this group--I call them the Peacocks--have extreme attitudes. Very difficult to work with. And since the men usually top seven feet, accommodations have to be tailored to suit them."

"Yes, they are tall. Where do they come from?"

"The Philippines. One of the inner islands, I forget which one."

This was a perfect lead in for another of her questions. "What about you, Kelvin? Where are you from?"

He lifted that quizzical eyebrow again. "Me? My family is originally from Ethiopia, but I've lived all over. Quite the wanderlust in my soul."

"Wow. Ethiopia. Very exotic." And unanticipated. Then again, so much about Kelvin was unusual. She dapped her lips with her napkin, then set it down. "So tell me, what was your favorite place on your Grand Tour of Earth?"

He also set his napkin down, signaling the end of the meal. "Petra, my dear girl. You ask the most interesting questions. Would you care for dessert?"

"No, thank you. The answer to my question?"

"Obviously it was the Bronx, in that junior high school where I first saw you." His deep grey eyes broadcasted his amusement.

She almost snorted. "Right. Sure. I believe you. I really do." He was a smooth operator. All fluff and no substance. Just like Bob.

As Kelvin laughed, he clapped his hand over his heart. "You wound me. But enough about me, Petra. What about you?"

She was saved from answering by the bald fellow who had sat with the amber gentleman. The man stood by the table and smiled at them.

"Greetings, sir, and lovely lady. 'Tis glad I am to see you enjoying your dinner, sir. I had feared my earlier news would disrupt your equilibrium."

Kelvin's nostrils flared. He glanced at her, and then calmly said, "Petra, this is Tarrnak, from... Venezuela. He's just returned from the Himalayas."

"A sacred journey. I am much pleased with the majestic mountains." Tarrnak bowed. "I leave you both now to continue your sumptuous repast."

The man scuttled back to his table.

Petra was being nosy. She knew it, but couldn't help it. "What bad news was Tarrnak referring to?"

Lines of worry etched Kelvin's forehead. He leaned in across the table and held her with his intense gaze. "In truth, this is something I wanted to discuss with you since it concerns Traynor. My nephew may be in some danger. You do understand this is just between you and me."

"Oh! Yes, of course." She hadn't expected anything like this.

"Good. The boy is my brother's sole heir. And Wilhelm, as you know, is our Taurus City Chairman. It is Tarrnak's opinion that the boy may come to harm. To that end, I have assigned two bodyguards to keep watch over him. You will see the officers tomorrow, however they will be inconspicuous and will not interfere with your teaching time."

He took both her hands and then trailed his thumbpads over the tops of her knuckles. She was so stunned by his news that she allowed him this privilege.

"You will be safe, Petra. I promise you."

Her mind reeled, and although she'd been comfortable before, now she felt frightfully cold. "Is there... is there anything I should do specifically? Any place on the island to stay away from?"

"The officers will oversee your safety. If a location isn't secure, they will let you know." His voice deepened and his grey eyes darkened to charcoal. "I don't want you to be worried. If you like, I would be honored to spend the night with you."

Was he serious? "I'm not worried. Not about myself, anyway." She pulled her hands away. "Thank you for dinner and for the information about Tray. I'll be sure to be on my guard."

She moved her chair away from the table. "Shall we go? Tomorrow morning will be here before we know it."

Kelvin smiled enigmatically, and then stood to help her from her chair. "As you wish, my dear girl. I look forward to tomorrow."

Petra wasn't so sure she looked forward to tomorrow. First, there was an intimation of danger. Second, a not so subtle attempt at gaining access to her bed.

As they walked out of the restaurant, once again, she regretted her decision to accept this position. What in the world had she gotten herself into?

Chapter Five

It was difficult to stay grumpy when surrounded by nature's beauty. After the morning lesson--focusing on some of Ecuador's customs, the country to which the Galápagos Islands belonged--Petra took Tray on an invigorating hike to a nearby hill. With a little huffing and puffing, they reached the summit.

The breathtaking views of the coastline were well worth the exercise. Below, the sparkling turquoise waters dazzled the eyes, but on land and in the skies the vistas were just as magnificent. Overhead, riding the wind, were large black birds--frigate birds--with their wings spanning over six or seven feet. In the breeding season, the males would balloon out their vivid red throat pouches to attract females. The mating season must've been over for their pouches remained deflated, but the birds were still glorious to watch.

Populating the ground a short distance away were the adorable blue-footed boobies with their large blue-webbed feet and long blue beaks. Every now and then a male, smaller than the female, would lift his feet high and spread out his wings--his mating dance. Oftentimes, the female would walk away, unimpressed.

Petra smiled. She should remember that. Just because a male tried to attract her didn't mean she had to take him up on his offer. But aside from nature's Love-For-The-Forlorn lesson, truly, this place was a birdwatcher's paradise.

But as it frequently happened, paradise contained a hidden snake. Danger... danger for Tray.

She glanced down at Tray, who was studying the progress of an on-the-prowl iguana, and then looked over where one guard, Bjorn, sat under a prickly pear cactus. He was a big man, crew-cut blond and sharp-eyed. He must've noticed her staring, for he lifted a large hand to acknowledge her.

She nodded back. Across from Bjorn was the second guard, Raulf. He was more restless than his partner, and had the slim body type to go along with it. Raulf paced the expanse of the summit, darting his dark eyes back and forth over the rocky protrusions.

Petra should've felt safe under the guards' protection. But feeling safe was all a matter of perception. A gunshot could ring out from a nearby cliff. Any number of unanticipated threats could occur. She kept her own vigil, keeping a watchful eye on her bright young charge.

She settled down in a cross-legged position. "Now Tray, let's go over what we just learned. When we meet someone from Ecuador, how do we greet them?"

"Buenas tardes," he replied without taking his gaze off the lizard.

"If it's afternoon, yes, wonderful. And if it's in the morning?"

"Buenos días."

"Right again. And at night?"

"Buenos nachos! With plenty of cheese!" The boy turned to her and grinned. "I'm hungry, Petra."

She had to laugh. "It's *noches,* silly. But I do understand. I'm hungry, too. How about if we have ourselves a delicious picnic lunch?"

She'd come prepared. Or rather Niko Starling, Taurus City's tall and rotund head chef, had prepared for her and Tray. Although she couldn't be sure, it seemed like every culinary delight possible was jammed into a very heavy portable cooler. It even contained cheesy nachos.

There was certainly enough food for her, a little boy, and two overgrown bodyguards.

Taking one more look around, Petra spread the lightweight blanket over grassy ground, half in the shade and half in the sun. Her tummy growled in anticipation. Surrounded by the island's gorgeous scenery, she looked forward to a picnic lunch that she'd never forget.

* * * *

Kelvin climbed this nearby hillside so often during his tour of duty here that he felt comfortable doing so without paying attention. Adjusting his sunglasses and setting his sports cap tightly on his head, he forged ahead on autopilot, his thoughts occupied by more important matters.

Matters like his talk with Will last night. As difficult as it had been to give his brother the Velan's message, Kelvin had had no choice. Will was at risk. Could be at risk, along with Tray and Kelvin.

Naturally, the news that Moira's death was, perhaps, not an accident caused Will to age ten years.

But Will hadn't panicked either, thank the stars. He'd gamely acknowledged the possibility of treason. Perhaps at the hands of the anti-establishment faction--the Continuers--that had grown exceedingly vociferous as of late. "I'll investigate this on my end. Clandestinely, of course. And you handle matters on Terra. Do you need reinforcements?" Will had asked.

"No. I've increased security measures. Sergio Iguana, our chief, is the best in the field. Two of his finest are guarding Traynor at all times."

"Take care of my son, Kel. He's all I have left of dearest Moira."

The anguish in his grieving brother's voice had nearly ripped Kelvin in two.

Sounds drifted toward him from over the summit. A child's giggle, a woman's laughter, and a man's deep chuckle.

Kelvin increased his pace to reach the top. A scene of domestic bliss greeted him. Tray and Petra laughed at the guard Bjorn's attempt at finger puppets using two of the disposable paper cups.

A stab of jealousy lanced through Kelvin. He should've been the one entertaining his nephew. And winning over the delectable Ms. Richardson.

As Kelvin walked toward them, he shook off his irrational emotion. The only thing that mattered was everyone's safety.

The other guard, Raulf, stationed on a high rock, acknowledged Kelvin's approach. Kelvin nodded at the man and then stood, looming over the seated trio.

"Good afternoon. I am glad you are enjoying yourselves on this fine day."

"*Buenas tardes,* Uncle Kel," Tray was quick to reply.

The guard dropped the cups and got to his feet, red-faced. "Sir," he mumbled. He then resumed his post at a nearby distance.

Petra watched him leave, then turned her smile toward Kelvin. "We just had lunch, but there's plenty left if you'd like to eat."

He sat in the vacated spot. "Thanks. I apologize for not joining you sooner. This and that came up. You know how it goes." He turned to Tray. "Good job with the Spanish."

The boy handed him a burrito roll. "I've learned a lot, Uncle Kel. As host, I say to you, *buen provecho,* enjoy! Now you're supposed t'start eating."

Tray sounded so mature. Kelvin sighed. Moira would've been proud. *"Gracias, muchacho.* A burrito is exactly what I wanted for lunch."

"Cool beans!" The boy's gaze darted in another direction. "I gotta go. I see a tiny dinosaur." Evidently he was hot on the trail of a marine iguana, *Amblyrhynchus cristatus,* warming itself on a ledge overhanging the summit.

"Certainly, Tray." Petra glanced at the boy as he scurried away.

Kelvin gestured to the nearer guard, Bjorn, to move in closer to the boy.

Petra released a long breath. "Good. Thank you. Your nephew can move very quickly. Sometimes he makes me anxious."

"Indeed. Tray is an impetuous child." Kelvin devoured the burrito. He then took the cup of iced tea that she offered. "My thanks. So, Petra, I thought we would do a little kayaking this afternoon. It's a fine day, and there's nothing more invigorating than paddling through these crystal waters amidst the island's abundant marine life."

Her eyes widened. "With Tray? Aren't the waters brimming with sharks?"

"Sure. Hammerheads and whites, beautiful creatures, really. Plus a variety of rays. But we'll be in the kayak, not the water."

As fast as a lightning bolt, Tray was back. He wrapped himself around Kelvin in a tight hug. "Oh, can we, Uncle Kel? I love kayaking! I love sharks! Can we?"

It was obvious from Petra's body language that she was reluctant. With her gaze lowered, she worried her lower lip. "Well, ah, are you sure it's safe?"

"Absolutely."

"Yay!" The boy freed Kelvin from bondage and then darted over to both guards to brag about the upcoming adventure.

Kelvin stood and held out his hand to help her up. "There's nothing to fret about, my dear girl. If, by chance, we do tip over, our life vests are highly rated. So buoyant, they practically lift a person out of the water."

In truth, the specially designed Taurus City life vests did elevate wearers completely out of the cold ocean, but Petra didn't need to know that.

"I'll make arrangements so the kayaks will be set up. One for the three of us, two for the guards. We'll bring provisions, too. Being on the water makes one hungry. And Tray does like to eat." Kelvin pulled out his cell phone. "In case we get soaked, which we will, towels and dry clothing will be waiting on shore. My assistant has our sizes. What do you say?"

Petra brushed wrinkles from her shorts. "I say okay then. Why not? Sounds like fun, except for the sharks."

Kelvin grinned. "You only have to worry about the ones that swim on the land." Giving her a wink, he pressed in Jade's number.

* * * *

All Petra could say was "Wow." Absolutely and totally wow. Leisurely paddling in calm shallow waters flowing between the sides of a high-walled lava gorge, she eagerly took in the beauty of her surroundings above and below the waterline. It was so peaceful and serene here. Every worry, every trouble vanished as if it had never been.

She inhaled deeply. She had no idea how long she, Kelvin, and Tray had paddled. Nor did she care. Each moment stretched out to infinity. It was a place she never wanted to leave.

"Look!" Tray crowed as he pointed down to the left. "I see a shark."

Was it? Could it be? A shiver traveled down Petra's spine, but she bravely glanced over in that direction to spot something--large and grey--swim past them.

"Yikes, that was huge," she managed to murmur as she straightened her position. One *never* leaned over the sides in a kayak. Leaning over meant taking a dive--literally.

"Just a baby. Probably looking for its mother," Kelvin, seated in front of her, replied.

He was kidding, obviously. That shark had to have been ten feet long.

"He was a baby?" Tray, in front of his uncle, asked.

"Well, okay, a juvenile then. Whites, or *Carcharodon carcharias*, can grow to more than six meters." Kelvin then added, "That's twenty feet," probably for her benefit.

Some juvenile. Petra chomped on her chewing gum. What if the shark had decided to bump into the kayak?

She peered over at Raulf, paddling in front, and Bjorn bringing up the rear. Given a shark's speed, they'd all be mincemeat by the time the guards arrived.

Calm down, Petra. The shark's gone. There's nothing but eagle rays, mullets, and sea lizards in the water.

Whoa. Something very odd looking just swam by. If she didn't know any better, she would've said it was one of those little pool cleaners, propelled by a thin rubbery hose.

"Kelvin." She bent forward to speak into his ear. "I just saw a small compact creature with a rubber-like tail swishing about in the water. What could it have been?"

He turned his head to speak over his shoulder. "Hmmn, let me think. Maybe it was a longtail stingray, *Dasyatis longa*. They often flock to this area to feed."

The thing she'd spotted hadn't resembled a stingray, but then again, she'd only seen it in a flash. And, given that this was the birthplace of Darwin's evolution theory, perhaps it *was* a type of stingray.

She shrugged. No matter. Time passed by in a haze. She enjoyed watching frigate birds and finches overhead and the sea lions and sea turtles sunning themselves on the nearby lava rock. When her courage held, she gazed down at the water show below.

They'd been fortunate not to get frequently splashed, so when unexpected wetness seeped onto the bottom of her feet, she yelped. "Oh! Omigosh, there's water bubbling into the kayak."

"The devil! You're right." Kelvin quickly anchored his oar, and looked down. "Where's it coming in? This is a fiberglass hull. There shouldn't be a leak."

But there was, of course. Petra found a small hole on the side by her right foot.

"Are we sinking?" Tray chirped. By his excitement, she knew he wasn't frightened. This was an adventure. If the kayak went under, well, that would be a thrill, wouldn't it?

Not to her.

"No sinking. Not today." Kelvin blew the whistle he had around his neck, attracting the guards' attention, then he signaled them to approach. Calmly, but with command in his tone, he ordered, "Tray, you'll go with Bjorn, and Petra, you'll transfer over to Raulf."

AN ALIEN PARADISE by Susanne Marie Knight

The boy stuck out his lower lip. He obviously wasn't pleased with the proposed arrangement. Petra was reluctant as well, but not for the same reason. The thought of transferring from one kayak to another-- mid-stream--scared the living bejesus out of her.

Bjorn arrived first. Kelvin explained, "We've got a slow leak. No danger, but take the boy. We're returning to the launch point."

The guard nodded his blond head and assisted Tray. Although the pout remained, the boy obeyed his uncle. The relocation was accomplished seamlessly. Handing Tray a paddle, Bjorn turned the kayak back in the direction they'd started from.

Good. Now she'd have some time to plead her case. Before Raulf pulled his kayak in alongside them, Petra placed her hand on Kelvin's muscular shoulder. "I have an idea. How about if I plug the hole with my gum? It'll slow the leak. Maybe even stop it."

"Excellent plan." As Kelvin smiled at her, his grey eyes crinkled. "You are quite resourceful, my dear."

She felt herself flush. "Well, I have a favor to ask. If you don't mind, I'd rather stay here with you. Crossing the great divide like this, with whatever is swimming below us, is scaring me silly."

"Nonsense. You'd do fine, but I confess I would miss your company. So while you plug the hole, I'll tell Raulf what's going on."

She removed the wad of gum, then felt the kayak's pinky sized hole. Not a problem, really, except... except that the edges of the opening were smooth, not jagged. Meaning that the hole was most likely drilled, bored through. Deliberate, malicious, with evil intent.

She shivered again. Just what in the world was going on in Taurus City?

* * * *

At the dock, Kelvin got off the boat first. Exiting out of a kayak took some practice. If not done correctly, a person could easily tip over, body and pride thoroughly dunked. He didn't want Petra to suffer through that. Before she had a chance to make a mistake, he leaned down, placed his hands on her ribs, lifted, and then set her down on the sturdy wooden platform.

"Oh, I didn't expect... ah, thank you." She stepped away, turning a glowing shade of rosy pink that almost matched her crimson hoodie.

His hands tingled from their contact. There was something about this

71

Terran woman that enflamed his every sensation, every blasted cell in his body.

He flared his nostrils. Now was not the time nor place to indulge in sophomoric romance. Not with evidence of sabotage right under his nose.

"Perhaps you should take Tray back to the house to clean up. I have a few things here to look into, then I'll join you for dinner around six."

She adjusted her sunglasses. "Sorry, I've already made plans to eat with Felicia tonight. Some other time, okay?"

"Certainly. Some other time." Kelvin fisted his hands. Hell, he'd handled that wrong, hadn't he?

He'd never had a woman turn down his invitations. And for what? To dine with another woman? Terran Felicia Alvarez, of all people?

Sobering.

Nodding dismissal, he then eased back down into the kayak. He watched Petra walk over to his nephew and give him a hug. Tray must've been tired for then she picked him up, his dark head resting against her slim shoulder.

Lucky boy.

But Kelvin had more important matters to think about. Removing Petra's gum, he felt the edges of the hole. Without a doubt, it had been intentionally drilled.

Hell.

He hadn't planned to go kayaking today. It had been a spur of the moment idea. No one knew of the plans except for him, Petra, Traynor, and the two guards. Along with Jade and whoever prepared the equipment.

He called his assistant, and learned Human Relation's Joe Hammer and Felicia Alverez, Operations' Owen Greenacre, and Team North America's Ellen B. had overheard the conversation. Which meant any or all staff members could have found out about the excursion.

Terminating the call, Kelvin then punched in Sergio Iguana's number. Security would have to be further increased. Especially with the diplomatic conference starting on Friday.

His decision was made. He would accept Wilhelm's offer of reinforcements.

Chapter Six

It was now Thursday afternoon, which meant, as Petra understood, most of the diplomatic conference members should have already arrived. Not that the big hullabaloo had anything to do with her. After all, she wasn't attending. Hadn't been invited. Not on the Christmas card list.

But oddly enough, irrationally, she couldn't help but feel left out.

She sighed. From where she sat in the great backyard of Kelvin's estate, no extraneous commotion could be heard. Ocean waves crashed on the nearby beach, sea lions honked up a storm as usual, and that was about all she heard. Yesterday and this morning had passed by quickly and peacefully.

And no additional threats to Tray's safety had occurred.

Thankfully. Tuesday's leaky kayak had raised several red flags of alarm, but she had no close friends here on the island to confide in and talk away her fears. Sure, she got along well with Felicia, and if she needed something, the Taurus City staff was happy to accommodate her. But open up to anyone about this apprehensive feeling she had?

Nope. There was no one. Not even Kelvin, whom she'd semi-fantasized about. Maybe she'd been mistaken but hadn't there been a hint of a romance developing with them?

Emphasis on "hint of." Ever since the aborted sightseeing trip, she hadn't seen him close up and personal. He maintained a chilly distance. Obviously she shouldn't have refused his dinner invitation quite so bluntly.

Then again, she had to be fair. Everything wasn't all about her. Kelvin, along with most of the staff, had their plates filled to overflowing as they prepared for this multinational conference.

Tray sat by her side under the shade of a leafy palm tree next to the lava rock wall. Usually, he liked to have his lessons out by the beach, but not today. Today, for some reason, he wanted to stick close to home.

From her supply bag, Petra removed a globe of Earth and held it out in front of her. She gave it a spin. "Okay, so far we've talked about Ecuador, Norway, Ethiopia--where your family is originally from, and the United States. Pick a place and we'll focus on that country next."

With his gaze dropped, the boy shrugged. A more accurate expression was that he drooped, which was very peculiar--for Traynor.

"Are you okay, honey?"

Nodding, he extended his lower lip in a pout.

She set down the globe, and then placed her hand on his forehead. Did he have a fever?

He pulled away from her touch.

"Do you want to tell me what's bothering you, Tray?"

It was as if he had been waiting for her to ask. With a leap, he got to his feet, then zoomed back and forth in front of her with his arms flying. "It's not fair. Not fair! He won't let me go."

"Who won't let you go where?"

"T'the conference." Tray said the words as if she should've known. "Daddy's the Chairman, and since he's not here, I should get t'go." He thumped his hand on his puny chest. "I'm t'be the next one. Next Chairman."

Then his small face twisted, almost bursting into tears, and yet the boy was able to tap down the emotion. "Uncle Kel won't let me. I'm gonna tell Daddy. I'm gonna tell Daddy now!"

Oh dear. Her young charge was working himself into a lather. What could she do to calm him?

She glanced over at the grand house a short distance away, seeking some kind of guidance. Surprisingly, she thought of something. "Tell you what, Tray. How about if I speak to your uncle and ask him if you and I can go to one of the seminars? One's enough, don't you think? These business meetings tend to be awfully long and boring."

She yawned into her hand for effect. "Hard to stay awake in them."

Tray's dark brows lifted, wrinkling his small forehead. "You've been t'the conference before?"

"Not this one, but most conferences are the same. Talk, talk, talk." She gave him a bright smile.

The boy chewed on his lip, clearly considering what she'd said. "Well, okay, 'suppose so. I thought you weren't t'know about, um, all the stuff."

All the stuff. What did that mean?

No matter. With lightning quickness, Tray left his funk behind. He flapped his arms and circled the rough trunks of the palm trees. "I'm Heckle and Jeckle!"

"Hey, kiddo," she called out to him. "We're not done for the day." Picking up the globe, she gave it a spin again. It twirled about, a mixture of blue, green, and beige. "Let's talk about where you live. Where's home?"

"Petra, you're silly! It's not there." He stilled, and then raised his small arms up toward the brilliant azure sky. "It's out here."

She blinked rapidly. What in the world? Was the boy being literal, meaning that of course he didn't live on a manmade globe? He lived out there somewhere, far away from the Galápagos Islands.

Or was the "out there" farther away, out past the sky, out into space, off planet Earth?

No bloody way!

She shook off that thought as a dog shook off water from an unwanted bath. She must've been going off the deep end to even consider such a thing. It was crazy, loony, and, yep, just plain silly.

But then again...

What if that were true? What if this Taurus City Travel Agency dealt with honest-to-goodness aliens? It would certainly explain some of the bizarre things she'd seen. Shimmering blue auras, eyebrows that had a life of their own, six identical women with the same first name... the list went on and on.

An approaching male figure attracted her attention. Petra narrowed her gaze. There could be no mistaking his appealing form. Kelvin Lacertus. But the billion dollar question was: was he human or was he an alien?

Whoa. She gulped down her notion so quickly that she started to cough. Okay, perhaps her imagination was going overboard here. Way overboard. She could admit that. After all, interplanetary visitors were certainly as far-fetched as anything she could imagine. But from now on, she would be on the lookout for anything strange and unusual.

And with that thought, she scrutinized her delectable host as he strode toward his nephew... and her.

She grinned. Maybe, with a little sleuthing, she could find out just what was going on here on this sleepy little outpost situated in the warm waters of the South Pacific.

* * * *

"Hey, squirt, I've been looking for you." Kelvin extended his hand and ruffled his nephew's shorn locks. He missed his daily get-togethers with Tray. He'd been busier than expected with this conference. Not only did he have to placate many high maintenance delegates, but also deal with unexpected security issues.

He also missed Petra.

Glancing over at where she sat, Kelvin took in her casual uniform of baggy grey sweatshorts and short sleeved hooded sweatshirt. No matter what she wore--laid-back clothes or formal attire--she increased his heart rate. Terran women had a tendency to do that to him.

Her hazel eyes were hidden, covered by dark green sunglasses. By the slight curve of her plump lips, he guessed she was glad to see him.

How gratifying. He smiled in return.

"I'm not a squirt." Tray pulled away, running his small hands over his head as if to brush away Kelvin's touch. "What's a squirt?" he asked Petra.

"A blast of cool water." She picked up her plastic water bottle, and then squeezed it hard in the middle. The liquid spewed out in a straight line, stopping only when it reached Kelvin's khaki chino pants. A dark stain spread across his thighs, just above the knees.

Tray burst into giggles first. Petra, after glancing at Kelvin, soon followed.

"Nice. Thanks." Kelvin brushed at the cotton material, but of course, the water would dry in its own time. "I'm sure the delegates will be curious to learn how this happened. Perhaps I should change."

She took a swig of water, then wiped her lips with her finger. "It'll dry. Don't be a baby."

"Cool beans! Uncle Kel is a baby!" Tray continued his fit of laughter as he hit the ground, and then rolled around on the grass. The next minute he jumped up. "I gotta go tell Georges." He spread out his arms, flapped them, and zipped back toward the house. Raulf and Bjorn left their positions to follow.

Kelvin processed the sight of his nephew's levity. It was a relief to see the boy so carefree. Not immersed in grief. His decision to hire Petra had been a good one. For Tray and for himself as well.

He took a seat on the bench. "Fine opinion you have of me, Petra."

Placing the cap on her treacherous bottle of water, she looked away from him. "Why does it matter what I think? Besides, I love babies."

"Indeed?" His heart beat faster. "Does that mean you love me?"

"What?" A delicious rosy blush crept across her cheeks, just as he knew it would. "No, of course not. Don't be silly. I hardly know you."

"First I'm a baby, and then I'm silly." Kelvin lifted his lips in a smirk. "You do realize you've dealt a serious blow to my self-esteem."

"I doubt it. Something tells me you've got more confidence than most of us mere mortals."

He couldn't help but laugh. "Oh, do you think I'm super human or something?"

"Are you?" She arched her eyebrow.

Interesting question. "Would you care to check my DNA? I assure you, I have twenty-three pairs of chromosomes just as you do."

"Hmmn," was all the answer she gave.

Kelvin glanced at his wristwatch, and then stood. "Well, my dear, it's time for me to head back. My thanks for the... refreshing conversation."

She also got to her feet. "Kelvin, something's come up with Tray."

He immediately analyzed her words and how she'd said them. Since she hadn't mentioned this earlier, it couldn't have been of paramount importance. He released a relieved breath. "Walk with me and tell me about it."

"Tray feels he should be able to attend this conference. Rather a strange whim for a five-year-old, but there it is." Keeping pace with Kelvin, she held out her hands. "Something about being a stand-in for his absent father."

"I see." He did understand. However the logistics of one so young at such a monumental conference...

Petra interrupted his reflections. "I told Tray I would ask you about it. I thought, maybe, he and I could go to one of the meetings. With Tray being as active as he is, I'm sure he'll get bored with having to sit still and be quiet. One seminar should prove to be enough.

Double hell. A throbbing built behind Kelvin's left temple. Without thinking, he rubbed the spot. Tray had a valid desire to attend the conference, true, and Petra would be the perfect person to watch over him. Rein him in if need be. But... how in the great spiral galaxy could the delegates--all the delegates--be persuaded to don Human skin suits?

Perhaps he could arrange an assembly with only agreeable, Humanoid aliens? Wn-Ganites, Velans, and Sirius natives, to name three friendly factions.

Kelvin nodded. "Let my nephew know that I'm giving it some thought. I'll see if I can set up a short seminar so that you both can have special clearance to attend.

"Clearance? Why do we need special clearance, Kelvin? Why's a travel agency conference so hush-hush?"

An array of clouds moved to cover the sun, momentarily darkening the afternoon. Petra set her glasses atop her head. Her cinnamon eyes twinkled in the waning sunlight.

He couldn't resist. He stopped walking, causing her to stop, too. Then he reached over and cupped her face in his hands. As slowly as he could, he grazed the sensuous outline of her tender lips with the pads of his thumbs.

Feeling her shiver, he leaned in closer, until their noses almost touched. Her warm breath and flowery fragrance teased his very soul.

"Petra," he murmured, "you ask too many questions. For once, just accept what I say."

He didn't give her a chance to reply. He kissed her, full and hard. But only for a moment. Pulling apart, he watched as her eyelids fluttered.

Good. She wasn't unaffected. No, not at all.

"I've been wanting to do that since I first set eyes on you, my dear girl. Way, way back, all those years ago."

When she gasped, he winked. "It was just as good as I anticipated."

"But--"

"But now I must head back to the conference. So hold that thought... and all your inevitable questions until later." He made a two-finger salute. "And be sure to let Traynor know I'm working on his whim."

Kelvin turned and strode toward the visitors' section. Acting on his desire had been a risk. By kissing her, he'd set in motion actions for future behavior. For future fulfillment. Whether that was a wise move or not remained to be seen.

Approaching the check-in entrance, he withheld his smile. It was his heart's desire to take the action to its logical conclusion.

* * * *

Insufferable man! Petra marched away toward a different destination than Kelvin. She headed for the house to collect Tray. But her tingling lips distracted her. They tingled from Kelvin's touch.

Stopping, she watched his receding figure, and then slowly traced the line of her lips with her fingertip. Maybe he wasn't so insufferable. Maybe he was wonderful. Pretty darn wonderful. Maybe that hint of a romance she'd fantasized about was about to develop into something more.

She smiled. A summer fling with the infinitely sexy and mysterious Kelvin Lacertus? Yeah, why shouldn't she indulge? He'd be the perfect balm to soothe the raw edges created by the aborted romance with Bob.

If it were meant to happen, it would happen. With those words of wisdom sloshing around in her head, Petra rang the front door bell.

Georges always opened the door right away. Today was obviously an exception. After two minutes, she rang the bell again... and waited.

She heard footsteps running on the hardwood floor. The door opened to reveal Georges, out of breath. His white starched collar wilted, a button on his steel grey vest hung by a thread... the man looked quite unlike his normal tidy self. How curious.

"*Mademoiselle*," he huffed. "I am glad you are here." He reached out to take her arm. "You must come. It is the young sir."

Tray? Her stomach dropped. Not wasting time in asking questions, she followed Georges upstairs.

Even before stepping onto the staircase, she knew Tray was having a tantrum. Goodness, his earsplitting screams could've been heard a mile away. As a result, her stomach twisted and her jaw clenched. Several deep breaths later, she entered the boy's bedroom.

A tropical forest motif greeted her--colorful wallpaper depicting a realistic scene of a long-billed toucan and two cute capuchin monkeys. A jungle beat added to the atmosphere, too, only the drumming came from Tray as he lay spread-eagle, pounding the floor with his fists and feet.

Conni, the young nanny, sat on the bed, with her chin sunk into her hands. Her long fair hair was askew, and her uniformed blouse was also missing a button. Whatever she'd done to calm down her charge had clearly not worked.

Tray continued screaming and yelling. He was so lost in his outburst that he didn't see Petra.

"What happened?" she quietly asked Georges.

He shrugged his broad shoulders. "*Alors,* it is so strange, *Mademoiselle.* His toy has vanished."

"Yes," the nanny confirmed. "Tray's favorite stuffed toy, the poomba, is missing."

"Poomba?" Petra tried to recognize the word. "Is that its name?"

Tray stilled his movements and looked over at her. His large eyes were filled with tears. "My poomba, Petra, my poomba is gone. I looked everywhere."

In a flash, he lifted himself off the floor and hurtled his little body against hers. The momentum caused her to stagger back.

"My poomba! My poomba!" He cried, hiccupped, and whined all at the same time.

Picking him up, she smoothed her hand down the back of his head, rocked him, and made soothing murmurs. "Hush, Tray. It's okay. Let's look for this toy together, okay?"

He clung to her and hiccupped into her shoulder. "My poomba."

Petra leaned her cheek against his forehead. "What's a poomba, Tray? A teddy bear?"

"No way! A poomba is a poomba. Not a bear, not a teddy." He lifted his head. One lone tear dripped down his chubby cheek. "Mama gave it to me."

That explained the reason for his temper tantrum.

"I see. It's a very special poomba then." She glanced at Conni. "What do you think happened to it?"

"I have no idea, ma'am. The toy is always on top of the bed, resting against the pillows. It was here when you arrived this morning to begin the boy's lessons. I am certain of this because I made up the bed myself. Then, a short while ago I heard Traynor's screams. I was in my room, just next door. Georges and I came running. We searched and searched but it's nowhere to be found."

Petra gulped. What the nanny had just spoken now took on a sinister meaning. Smoothing her hand in soothing circles on Tray's back, she walked over to Georges. "Who had access to this bedroom today?"

"With the exception of the staff, *Mademoiselle*, no one visited the second floor. Today, we had business visits from..." He ticked off names on his square fingers. "Josephus Hammer, Felicia Alverez, Owen Greenacre, Sergio Iguana, and Team Europe's Ellen E."

Basically the same folks that had known about the kayaking outing. Except for the security chief and a different Ellen. Interesting.

Georges lifted a thick eyebrow. "However, I was not in the house the entire day. Others may have gained access."

Which meant, as before, that no finger of blame could be firmly fixed to any one person.

Tray had quieted down. Settled against her, he sniffed every thirty seconds or so. He also made sucking motions, although his thumb and fingers were tightly captive, curled up in his small fist.

"Would you like to look for the poomba now?" She tried to lower the boy to his feet.

"No!" came the definite answer. "No. Don't wanna move. Don't want you t'go. You stay. You sleep here with me."

Oh dear. This was not how she'd envisioned her evening... nor her night.

She glanced over at Georges, who nodded, and then said, "I shall prepare a room--"

"No, Petra stays with me." Tray's lower lip extended in a pout.

"A cot, then. Is that agreeable, *Mademoiselle?*"

"Sure. Great." She hefted the boy a little higher, and then headed for a comfortable rocking chair in the corner of the bedroom. "Tray and I will be fine now. Why don't you both get on with your day?"

After Georges and Conni left, Petra sat, then murmured into Tray's ear. "Tell you what. How about if I read you a book? One of your favorite stories, okay? Then, after dinner, we'll go to my place. I've got to pick up pajamas, change of clothes, things like that. Deal?"

"D-Deal." His eyelids fluttered closed. His tantrum apparently had taken a lot out of him. It was a sure bet he would fall asleep soon after she began the book.

And that was a good thing because she needed time to think. She needed to tell Kelvin about what happened. After all, he'd told her not to worry--that additional security was in place.

Well, maybe it was for the conference, but more was definitely required at the house. Someone had known exactly what to make off with in order to wreck havoc with Tray.

Poor little guy.

A shiver traveled down her spine. She didn't feel safe. Not for Tray, and not for herself.

When Kelvin would arrive home was anyone's guess. She'd ask Georges to let her know when his boss came in. If she didn't see Kelvin tonight, then she'd be up first thing in the morning to catch his ear.

She picked up a book about a friendly dinosaur, and then softly read aloud rhyming verses about the triceratop's prehistoric adventures.

* * * *

All in all, it had been a helluva day... a helluva night. With a heartfelt sigh, Kelvin pushed back his overhang of hair. He glanced around the entryway in his house. Everything was in its place. All was quiet.

Not so at the conference's icebreaker. The yammer of dozens of different speech dialects... and vocal apparatuses had taken a toll on his equanimity. Along with troublesome aliens. The Phi Pavonis faction had been predictably aloof, the Brhites uncouth, and Hunt, the ambassador for the Uortzks, had been downright antagonistic. No surprises there.

However, Georges' communication about the missing poomba had caused Kelvin's blood to boil. Of course there was the real possibility that the stuffed animal could have just been misplaced. But he didn't think so. Not with Tray's attachment to the toy.

No. Security at the house had been lax. Which meant Sergio Iguana's neck was on the chopping block. As late as it was, the man was now engaged in interviewing those staff members who had visited the house today. The ultimatum was this: if the culprit wasn't discovered by noon tomorrow, the security chief knew his head would roll.

Figuratively speaking, naturally. But as much as Kelvin supported Sergio, he'd have no qualms with sending the man back to his home world on Capella 8, and appoint a new chief of security.

Rhythmically moving his shoulders to release pent-up tension, Kelvin checked to make sure the new tachyonic particle system was online. It was. Good. With the house now in a protective invisible bubble, no one could enter or leave the premises without clearance.

He then slowly made his way up the staircase. He'd look in on his nephew, and then hit the sheets for some much needed sleep.

Kelvin made his way inside the jungle-themed bedroom and over to the bed. It was difficult to see in the darkness, but there Tray was, scooted over to the edge of the mattress. His newly cropped head of hair barely peeked out from under the blankets.

Kelvin took a step closer, and then froze. The boy leaned his head against another head, one with masses of dark hair scattered every which way.

Petra's head. She slept in a cot butted against the bed. Her slim arm had snaked out from her cover to curve around Tray's tiny waist.

For a long moment Kelvin took in the sight of her nestled so close to his nephew. Her shoulder, nearly bare except for a thin strap, tantalized him with smooth, tanned skin, just begging to be touched. She lay on her side, facing Tray, with her sweet form unfairly hidden by the blanket.

Kelvin steadied his suddenly increased breathing. Obviously Georges hadn't given him a full report. He hadn't expected to find Petra here, under his roof. She would prove to be an impediment to a good night's sleep. Unless...

He flickered his gaze over her. No. As much as he would like, he couldn't take her away from Tray's side. The boy had had one of his tantrums. Petra must've agreed to sleep next to him to calm him down.

My turn next! Kelvin grinned. Maybe once this infernal conference was over, he could convince her to slip into his own bed.

About to leave, he saw Petra, still sleeping, pull her thin blanket higher to cover her shoulder. Perhaps she was cold. He walked over to the closet and removed one of the spare comforters. When he carefully draped it over her, a small smile lifted her pink lips.

A sharp sensation pierced his chest. Sharp and yet not unpleasant. Something like Cupid's arrow?

Ridiculous!

Kelvin withheld his snort of laughter as he quietly left his nephew's bedroom.

Chapter Seven

Petra woke up with a start. The first thing she saw was impossible: a grey elephant with a monkey curled up in its trunk staring at her. *Omigosh!*

Rubbing her eyes, she suddenly remembered. The huge pachyderm was only wallpaper. She'd slept in Tray's bedroom last night.

She exhaled relief, and then glanced over at the boy. Still sleeping, he had moved over on the mattress as far as he could go. One more inch and he'd be on her cot.

Which brought back memories of the poomba. What in the world had happened to it? Maybe someone hadn't taken it. Maybe it had been misplaced.

Petra quietly pushed aside the covers, got up and then stood barefoot on the carpeted floor. Her first puzzle of the day was that an extra comforter had inexplicably appeared on the cot. It hadn't been there last night. *Where did that come from?*

No matter. She focused on the important puzzle. *If I were a poomba--whatever that looks like--where would I hide?*

Easy. The first place that came to mind was under the bed. She crouched down, lifted the hanging covers, and peered underneath. Several nebulous items were scattered haphazardly under the bedskirts. Most objects were on the far side of the bed.

Might as well be thorough. She walked over to the other side and stretched out on the floor. Sticking her arm under the bed, she then swept the nearest debris out from the murky depths. Her booty consisted of two balls, a pair of socks, and a few building blocks. No stuffed toys.

She reached in again, this time closer to the end of the bed. Only one thing came out to see the light of day. But it was an important one--a stuffed animal with shaggy wooly hair, six short, clawed feet, and round purple eyes. Not exactly a teddy bear for sure, especially with fangs, also purple, as long as a walrus'.

This had to have been the poomba.

A quick check of the time revealed it to be five minutes after seven. Georges had told her Kelvin planned to leave at seven thirty. She didn't have much time.

She slipped into a short grey robe to cover her tank top and pajama shorts. After belting, she then pulled down on the back bottom hem. The robe had the unfortunate tendency to ride high, just under her derriere.

Still barefoot, she grabbed the stuffed animal, and then exited the room. She zoomed down the stairs, huffing and puffing as she looked around the entryway. Where would Kelvin be? Where was Georges?

"Mademoiselle," the butler said from behind.

Goodness, where'd he come from?

Since Georges was immaculate as usual, he must've recovered from yesterday's ruckus. His gaze lit upon the toy. A relieved expression covered his handsome face. "You have found the young sir's poomba! Where was...?"

His features lost animation as he shook his head. "No. No time. You must come with me to Master Kelvin."

Petra followed behind, biting her lip all the way. She hadn't bothered to check the way she looked this morning. No washing the face, no combing the hair... thankfully, she'd covered her skimpy pajamas. But she was *barely* covered. Darn it all, what had she been thinking?

She waited while Georges opened the door into a room she'd not seen before, and then shrugged off her embarrassment. Perhaps Kelvin would be so pleased to see the poomba that he wouldn't pay attention to her appearance.

* * * *

Sergio sat in front of Kelvin's desk, a serious expression on his dark face. Which was no surprise. Kelvin's expression had to have been serious as well. As yet, yesterday's security breach in the house remained unsolved. The chief of security had nothing positive to report.

Hell.

The deadline was looming. If the intruder remained at large, then Sergio would be relieved of duty and shipped off on the next transport to Capella 8.

A bleak prospect for both of them.

Georges' distinct knock sounded on the door.

"Enter." Kelvin shut his eyes and rubbed the bridge of his nose. Double hell. It was going to be a very long day.

A sweet fragrance invaded his senses. He opened his eyes and saw who had entered with Georges... and how she was dressed.

He sat up ramrod straight. "Petra... good of you to visit, my dear." Then he saw what she was holding. "You found the poomba?"

She rubbed the back of her left calf with her bare right foot, obviously nervous. "Oh, I'm so sorry to interrupt. I just thought you'd like to know I found Tray's toy."

"Where?"

"It was under the bed." Her gaze darted from him to Sergio, and back again.

"*Voyons!* This cannot be!" Standing by her side, Georges lost his stiff demeanor. "*Alors,* that is the first place Conni and I looked."

Sergio got to his feet and then placed himself squarely in front of the butler. "You and the nanny both checked under the bed?"

"Indeed, yes. At the same time we pulled up the bedspread and cleared out whatever was hidden beneath." Georges gestured with his hands to convey what happened. "Many dust bunnies were stirred up, causing us to cough."

"There can be no mistake?" Kelvin also stood and walked over.

"*Non,* not at all, sir. We then returned the mess to under the bed and searched elsewhere."

Kelvin caught Sergio's speaking glance. He nodded slightly. "Georges, bring some coffee for us. And see that we're not disturbed."

"*Certainement.*" The butler clicked his heels together and left to accomplish his task.

"Petra, please, have a seat. You'll be more comfortable." Kelvin led her over to the couch, waited until she complied, and then sat beside her.

She fingered the front edges of her delightfully short robe. "I'm afraid I'm much too comfortable as it is. I rushed right downstairs without, you know, thinking about my...." She shrugged.

"You look charming." He gave her a wink.

"Almost combustible," Sergio added. The security chief sat across from them in a lone side chair.

As she lowered her lashes, a faint blush spread across her cheeks.

Kelvin smiled. She truly was charming. But back to business. "So, these are the facts--the poomba was discovered missing last night at around four p.m. Conni, Georges, and Tray conducted the search, including under the bed. This yielded nothing." He lifted his brow at Petra. "Is this so?"

"I didn't actually see the search, but when I arrived at the house, right after you left yesterday, Georges brought me upstairs. He and Conni, and of course Tray, were all definitely distraught."

Sergio leaned forward in his chair. "Did you stay in the bedroom the entire time until the sizzling sunrise?"

She shook her head. "After dinner, which we had in the room, we went to my place to pick up a few things. We probably weren't gone more than thirty minutes. And... I remember now, when we got back to the house, Tray looked under the bed again, just in case, he'd said. But the poomba wasn't there."

"Good to know. Thank you." Sergio continued his questioning. "Bjorn and Raulf accompanied you outside, correct?"

"Yes, they followed us."

Sergio narrowed his dark gaze at Kelvin. "By that time, the protective system was in place. Meaning no unauthorized entries or departures. I've checked the security cameras. The cook and Juanita and Inés, the household staff, are all accounted for. During the time of Petra and Traynor's outing, only two personnel were in the house."

Kelvin nodded. "Georges and Conni."

"What protective system?" Petra piped up.

"An extra security measure. Nothing for you to worry about," Kelvin said smoothly.

She frowned at him.

Sergio checked his portable tablet. "And after you and Traynor returned, the number of house occupants remained at six for the night, until Kelvin came back at midnight."

"Wait a minute." Petra's hazel eyes grew wide. "I know for sure someone came into the bedroom last night. I woke up covered with a comforter instead of just the blanket that Georges had given me."

Kelvin chuckled. "No mystery there. That was me. You looked cold so I added the extra covering."

"You watched me while I slept?" Her voice was indignant.

"I checked on my nephew, Petra. As a matter of fact, Georges neglected to tell me you were staying with us." Kelvin lifted his eyebrow. "Imagine my surprise."

The faint blush turned deeper. Very gratifying, indeed.

Sergio stood, then paced about the study with restless energy. "The poomba was returned some time during the night. On one side of Traynor's bedroom, with no adjoining door, Bjorn and Raulf slept. On the other side are the bath facilities, shared by the nanny's bedroom. The door, is it locked?"

Petra tugged on her lower lip with her teeth. "I don't know about Conni's door. The one between Tray's and the bathroom was ajar."

Kelvin heard noises from the corridor and jumped up to open the door. "Here's Georges. He'll know."

The butler carried in a tray filled with mugs, a large coffee pot, fresh scones, milk, and sugar. "You have a question for me, sir?"

"Yes, is the door between the nanny's room and the facilities kept locked?"

"Not usually, sir. And the lock is only for Conni's bedroom, so that the door cannot be locked when one is inside the bath."

Kelvin nodded. "Thank you, Georges. You may go."

Once the butler left and the door was closed again, Sergio pounded his fist into his hand. "Sizzling suns! You do see that it is the nanny who has the easiest access to Traynor's room?"

Petra shook her head, sending her loose hair flying. "But that's just circumstantial evidence. Someone could've simply entered through the main bedroom door."

"As I did." Kelvin briefly smiled. "However, to be honest, we do have a security camera right outside Tray's bedroom door. If anyone else entered, we'll have a record of it."

Sergio shot across the room. His hand on the doorknob, he called over his shoulder. "If you both will excuse me. I've got a scorching need to check this out pronto."

And that left Kelvin alone with the provocatively dressed Petra. "Let's have some coffee." He picked up the pot and poured into two mugs."

She demurred. "No, thanks. I should go upstairs before Tray misses me."

"But then I'll miss you."

"Right." She made a face at him. "Seriously, I don't understand. If it was Conni, why would she do it? Why would she want to upset Tray?"

He took a sip of the hot Ecuadorian coffee. It was fine, very fine indeed. "No idea. Sergio will pry it out of her, though. As I recall, she hasn't been in my brother's employ very long. In fact...."

In fact Tray's previous nanny had succumbed to an infectious disease right about the time of Moriah's goodwill mission. A coincidence? He thought not.

A special questioning was in order with Ms. Conni... what the devil was her last name?

Setting his mug down, he turned to Petra. "Why don't you finish your coffee? Have a scone. I'd love to stay and chat but I've got to change before I head over to the conference."

Before she had a chance to reply, he stood. "Also, I meant to tell you I've arranged clearance for Tray, and you, of course, to attend a short seminar at the conference. Business formal so dress yourself and Tray accordingly. Starts at one thirty this afternoon, right after the lunch break. Should only last an hour. Tell the reception committee and they'll escort you to the correct location. I'll be waiting for you out front."

"But--"

He grinned. "See you then." Outside the study, he dropped his smile. Sergio would have reviewed the surveillance records by now. Chances were high that no one, other than Kelvin himself, had entered the bedroom.

Fisting his hands, Kelvin prepared for an interrogation that promised to be very enlightening indeed.

* * * *

Holding the poomba and a mug of coffee, Petra took the stairs and went back to Tray's bedroom. Her thoughts zipped about, going a thousand ways at once. Could Conni have intentionally wanted to upset Tray? But why? And why bother to return the stuffed animal after all that fuss?

She entered the room and looked over at Tray. Thankfully, he continued to sleep. She slipped the poomba next to him. He must've subconsciously known his toy was back for he curled his arm around it and snuggled his face in its fur.

Now what? She glanced at the bathroom door. Maybe she should talk with the nanny.

She walked through, and then rapped on the connecting door. "Conni? Conni, are you up?"

Nothing. She tried again with no results so she turned the doorknob. The door wasn't locked.

"Conni?" Petra stuck her head in. She took a quick look around. The bedroom was spacious, as large as Tray's, but it was also empty.

She glanced at the rumpled bed. Where had the nanny gone? Had she left early? But how could she have, with that "protective system" in place? Or perhaps Conni had been summoned by Sergio? And maybe seeing the nanny was something Kelvin wanted to do before going to the conference.

Petra closed the door. It was late and she needed to start the day. As she turned on the shower faucet, a sudden thought hit. Kelvin had instructed her to dress Tray in business formal. But that was Conni's responsibility, not hers. Not hers unless Kelvin had already decided that the nanny was guilty.

The warm gush of water eased her tensed-up shoulder muscles. But even with this shower massage, she couldn't help but feel uneasy. Despite bodyguards, a protection system, and surveillance cameras, security was still illusive. There was no doubt about it; she just didn't feel safe.

* * * *

The nanny wasn't cooperating. She sat in front of Kelvin and Sergio with her shoulders hunched and arms crossed, tightly pressed against her chest.

Sergio stood and pointed an accusing finger at her. "Why did you take the poomba?"

She glanced at him, and then lowered her gaze to the floor. "I didn't. You have no evidence against me."

Kelvin studied the tense young woman. Her nonverbal signals flagrantly broadcasted deception. Clenched jaw. Compressed lips. Flared nostrils. Facial tick. She and Sergio went back and forth and back again, making no progress.

With each answer she gave, her voice grew louder. "You have no right to accuse me," she sneered.

"I have every right," Kelvin interrupted. He stared at her until she flushed, a mottled blotch of red disturbing her pasty cheeks.

"Why would I bother with an insignificant stuffed toy?" she mumbled.

"Why, indeed? As the Lacertus in charge here, in case you have forgotten, I do accuse you. You are responsible for taking care of the Chairman's only son and heir. Traynor's health and happiness are of prime concern to all of us at Taurus City. You have failed in your duty."

"My duty is not to you, you Lacertus locust! You pompous--" She shot him a look brimmed with hatred, and then looked away again.

Kelvin lifted an eyebrow. He hadn't expected hostility. Definitely a point worth pursuing. Conni's resentment showed that there was a very real possibility that she was part of the anti-establishment faction, the Continuers.

Even though the Lacertus line had stewardship of Terra since the beginning--or perhaps it was because of this--certain Tau Cetians clamored for a change. The primary protesting group was known as the Continuers, so named because they continued to press for their own people to depose of the status quo and assume the mantle of rulership.

Was the disruption of Traynor's routine--the disappearance of his poomba---part of the Continuers' scheme to chip away at the Lacertus family? Perhaps to show that even with increased security, Traynor wasn't safe?

Sergio removed metal restraints from his security belt. He rhythmically hit them against his open hand. The clanging sound grated. "Sir, I strongly recommend we adjourn to the detention area and conduct a more extensive interrogation."

Sweat beaded on the woman's narrow forehead. She darted her gaze and licked her thin lips.

A thought resurfaced. Kelvin paced in front of the woman's chair.

"Conni, what's your last name?"

Sergio made as if to answer, but Kelvin held up his hand. "Conni? Chief Iguana will tell me if you don't."

More perspiration flowed. She stuck her hand in her pajama pocket, and then put her hand on her mouth. "It's... my name is True."

"Conni True." He thought a moment. "That's an anagram, isn't it?"

"Sizzling suns!" Sergio stared at the woman. "It is! The letters form the word--"

Kelvin held up his hand again. "Conni, would you mind telling us what the anagram is?"

Rapidly blinking her pale eyes, the woman managed to utter, "Continuer." Then, quite dramatically, she tumbled over as if she'd lost consciousness. Her mouth half open, her gaze unseeing, she remained motionless on the floor.

"She's had a meltdown! She's down for the count," Sergio exclaimed as he pressed his fingers against the inside of her wrist. "I barely feel her pulse."

The next second, Conni went into convulsions.

Kelvin grabbed his cell phone. Fortunately, Cornwell Young quickly answered. "Doctor? My home office--stat! Conni True is convulsing on the floor."

There wasn't much that could be done while they waited for the doctor. Her involuntary spasms were violent. To prevent her from doing more injury to herself, Kelvin and Sergio held her arms and legs down.

Thankfully, Cornwell appeared in record time. "What happened?" He knelt by her side and examined her face.

"Not sure. She passed out and then started convulsing. Doc, just so you know, she's one of the Continuers."

"Blast. Smells like bitter almonds. Cyanide." He pulled out a tiny glass vial from his medical bag. "Amyl nitrite," he muttered.

Then he prepared an injection, and jabbed it into the woman's arm. "Sergio, c'mon, we've no time to lose. Let's get her to the lab. I'll have to pump her stomach."

The security chief nodded. He lifted and carried the thrashing Conni

True out the door. Cornwell closely followed behind.

"Keep me posted," Kelvin called out after them. He took a moment to inhale and exhale deeply. Hell, as he'd thought earlier, it was going to be a *very* long day.

Chapter Eight

Although what happened earlier had thrown a pall over her emotions, Petra did look forward to attending the conference, as did Tray. He looked adorable in a white long sleeved shirt, dress pants, and matching vest. Oddly enough, he'd insisted on wearing a tie.

She smiled. He was quite the little man.

But no matter how grown up he dressed, he still was clingy. He insisted on accompanying her to her place while she changed. As for the poomba, it was figuratively glued to his side.

The dear boy. The temporary disappearance of his beloved poomba obviously stirred up his sorrow over the loss of his mother.

Petra blinked back sudden tears. Holding out her hand, she said brightly, "So, what do you say we head back to the house for a quick lunch?"

"I'm not hungry." Tray stuck out his lower lip. Waiting for her to finish dressing had stretched his limited patience to the max.

"Not hungry? That's too bad. I heard Chef Niko made chicken bits covered in honey just for you."

"Cool beans! With curly fries?"

"Of course."

The boy grabbed her hand. "C'mon, Petra! We don't wanna be late. As soon as we eat, then we get to go to the conference, okay?"

"Sure." Hiding her smile, she let Tray lead the way. Once outside her bungalow, she signaled to Raulf and Bjorn. Truth be told, she wasn't hungry either, but she'd manage to eat a few bites to insure her tummy wouldn't start bellowing at an inopportune time.

She drove back to Kelvin's estate with the convertible top up. Insurance of another sort. She'd spent too much time on her clothes, makeup, and hair, hence Tray's earlier bad mood. But for some reason, she felt the primping was necessary. Her intuition told her that a great deal was riding on this conference. The last thing she needed was to show up for the event looking windblown and unprofessional.

Petra glanced over at the little gentleman by her side. All she had to worry about was to make sure no remnants of lunch found their way onto his... and her picture-perfect clothes.

* * * *

The ride to the convention location was quick and silent. As the car approached the somber, steel grey wall, shivers of apprehension vibrated down Petra's spine. She hadn't been this close to the eerie wall before. Thankfully, Georges insisted on driving. She was glad to have his escort.

After parking, he quickly left the car and opened the doors. Raulf and Bjorn pulled up alongside them.

"Allow me to check you in, *s'il vous plaît, mademoiselle.*" Georges clicked his heels together, and then approached an automated station.

She placed her hand on Tray's shoulder while they waited for Georges. A few words, a whirl of lights and sounds later, he stepped back and a door silently and seamlessly slid open. Wanda Cropper, the Reservations and Accommodations Manager, stood on the other side.

"Hey there! How are you guys doing?" Wanda reached out to ruffle Tray's hair.

"We've gotta hurry, Miz Wanda." Tray shook off the woman's hand. "We don't wanna be late for the conference."

"Certainly not, young Tray." Wanda nodded at Georges. "I'll take it from here."

Georges returned her nod and then looked at Petra. "When you are ready to leave, *mademoiselle,* give me a call."

"Thank you, Georges."

"C'mon!" Tray stamped his foot.

Petra withheld her sigh. Little Tray had been so good, but now his patience was sorely tried. She took the boy's hand. "Okay, let's go."

As they briskly walked down dark corridors with the bodyguards following, a cool breeze and scents of fragrant island blooms traveled with them. Wanda kept up a travelogue about the building with its many sections, and busy personnel smiled in greeting as they passed by.

Soon they stopped in front of a closed double door. Sentries were stationed on either side. Wanda checked her watch. "Eight minutes to spare. Bonus!" She grabbed two brochures from a nearby table, and handed them out. "You guys picked a great seminar to attend."

Petra glanced down at the colorful and shiny brochure. She read: *New Attractions and Visitor Favorites. Don't miss these scenic sights.*

"Sounds good. Maybe the next trip I plan, I'll plan it with Taurus City."

For some reason, Wanda looked surprised at Petra's comment. The woman brushed back a wandering lock of frizzy hair and then pointed down the very long corridor. "Lor, here's our CEO now. Record time for Kelvin."

Petra spotted some figures but couldn't make out which one was Kelvin. Wanda certainly had good eyes.

Once Kelvin came into view, Tray couldn't hold still a moment longer. He dashed down the walkway to throw his arms around his uncle's legs. "Uncle Kel! We're not late!"

Exuberance must've been the boy's middle name. Hopefully Kelvin didn't mind the high-spirited hug. Petra crossed her fingers.

Wanda poked at Petra's arm. "I'd better get back to my post. Hope you enjoy the session." With a wave, the blonde then trotted away.

Petra turned back around. Oh good gosh. Kelvin looked absolutely dreamy in his dark blue, impeccably tailored suit. She was no expert on men's attire, but she'd be willing to bet this suit was from the Armani collection. Italian wool twill material, shimmering dark silk tie, brilliantly white classic shirt. The blazer jacket hugged his broad shoulders to perfection, and then tapered down to show off his slim waist and hips.

She trailed the tip of her tongue over her lips. Goodness, but he ignited a fire in every part of her body. Thank heavens she'd taken extra time with her appearance. Wearing a repeat--the same long flowing skirt, camisole top and matching three quarter length sleeved covering that she'd worn the day she arrived on the island--she changed the sandals to her high heeled pumps. Her hair was pulled back into a loose top bun, showing off her only pair of dangly earrings.

All in all, she looked professional and attractive. More important, she felt confident. Around Mr. Finger-Licking-Good, that was a must.

Kelvin lifted his nephew, settled the boy on his hip, and then carried him over to her. "Petra, my dear, you look subliminal."

"Subliminal?" That was surely a strange description.

He leaned close and whispered in her ear. "Subliminally sexy, naturally.

I'm having a difficult time keeping my hands off you."

Tray heard, though. "Here, Uncle Kel." The boy grabbed Kelvin's hand and pulled it until his fingers reached Petra's shoulder. "She's always holding my hand and giving me hugs. She won't mind you touching her, silly."

Kelvin flashed a dazzlingly white smile. "Out of the mouth of babes, hmmn?"

Flushing, she took a step away. "Um, perhaps we should go inside and find seats?"

His smile deepened. "Of course." Setting Tray down, Kelvin nodded to one of the sentries who then opened a door for them. "After you, my dear."

As predicted, Petra took Tray's hand, walked inside, and then looked around. She gulped down hard. Wow. This room was enormous--two stories high, at least. At the front, a huge wall mural hung. Two views of Earth shimmered at her: one showing North and South America, along with the poles, and the other of Asia, Europe, Africa, Australia, and the poles.

The picture looked so clear, so real. As if what was shown on the mural were actual shots of Earth. Minus the clouds, of course.

Tearing her gaze away from the sight, she focused on the people already seated. Their conversation buzzed around the tremendous room. On a dais, behind a long rectangular cherrywood table, stiffly sat Valli Proximus, the Travel Director, and her staff, the six Ellens and Maizie. No conversations volleyed back and forth among the travel department.

Six Ellens. Goodness. Petra couldn't help but blink her eyes. Seeing six identical people assembled in a row was truly blowing her mind.

In front of the dais was a horseshoe table, also made of cherrywood. Seven people sat behind it. Nameplates were stationed in front of each position. She strained to read the closest one. "Ambassador Hunt" it read. Sure enough, the hirsute man she'd seen at the welcome party at the beginning of the week pawed through papers set near him. He looked up and caught her gaze. Hunt snorted, and then inclined his massive head as if in greeting.

Petra gave him a tremulous smile.

"Let's sit behind the ambassadors," Kelvin spoke in a low tone. "There are a few empty spots in the second row.

She nodded. The first row of seats was filled with people who resembled the ambassador in front of them. The woman Kelvin had said was British, only Cornwell Young called a Brhite, sat behind a similarly tattooed man. A very tall and thin man, from the Philippines according to Kelvin, sat behind a woman ambassador with the same body structure. And so on. However, the chair behind Hunt remained empty.

Kelvin waited for Petra to sit first. Tray sat between them. She found herself behind Dutto, the man with the strange white eyebrows. In front of Tray was Tarrnak from Venezuela, and Kelvin had Oblan in front of him.

With a gavel, Valli rapped on the table, the sound of which could easily be heard over the various conversations. "Order! We will begin the meeting."

The woman's monotone voice brooked no disobedience. Very soon silence filled the room. She welcomed the guests, introduced herself along with a brief mention of her staff. She then gave an overview of what scenic sights--listed by continent--that they would discuss.

Petra felt her attention fade. Valli Proximus was the type of speaker that would soon have her audience snoring.

Tray tugged on his uncle's jacket sleeve. "Uncle Kel, can I sit up there, with all those Ellens?"

"Certainly, Tray. However, you must leave the poomba with me."

The little boy stuck out his lower lip, but he also nodded.

Before Valli continued with the program, Kelvin stood. "Pardon my interruption, honorable ambassadors and visitors, I wish to present Chairman Lacertus' son and heir, Traynor."

Smiles, applause, and low murmurs came from all the attendees... all except Valli Proxiumus. Her expression remained impassive.

"May our young chairman-to-be sit on the dais with you, Valli?" Kelvin asked.

"But of course," the woman said smoothly. "Young Traynor can sit next to me."

"Yay!" Like a shot, the boy was up on his feet.

"Slowly," Petra advised.

"As a Lacertus," Kelvin murmured.

Obviously, Tray got the message for he carefully walked up to the front platform as if walking on eggs. Valli had already placed a chair next to her and smiled at him in greeting.

Kelvin picked up the discarded poomba, and then sat back down in his nephew's vacated chair.

With Tray settled in, Valli continued with the agenda. As she mentioned a travel location, a light on the mural behind her flickered on the corresponding continent. Vivid pictures of the tourist attraction filled screens on either side of the two hemispheres of Earth.

Petra listened for ten minutes. She noted an interesting trend. Geographic locations were featured, nothing else. Places like the Himalayas and Mount Everest; the beautiful Victoria Falls in southern Africa; the lush Amazon Rainforest; and the Grand Canyon.

She frowned. Why weren't cities mentioned? Paris, New York, Rome, Beijing were sightseeing meccas in their own right. Or archeological sites like Stonehenge, the Pyramids of Egypt, and the Taj Mahal. This omission was very strange.

The more she thought, the more she simmered with questions. Since Taurus City was a travel agency, why were the people seated around the horseshoe table called ambassadors? And Hunt, or rather Ambassador Hunt, had told her he was attending a diplomatic conference, not a travel conference.

What did it all mean?

"You're frowning," Kelvin said in a low voice. "Is there a location you disapprove of?"

"No, it's not that."

"My nephew being a little too fidgety?" He persisted in talking.

"No, I--" She stopped short when Valli's hard gaze landed on her. "Ah, I'll tell you later."

"I'll hold you to it, my dear." Kelvin turned his attention back to the front screen now showing the interior of an active volcano.

The session ended with the floor open for suggestions. Future tour sites were being discussed. Dutto, the white eyebrow fellow, raised his hand. "Madam Chair, we have been asked by a member not in attendance about the possibility of reopening Australia's Great Barrier

Reef to our assemblage."

Valli nodded. "You speak of the aquatic aficionado..." She cleared her throat. "Mr. Nephros, do you not?

"Precisely," the man answered.

"Please give him my wishes for a speedy recovery." A small smile lifted her lips. "Ellen F. of Team Australia will brief us on the Great Barrier Reef's status."

Petite, slender, and severe, like all the other Ellens, Ms. F. stood and gave a report on how the reef continued to be under strict protection by the locals to limit the potentially detrimental effect of sightseers on the living coral.

Petra leaned over to Kelvin. His unique scent of sandalwood, leather, and musk played havoc with her senses. She inhaled deeply, steadied herself, and then asked, "What happened to Mr. Nephros?"

"A slight accident with a crocodile."

When she gasped, Kelvin patted her left hand and then held it. "Not to worry. Mr. Nephros has been completely rehabilitated. Better than before, actually. Doc Young is a miracle worker, to be sure."

She received another glare from Valli. Petra removed her hand from Kelvin's. Ms. Proximus seemed to have a thing for her boss.

Then again, most likely the entire female staff had a thing for Kelvin. Felicia had all but said as much.

Folding her hands in her lap, Petra tapped her foot as she waited for this meeting to finish. Rather than providing answers, the seminar only stirred up more questions.

* * * *

Tray had been on his best behavior while seated on the dais. His attention had wandered only a little, so, if there was one thing Kelvin knew about his nephew, it was that the boy required an immediate outlet to release his pent-up energy.

The seminar now over, Kelvin signaled to his nephew to join him and Petra at the back of the conference room.

The boy grinned, and then very politely shook Valli's hand. He must have been thanking the travel director for letting him sit beside her.

"He's a wonderful child," Petra murmured.

"Yes, he is." For a moment, sadness swept over Kelvin. Not only did the boy have to handle sorrow concerning his mother's death, but someone, or a group of dissenters like the Continuers, wanted to harm him. Harm the entire Lacertus family.

Double hell.

Kelvin had to change the subject. "How did you enjoy the seminar?"

"Truthfully, I found it sort of, ah, curious. I've got a lot of questions--"

"Petra." Tray reached her side. "You were right. The conference is pretty boring. I wanna go now."

"Boring?" Kelvin lifted an eyebrow.

She had the good grace to blush. "I was telling Tray that he'd only want to go to one meeting. That all the meetings would be almost the same."

"Perhaps." Kelvin withheld his smile. He returned the poomba to its rightful owner and took his nephew's free hand. "I don't have anything scheduled for the next hour. How about if we grab a cone at the ice cream hut and then throw the ball around outside?"

"Yummy ice cream!" Tray rubbed his belly.

"Am I invited?" Petra asked.

"Certainly, my dear. I need to impress you with my physical prowess."

She rolled her eyes. "You're joking, of course."

"But of course." He leaned over to take her hand, too, but she avoided him by walking next to Tray's other side.

They traveled out into the corridor. Tray then piped up, "I wanna play light sabers instead."

Petra laughed. "Like Darth Vader?"

"Who?" Tray blinked in confusion.

Her mouth dropped. "Darth Vader? Star Wars?"

Kelvin hurried to explain. "Tray doesn't watch many movies... or TV, either."

"Oh."

More questions formed on her sweet pink lips. Kelvin knew exactly what she was thinking. If Tray didn't know Darth Vader, then how was he acquainted with light sabers?

The answer was simple. Light sabers were real; Darth Vader, however, was only a fictional character. A wildly popular fictional character, true, but one the boy wasn't familiar with.

Before she had a chance to ask her question, Kelvin spotted a somber trio heading their way. His way. Joe Hammer, Sergio Iguana, and Cornwell Young looked as if this system's sun was about to go supernova.

Kelvin sighed. Obviously the vacancy in his schedule just filled up.

"Gentlemen," he addressed his staff. "I take it we have something to discuss?"

"Indeed," was Joe's temperate response.

"Sizzling suns! You're spot on," exclaimed Sergio.

"Blasted waste of a day," grumbled Cornwell.

Tray whimpered beside him.

Kelvin ruffled the boy's hair. "Not to worry, Tray. You won't have to sit through another boring meeting." He nodded at the HR Director. "Joe, you enjoy throwing the ball around, don't you?"

Joe's green eyes crinkled. "I most certainly do. And I would be happy to test young Tray's pitching arm, especially if Petra joins us."

She dimpled a smile. "I'd be delighted."

Kelvin watched as the three of them walked away. He sighed again. Joe had the audacity to curve his arm around Petra's slender shoulders. Anger... or jealousy built behind Kelvin's eyes.

But such emotions weren't appropriate. Releasing his regret, he turned his attention back to his remaining two officers and walked into a nearby empty room to hear whatever dire news they carried.

"Okay. What gives?" He took a seat at the head of a conference table.

Cornwell sat to his right. "Well, you're not gonna like this, but our Continuer infiltrator is dead."

Kelvin lifted his eyebrow.

The doctor scratched at his short salt and pepper Afro. "Self induced poison. The old cyanide pill in the mouth scenario." He paused a moment before adding, "A particularly painful way to go."

Painful, yes, but by her own hand. Kelvin darted his gaze to his chief of security. "Sergio?"

"Investigation on this end in Taurus City has fizzled, sir. Conni True had no ties to anyone here at the Agency. No known ties, at any rate. Back at Tau Ceti, Headquarters is still scrutinizing her background."

"She couldn't have been working alone. Conni True was merely a cog." Kelvin couldn't remain seated. He pushed away from the table, and then paced the length of the room. "No, gentlemen, we have an upper level traitor in our midst. Someone we trust. But who?"

Naturally, no one had the answer.

Giving additional instructions to both men, Kelvin remained in the room and then locked the door after they left. He continued to walk with his hands clasped behind his back. This solitary pacing usually helped him to think, to analyze, to solve problems. He needed every form of help possible. The urgency of this dilemma overwhelmed him.

May the stars shine down on this Terran paradise and allow me to find a solution.

Chapter Nine

As Tray splish-splashed in the bathtub, Petra propped herself up against the pillows on his bed, giving him privacy while she waited for him to finish. Her mind zipped in a million different directions. She'd wanted to ask Georges about what was happening with Conni, but somehow time had just slipped away. Now here it was, bedtime, and she still wasn't sure what was going on. Was she expected to take over the nanny's position? Stay here at the house?

She rubbed her forehead. She was filled with so many questions, she was sure she'd burst.

When a knock sounded on the open hall door, she got up and opened the door. Georges entered, and then bowed. Despite the eight o'clock hour, he looked as fresh and as formal as he had at the beginning of the day.

"A thousand pardons, *mademoiselle.*" He walked over to the bed. Darting his sharp gaze to the ajar bathroom door, he then lowered his voice. "I have heard from Master Kelvin. He desires that you move your belongings into this house. Into the nanny's bedroom to take her position, so to speak. The room has already been refreshed and prepared. *Naturellement,* you will be compensated for this additional duty."

Extra money was nice, she supposed, but not foremost on her mind. "Tell me, Georges. What happened with Conni?"

His Adam's apple jumped. "It is sad, *mademoiselle.* The woman, she was not a friend, *comprende?* She, er, by swallowing a pill, she is no more."

Omigosh. Petra gulped down surprise. "Conni committed suicide?"

"Yes, *mademoiselle.* It is so."

Petra rubbed her forehead, again. What in the name of heaven was going on here?

"*Mademoiselle?*"

"Oh, ah, yes. Yes, I'll definitely move in here. Now with the extra security, it'll be safer, won't it?"

"Indeed." He inclined his head. "I shall instruct the staff to pack up your possessions."

"Ah..." She hesitated, balking at the thought of strangers, particularly male strangers, pawing through her undergarments.

Georges must've read the expression on her face for he added, "Our female staff, *mademoiselle*. You have met Juanita and Inés?"

Petra smiled. "Yes, they've been very helpful."

"That is good. I shall make the arrangements. All should be complete within the hour." He turned to leave.

She delayed him. "Georges, I need to talk with Kelvin. Could you let him know when he gets in no matter how late it is?"

"But of course, *mademoiselle*." Georges clicked his heels and then walked out into the corridor.

Gnawing on her lower lip, Petra sat back down on the bed. Tonight she would get some of her questions answered, one way or another. Kelvin owed her that much.

* * * *

Kelvin impatiently waited by his front door for the new security system to clear him. The hour was late, or early depending on how he looked at it. Three o'clock--only four hours to go before he had to start the new day.

He ran his hand through his weary hair. Perhaps he should assign the morning meet-and-greet to his assistant, Jade. She'd been eager to offer her services only an hour ago. For pleasure, not for work. She hadn't been the only one. Sage, the skinny ambassador from Phi Pavonis had also hinted at a midnight tryst. As did Napa, the tattooed warrior.

A shiver skipped down Kelvin's spine. Who knew if it was because of the cool night air or the thought of coupling with the savage Brhite?

A position of power always engendered lust... and envy in those who desired authority. This evening Valli Proximus' dark violet eyes had darkened further as she'd watched him mingle with the ambassadors. Even Wanda Cropper's eyes--natural and bionic--had lingered on his lips.

By the stars, sex was the last thing on his mind, no matter who the partner.

A vision of Petra intruded. She'd smiled at him earlier in the day, causing his heart to beat faster. He grinned. Then again, a tangle between the sheets did have appeal.

The door finally opened, and Kelvin stepped inside the entryway. Like a faithful dog, Georges waited for him.

"You didn't need to stay up, Georges."

The butler blinked tired eyes. "But sir, I have a message for you."

"A note would've been sufficient." Kelvin braced himself for bad news. "What's the message?"

"It's the *mademoiselle*, sir. Ms. Richardson wanted to speak with you no matter the hour."

"Indeed? Do you think it's urgent?"

The butler made a continental shrug.

"All right. You go to bed. I'll look in on Tray, and then I'll see if Petra is still awake. Thank you, Georges."

With a nod, he and the butler went their separate ways. As Kelvin took the stairs, he loosened his tie, and then shrugged out of his blazer. As late as it was, he felt rejuvenated. Anticipation lifted his steps. Was Petra waiting for him? Should he wake her up?

He opened the door into Tray's darkened room. The boy snuggled in bed, curled next to his poomba. Kelvin leaned down and gently placed a kiss on his nephew's forehead.

Tray softly grunted.

Smiling, Kelvin walked through the connecting bathroom into the room Petra now occupied. By her bedside, a small lamp dimly lit the darkness.

She wasn't in her bed. Instead, she kept her vigil in an armchair with her slippered feet propped up on an ottoman. Baggy sweats and an oversized shirt were her pajamas. She was asleep, of course. Her head tilted awkwardly against the plush upholstery and her hair, long and loose, splayed every which way... across her eyes, on her shoulder, and hanging down over the chair's edge.

She was Beauty personified.

Something intangible tugged on his heartstrings. Something warm. Something piercing. Something that quite possibly could be love.

His breath caught in his throat. Could this be true? The answer was staring him in the face. Yes, it was true. He was in love with Petra.

She sighed in her sleep. Perhaps she somehow could perceive his thoughts.

He snapped to attention. She must've been uncomfortable. He dropped his blazer, carefully scooped her up in his arms, and then carried her over to the bed. Setting her down, he removed her slippers and then pulled blankets over her.

Gazing down, he felt his heart rate increase, hammering out just how much this woman affected him. But it was late. He was tired. He should go. Emotions such as love should not be dwelt upon... or even discussed in the cold pre-dawn light.

He turned on his heel, but a murmur from the bed stopped him.

"Kelvin, you're here." Rubbing at her eyes, Petra sat up. "Goodness, what time is it?"

For a moment, his new revelation stilled his words. He swallowed down desire. "Petra, I do apologize. I didn't mean to wake you."

"Then we're even. I didn't mean to fall asleep." She brushed her hair out of her face, and then glanced at the clock. "Omigosh! It's after three. You should be in bed."

"Good idea." With that, he tossed back the covers and scooted in, sitting beside her. Glancing at her now thinned lips, he grinned. "What?"

She folded her arms across her chest. "I didn't mean in here."

"I know, sweetness. It's just been a very long day." He propped up a pillow and then leaned against it. "Allow me to relax for a few minutes. You can tell me why you wanted to see me, and then I'll leave. Deal?"

"Deal. But first, take off your shoes."

"Gladly." Dropping his oxfords on the floor, he lifted his eyebrow. "Anything else you'd like me to remove?"

She wrinkled her nose. "Funny. So, are you ready for my barrage of questions?"

"One moment." He pulled out his cell phone and left a message for Jade and Owen Greenacre to take the morning shift. Kelvin then closed his eyes. "Fire away."

"Okay then. First, Georges told me Conni, ah, committed suicide. Why would she do such a desperate act? It's incomprehensible. And it certainly wasn't because she hid Tray's stuffed animal."

"No." Kelvin massaged the bridge of his nose. "Far more than that, I'm afraid."

He'd reveal some of the truth without mentioning the extraterrestrial connection. "I told you about our concern for Tray's safety. It turns out that Conni True was a member of a rebel group called the Continuers. In fact, Conni's name is an anagram of the group. We're still investigating her background to determine her real name and to discover her associates. What I fear is that there is a traitor among us. Perhaps there is more than one."

Petra placed her hand on his upper arm. "That's awful. I'm so sorry, Kelvin."

He clasped hands with hers. "We'll get to the bottom of this. Hopefully sooner rather than later. Next question?"

"Well, here goes. This is a big one. Things don't add up here, Kelvin. This place is so strange. Is the Taurus City Travel Agency some kind of secret society? Why are your travel conference attendees called ambassadors? Why did Hunt tell me this was a diplomatic conference, not a travel conference? And why were all the sightseeing spots covered by Valli Proximus geographic locations, with not one mention of a city or an archeological site?"

Kelvin couldn't help sighing. His creative thinking ability would be put to the test. He gave her hand a little squeeze. "Very perceptive of you, my dear. We, at the Agency, are not a secret society, per se. However we do cater to a select clientele. Extremely select. Big egos are the norm, hence the titles of ambassadors."

He glanced at her. Was she buying this? Her closed expression revealed nothing.

"As for diplomatic versus travel," he continued. "I suspect Ambassador Hunt was referring to the renewal of contracts that we'll be handling later in the conference. Believe me, massaging such massive egos come contract time is no uncomplicated diplomatic task by any means."

"Hmmn."

A noncommittal response. Was he succeeding or failing her interrogation?

Petra wouldn't let him off the hook. "And the geographic locations?"

"That's the easiest one to answer, my dear girl. All our clients prefer to explore Earth's natural beauty. They compare it to a pleasure dome."

"That's what Hunt had said. Pleasure dome and Xanadu--words from Samuel Taylor Coleridge's poem 'Kubla Khan'. How odd."

"Not really. Perhaps one of our clients gave Coleridge the inspiration."

She frowned. "'Kubla Khan' was published in 1816. Has the Taurus City Travel Agency been around that long?"

Without meaning to, Kelvin yawned. "The Agency goes back quite a ways." He slid down to rest his head on the pillow. "And I have a question for you. Why the difference in your nighttime apparel?"

"From yesterday's short robe to these sweats?" Laughter lightened her voice. "Obviously it's because I was expecting you tonight."

"Obviously." He yawned again. His hold on consciousness was slipping. He'd better head over to his bedroom while he was still able. He flipped back the blankets. "Before I forget, thank you for taking over Conni's position. I feel better with you staying here. Tray does, also."

Before he had a chance to sit up, Petra reached over and pulled the blankets back over him. "I feel better with you staying here, too. Have a good sleep, Kelvin." She turned out the light.

By the stars! Petra wanted him in her bed? He was the luckiest man alive. He was also the sleepiest. Too bad he couldn't take advantage of this unexpected situation.

Kelvin closed his eyes, took Petra's hand once again, and then promptly fell asleep.

Chapter Ten

When Petra awoke, she was aware of a soothing pulse under her ear. Mmmm, so relaxing. Her arm curved around a hard but warm pillow. Content, she inhaled deeply. Scents of bay rum, coffee, and musk filled her lungs.

Her eyes popped open at the same time her memory returned. Her hard pillow was Kelvin! He'd been so exhausted last night after he'd answered her questions, she hadn't the heart to make him seek his own bed. And as soon as she'd turned off the light, he'd surrendered to sleep.

He slept still. Slowly, carefully, she eased out from his unconscious embrace and studied him. His dark hair, usually brushed back, now haphazardly fringed his forehead. The sharp lines cut around his mouth, along with the crinkles by his closed eyes were softened in the morning light. His lips, so full and sexy, slightly pouted as he dreamt.

He looked divinely kissable, but she resisted. She had to. Kelvin had a busy day ahead of him as did she. Besides, if she did kiss him, she preferred the event would be a long and lingering one, leading to more, much more. Her reality here was that any minute Tray would be waking up.

Once out of bed, she grabbed some casual clothes and entered the bathroom. There was only one lock--this one was attached to the door to Tray's bedroom. Unfortunately, the door to her bedroom didn't have a lock. She'd have to chance it that Kelvin wouldn't wake up and open the bathroom door.

As she showered, she allowed her thoughts to wander. What Kelvin had told her last night hadn't completely relieved her mind. She still believed the Taurus City Travel Agency was a secret society. No matter what Kelvin had said, something strange was going on here; there was some kind of hidden agenda.

Then again, maybe it wasn't any of her business. As long as she took care of Tray for the duration of her contract, she really didn't need to know the Agency's deep dark secrets. She would earn a nice little nest egg for herself. As a side bonus, maybe, just maybe she and the delectable Kelvin Lacertus would indulge themselves. Indulge in hot, passionate nights. He wanted her. She knew he did. So why shouldn't she enjoy a brief affair while she had the chance?

And then, come the end of August, she'd leave this place and return to the dubious delights of teaching middle school. When the frigid days of winter arrived back in the city, she would have memories of their lovemaking to keep her warm. Fingers crossed!

Holding that thought, she dressed, wound her damp hair into a topknot. She couldn't resist taking a quick peek at Kelvin. He'd turned in the bed with his strong arm now flung over a pillow.

He missed her. No thought could've been more pleasing. She smiled.

But another Lacertus had to claim her attention now. She unlocked the bathroom door to Tray's room. He also hugged something--his poomba. He stirred under the covers. It was a sure bet that soon he'd be raring to go.

A knock sounded at the door. Georges leaned his closely shaved head inside. *"Mademoiselle,* you are up." His gaze flickered to the bathroom door. "Have you, perchance, seen Master Kelvin? He is nowhere to be found."

"Oh. Yes, actually he was so tired last night, he fell asleep in my bed." Goodness, her cheeks probably flushed pure pink.

For a split second, Georges' lips lifted in a smile, but then he was solemn once again. *"Merci, mademoiselle.* You relieve my mind. I shall attempt to roust our slumbering CEO." Withdrawing from the bedroom, he closed the door with a soft click.

Petra waited a moment. She fanned her face with her hand to drive away embarrassment. The humor of it all then struck her and she broke out in a huge grin. Well, so much for a little privacy. Even though Georges was probably the soul of discretion, she'd wager that rumors would be flying around the household staff about her and Kelvin.

She crossed her fingers. Hopefully soon, very soon, the rumors would turn into fact.

* * * *

The morning passed by quickly. Tray had been on his best behavior through lessons on the People's Republic of China, the history of the Great Wall, and practicing his ABCs along with a touch of penmanship. The carrot dangling before him was an afternoon picnic by the beach.

The ever-present sea lions had been glad to see them. Tray singled out his friend Heckle--or so he identified the animal. Noisy greetings between the two then followed.

Since all sea lions looked alike--at least to Petra--she assumed Tray thought he was fooling her. Then again, maybe he *could* distinguish one sea lion from another.

Now that they had finished lunch, Tray busily dug in wet sand close to the shore. Looking for treasures, no doubt. Or for tiny fish to feed his sea pals. Raulf and Bjorn kept a vigilant watch. Allowing her mind to wander, she closed her eyes. All sounds seemed to fade in the distance--the honk of congenial sea lions, the rush of island scented breezes, the occasional splash from the water.

She must've been lulled to sleep because one moment she drifted in between dreams and the next, she heard a high-pitched squeal.

Without even thinking, she jumped to her bare feet and ran over to Tray. As she did, Bjorn and Raulf joined them.

"Ooh! Lookee what I found. It just washed up by my toes." With his shovel, Tray poked at a beige rubbery mass.

Petra dropped to her knees to examine the strange object. Gingerly touching an edge, she lifted an extremely lightweight casing or covering. It reminded her of what was left behind when a snake shed its skin.

"What in the world is this?" She turned to the guards for an answer.

Both men shrugged. Obviously they didn't consider this a dangerous object. "Nothing to worry about," muttered Bjorn. The blond guard turned back to his perch on a sandy rock. Restless Raulf pulled out his cell phone and, pacing around their perimeter, made a call.

She continued to lift the skin, or whatever it was, so that it reached about five feet in height. It was all one piece, then it separated into two thin tubes attached to the main trunk near the top. The main trunk then split into two.

Her mouth dropped. Two arms, two legs, and a small area for the head. "Omigosh. This is... this is..."

Words failed her.

Tray gave the skin a once-over. "I know what it is. It's for the visitors. They wear it."

Letting go of the thing, she ran her hands through the turquoise waters lapping the shore. If she'd had a bar of anti-bacterial soap, she would've scrubbed up as intensely as a surgeon. Several deep breaths later, she struggled to contain her panic. Tray was so matter-of-fact about this skin; she certainly didn't want him to get scared just because she was out-of-her-mind terrified.

"W-Why do the visitors wear this?" She swallowed a bit of bile.

He scrunched up his little nose. "So they look like us, silly."

Naturally. Why else?

Her lunch threatened to make a reappearance. Holding her fist over her mouth, she concentrated on slowing her breaths. In, out, in, out.

Good. Maybe now she could ask him more questions--

A loud splash interrupted. It came from the bay, about twenty feet from where she and Tray sat. The sun shining down brightly, she had to squint. Her gaze riveted on something green. A green head with blinking green eyes.

No bloody way.

The thing, the head, disappeared under the water.

Petra stood. "I think we should go now." She held out her hand for him to grab.

"No, I don't wanna. We just got here."

Her stomach heaved again. "I have to go to the bathroom, Tray. I guess you can stay with Bjorn and Raulf."

Evidently that wasn't okay with Tray. "I gonna come with you. I gotta go, too."

Thank goodness that was easy. She signaled to the guards, and then, holding Tray's hand, trudged through the uneven sands back to the house.

Her mind swirled with the implications of Tray's words and the evidence of her own eyes. She couldn't be mistaken here. Something momentous had just occurred. Something that Kelvin and company would not be able to explain away.

She'd learned, reluctantly and first hand, that Humans were not alone.

* * * *

Kelvin pocketed his cell phone. Double hell. There was no time to dwell on the security guard's report, however. Instead, he gave his

114

regrets to the Kykanophians--Ambassador Kamtos and Citizen Korpos--for having to end their conversation, and then motioned to Valli Proximus and Owen Greenacre. While he waited for his staff members, he placed a quick call to Felicia Alvarez. Petra would, no doubt, be upset after her discovery. Perhaps the cheerful HR assistant would be able to take Petra's mind off of what she had found.

"What's going on?" Owen, elegantly attired as usual, straightened his purple silk tie and then smoothed back gleaming silver hair.

Valli, ever watchful, withheld her questions.

Kelvin kept his reply short. "Come with me." They left the conference room and strode in silence down the corridors.

He waited until they exited the visitors' section before explaining. "There's been a breech in protocol."

"Since you are informing me, I assume the offender is one of our visitors." Valli looked down her regal nose as if the alien in question had committed a personal affront. "Who is it?"

"Tarrnak from Vela. He and the Sirian Dutto decided to take a swim in the bay within the boundaries of the compound... sans their skins."

Owen slipped on sunglasses. "There is no protocol against swimming, Kelvin."

The man's superior tone rankled. "True, Owen. Tarrnak's breech was inadvertent. He'd left his skin too close to the shore where, regrettably, the incoming tide swept it away."

Owen shrugged. "That's unfortunate, yes. But, using the local vernacular, 'no harm, no foul.'"

"You are wrong." Kelvin took perverse pleasure in taking his operations director to task. "The discarded skin washed up on shore... in the natives' section of the island. As you may have surmised, a Terran discovered the skin. She actually examined it."

Owen's mature face drooped while Valli raised a dark eyebrow.

"And not only that," Kelvin continued, walking toward his office. "In an attempt to recover his skin, Tarrnak swam along the coastline. Without a doubt, the Terran spotted his green head."

Valli's violet eyes flashed annoyance. "Who is the native?"

For some reason Kelvin was reluctant to mention Petra's name. "That isn't important. I will see to damage control. It's Tarrnak I'm anxious about. Perhaps we should impose a fine? Your thoughts on this, please."

Once inside the building, Owen removed his sunglasses. "The Human skin will have to be refreshed or, if that's not possible, Tarrnak will need a new one. Either way, the extra expense will be great. Would that be punishment enough?"

"I disagree, Owen. Something more stringent should be invoked. The rules are firm on this issue. Because of the Velan's negligence, a Terran is now aware of extraterrestrial life." Valli turned to Kelvin. "I fail to see how you can adequately handle damage control."

"That is *my* concern." Kelvin opened the door to his office suite, and then ushered Owen and Valli inside.

Tarrnak and Dutto already sat inside with a security guard watching over them. The Sirian, normally light blue, wore his Human skin. His hair remained startlingly white.

If there was a word to describe Dutto's mood, it would've been bubbly. By contrast, Tarrnak sat, without his skin and with his bald green head lowered. By the unpleasant earthy odor in the room, it was a certainty a shroud covered his face, emitting the smell.

After greetings were exchanged, Kelvin and his staff sat in the available chairs.

Dutto jumped to his feet. "I cannot contain myself, grand sir, Mr. Greenacre, and Ms. Proximus. I am in alt. Simply in alt."

"Why is this, Dutto?"

The Sirian clapped his hands together. His expressive eyebrows almost clapped as well. "The swimming in Xanadu's waters, grand sir. So very restorative. So very delightful. It is a spiritual event I crave to experience again and again. I shall inform all my fellow Sirians that this planet's reputation is well deserved. Xanadu is beyond compare."

It was always good to hear from satisfied customers. Smiling, Kelvin thanked the Sirian. His gushing about swimming was easy to understand. Whenever Dutto's race became overstressed, to use a Terran term, their skin tended to lose moisture, making them smaller, harder. To recover, they had to immerse themselves in water. Although Dutto wore a Human skin, he appeared far plumper than he usually did.

Kelvin stood and escorted the Sirian to the door. "If you'll excuse us, we need to confer with Tarrnak."

Both aliens exchanged a glance. Dutto nodded, and then ducked out the door.

When Kelvin returned to his chair, Tarrnak lifted his shrouded head. His breathing rate increased. "I speak with only you, most hallowed sir."

Owen got to his feet. He held out his hands, palms up. "That's fine with me."

Valli, though, disapproved. Her thin lips tightened. "As Travel Director, I strongly believe I should be included, Kelvin."

Owen placed his hand on her arm and helped her up. "If Kelvin needs us, he'll call, won't you, Kelvin?"

"Of course I will." Kelvin watched as the master manipulator--Owen--worked his charm.

Owen smiled his one hundred watt grin at her. "How about if you come with me and we go get a drink?"

By the pull of her lips, Kelvin knew she wasn't happy. Valli straightened her suit jacket, and nodded. "I certainly could use one."

Kelvin gestured for the security guard to also leave.

As soon as only Kelvin and Tarrnak remained, a ripple flowed through the Velan's velvety skin. The shroud covering his face also disappeared.

He blinked vivid green eyes. "My thanks, most hallowed sir. I prefer to face disgrace in private. There can be no excuse for my carelessness."

Kelvin massaged the bridge of his nose. He was torn. On one hand, the Velan's actions broke the number one rule on the planet: keep native Terrans ignorant about extraterrestrial life.

On the other hand, Tarrnak had acted innocently enough. His planet didn't have a moon. Vela's oceans weren't subject to gravitational tides.

Kelvin sighed. What should he do?

"You love her, sir. You should tell her."

By the stars! That was his answer, wasn't it? Only that wasn't the question he was asking. Then again, he would be unwise not to heed a Velan's psychic recommendation.

He withheld his smile. "Thanks for the advice, Tarrnak. However, we need to settle your transgression, not discuss my love life."

"'Tis foremost on your mind, sir."

"Perhaps." Kelvin allowed himself to smile. "So, here's my ruling. You will purchase another skin. Chances are high that seawater ruined the original one. In addition, you will forgo swimming for the duration of your visit, and you will forfeit one thousand credits."

The Velan bowed his head. "A fair judgment, most hallowed sir."

Kelvin stood. "Good. I'm glad we agree." He made arrangements for Tarrnak to be escorted back to the visitors' section without being seen.

All that remained was to somehow explain to Petra about the Human skin suit.

And to tell her he loved her.

Chapter Eleven

After splashing cold water on her face, Petra stared at her lackluster image in the bathroom mirror. Her ponytail hung limp as if the life had been sucked out of it. No shine, no bounce, no pizzazz. Her hazel eyes seemed sunken, her complexion pasty. Deep breathing didn't help to restore her composure. Nothing helped. All she could think about was that the Taurus City Travel Agency was a hotbed of extraterrestrial activity.

She leaned against the granite countertop and closed her eyes. Unfortunately, her thoughts just kept coming. Why were these beings here? What did they want? Fear weaved its insidious way through her body. Her heart pounded out its terror. Her teeth chattered. Clammy sweat iced her hands. She was an emotional mess.

Wait. Cold reason intruded. Should she really be afraid? Afraid of what, an alien invasion?

These... people, the ones she'd met, the ones that might possibly be aliens, seemed more like tourists than invaders. Sightseers, pleasure seekers.

Yes, that brought to mind what Ambassador Hunt had told her: pleasure dome. Xanadu. A paradise for aliens. Nothing menacing there. Surely there could be no harm for them to just visit Earth's attractions?

A series of knocks sounded at the door. "Petra? Are you done yet? C'mon! I wanna go outside."

She took another deep, calming breath. Tray was just a little boy. Wherever he was originally from, she had nothing to worry about with him. And maybe, she had nothing to worry about, period. Aliens or no.

Okay. I can do this.

"Be right out," she called to him.

As soon as she opened the door, Tray grabbed her hand, pulling her into the corridor. "C'mon! Miz Felicia's here to see us."

Petra allowed herself to be dragged, but her mind refused to be stilled. Everything took on a sinister tone. Why was Felicia--out of the blue-- paying them a visit?

"Hi! Golly, it seems like ages." Felicia jumped up from the room's white couch, rushed over and gave Petra a hug. "How're you doing, girl?"

Petra gave a weak smile and submitted to the friendly squeeze. It was easy to get swept up in Felicia's enthusiasm. "Fine. Good. How about you?"

As Felicia rattled on, Petra gave the woman the once-over. Was she an alien? Or was she like Kelvin? Was she originally from Ethiopia, too?

Georges entered, rolling in a treat-ladened cart. "Pardon the interruption, *mademoiselles*. The young sir looked in need of nourishment." He lifted a gleaming teapot. "Tea?"

While Tray hopped and skipped around the food, Petra observed Georges. Was *he* an alien? But how could that be so? He had a French accent.

Stop!

She'd go crazy if she questioned every person she came across.

After the butler left, she sat next to Felicia on the couch and sipped at her orange-spiced tea. "Any particular reason for the pleasure of your company today, Felicia?"

"Well, Kelvin called and asked me to stay with Tray." She tossed a hank of tightly curled hair over her slim shoulder. *"You* and Tray."

She then leaned closer and lowered her voice. "I think he's got the hots for you, girl."

"Ah, no." Petra's denial was automatic. "He's considerate of everyone." She called a halt to Tray's wholesale demolition of cookies. "Tray, let's go outside now. I'm sure you feel like running around."

Felicia giggled. "Great idea! All that sugar would make me hyper, too."

Felicia being hyper just didn't bear thinking about.

Once outside in the late afternoon air, all worries seemed to downsize. Palm trees swayed from ocean breezes, Tray zipped up and down the compound grounds playing his favorite game of pretending to be Heckle and Jeckle, and an easy conversation with Felicia as they sat on a bench made everything as normal as could be. Nothing was out of the ordinary. Everything was peaceful and serene.

Petra exhaled a grateful breath. Thank goodness. Being so emotionally keyed up certainly wasn't healthy.

After an hour enjoying this island paradise, she noticed Georges making his way toward her. *"Mademoiselle,"* he inclined his shorn head. "Josephus Hammer is here to see you."

Hmmn. Again, here was something unusual. "Thanks, Georges. He can join us out here."

Felicia made one of her trademark squeals, and then sat up straight. "Golly! I haven't seen my boss in ages. He's been so busy with the conference."

Petra smiled. "It seems to me that you have the hots for Joe."

"Who wouldn't?" Felicia fussed with her hair, and then fluttered her eyelashes in Joe's direction.

The HR Director, tall and lanky, approached them with a folding chair in his hand. He set it up in front of their bench, and then sat. "Good afternoon, ladies. I trust you are both relishing this fine weather."

Her dark eyes wide, Felicia nodded vigorously.

"Yes, thank you." Petra cut to the chase. "And what brings you here, Joe?"

"Two reasons, actually." He folded well-manicured hands on his lap. "First, Kelvin would like to take you to dinner, Petra. He made reservations at the Shining C for six thirty, and plans to pick you up around six, if that's convenient."

"Yes, it's convenient. But, well, isn't he occupied with the conference?"

Joe's lined face creased with more wrinkles. Or rather, in his case, character lines. "Since it is Saturday night, there is a special off-island trip scheduled for the attendees."

Felicia found her voice. "Ooh, yeah. It's to Isabela Island, isn't it? The largest island in the Galápagos."

Joe nodded. "Indeed. Many attendees expressed a wish to see a volcanically active location--especially at night. Isabela Island has six volcanoes, five of which are still active."

This trip fit in with what Kelvin had confirmed--his clients were interested in geographic settings.

"I see. So Kelvin doesn't have to accompany them?" she asked.

"No. We have more than enough personnel to handle the tour. Valli

Proximus, of course, will head it, assisted by Ellen D. who manages Team South America. Also, several members of the staff, and I believe Owen Greenacre might assist as well."

The conversation lulled. Felicia continued to make goo-goo eyes at her boss.

Petra withheld her amusement. "You mentioned two reasons, Joe."

He cleared his throat. "Yes. Indeed. I was hoping you, Felicia, would join me for dinner at the Agency Café."

"Me?" Felicia's voice lifted a few octaves. So much so that Tray stopped his endless run about the grounds.

He peered at her. "You sound like a chattering magpie, Miz Felicia." He then continued his wingless flight.

Felicia's mocha complexion reddened.

Joe cocked his head. "Felicia?"

"Oh, um, yeah, of course. Golly, I'm honored." Standing, she restlessly brushed at her long sleeves and her cotton slacks. "I'll go change, okay?"

Petra also stood, as did Joe. "You know, I think Kelvin and I should have dinner here. So Tray isn't alone."

Joe's green eyes crinkled. "Kelvin was right. He thought you might say that. I will get one of the Ellens to watch the lad. Between her company and Georges', Traynor will be fine. Not to mention the bodyguards, of course."

Joe gave them both a smile. "Ladies." He then turned toward the house.

Felicia winked at Petra, and then hurried to take his arm. "So when are you picking me up, Joe?"

His answer was too low for Petra to hear. She watched as they both headed for their cars.

Petra sat back down, her thoughts swirling. A date with the mysterious Kelvin. Maybe she could learn what *really* was going on here. Now that she had some ammunition.

* * * *

Joe Hammer was as good as his word. A half hour later, one of the Ellens knocked at the door. Petra rushed down the stairs, but Georges answered it first.

"Greetings," this Ellen murmured, dressed in a dreary grey shirt and matching slacks. "I am here to watch over young Traynor."

As soon as Petra approached, she knew exactly which Ellen this was-- Ellen F. who handled the Australian travel team. The scent of peppermint was unmistakable.

"Thanks so much for coming, Ellen. I appreciate you looking after Tray for us."

"Not at all." The woman's sleek black hair gleamed under the house lights. Not a strand was out of place. Not an imperfection marred her cold beauty.

Petra shivered. Truth be told, Ellen F.--actually all the Ellens--looked more like mannequins than actual people.

"Tray's in his bedroom, having fun with his toy soldiers." Petra gestured for Ellen to follow her up the staircase. "He's fine playing by himself. Dinner is around six, and then bedtime's at nine. Once he's asleep, you can let Georges know, and then go home. Does that work for you?"

"Perfect." Ellen's toneless voice echoed up the stairs. "I love children."

Another shiver scurried down Petra's spine. This woman had near zero personality. It was as if one person's individuality got split six ways between the Ellens. Or maybe, since this one was the youngest, being "F", she got gypped on the Ellen personality.

Tray barely looked up from his army men's battle to acknowledge Ellen. The woman smiled--a chilling sight in itself--and picked up one of his books to read.

Petra contained her shudder. "If you need me, I'll be in the next room getting ready." Without meaning to, she hurried through the bathroom, closed the connecting door to her bedroom, and then leaned against it.

Goodness, she was a bundle of nerves, wasn't she?

It didn't take long to dress. Since she'd only packed two skirts, and she'd worn one yesterday, the choice was easy. Her patterned chiffon skirt billowed down to the floor. To glamorize it, she chose a silky black top with spaghetti straps. A fringed black scarf would do double duty as a shawl. The same dangly earrings and the same high heeled pumps... again, that would have to suffice.

She released her hair from its ponytail and brushed some life into it. Long and free, it covered her shoulders. Twirling in front of the mirror, she approved of her sexy image. Now she had even more ammunition to hit Kelvin with. And that thought made her smile.

On the dot at six o'clock, there was a knock at the bedroom door. As she opened the door, she tapped down her excitement. But instead of Kelvin, it was Georges.

His dark blue-eyed gaze quickly roamed over her. *"Mademoiselle."* He inclined his head. "Master Kelvin is downstairs for you."

"Thank you, Georges." She grabbed her scarf and then went next door to say goodnight to Trey and Ellen F. After that, Petra carefully walked down the staircase. Three-inch high heels tended to slow her down.

"Petra." Kelvin joined her at the bottom of the stairs. He took her hands and smiled. His touch was warm, exhilarating. "You look wonderful."

"So do you." Heart-stoppingly wonderful. She couldn't help but lick her lips. In a black-checked blazer and skinny black tie, he dressed dashingly retro. A curl of dark hair fell onto his forehead. Oh, she was so tempted to smooth the renegade lock back into his hair.

A crooked smile lightened his face as he placed his arm around her shoulders and hurried forward. "Well, come on then. We don't want to waste a moment, do we?"

The way he speed-demon drove to the Shining C, it was apparent *he* didn't want to waste a moment.

The restaurant was completely empty except for the wait staff. Petra chose to sit outside this time, at a small bamboo table, under the twinkling expanse of stars.

"Where is everyone?" she asked, sipping on her chi chi. "Are we that early?"

"Not at all. Tonight I reserved the entire restaurant for us, to insure our privacy." He winked.

Her mouth dropped. "Wow. You certainly do things in a big way."

He smiled confidently at her. "One of the perks of the job, my dear."

Hmmn. They were virtually alone--no one to overhear, which meant it was a perfect time for her to question him. But how could she casually bring up her suspicion that there were extraterrestrials running around?

She dug her top teeth into her lower lip. So this was what it felt like to be a candidate for the nut house.

He leaned in across the small table and lowered his voice to an intimate whisper. "I've been told you found something... interesting today."

"Yes, you could say that." Something interesting that changed everything. Something that, if known, would rock the world.

"How are you holding up?" He lifted an eyebrow. "Are you petra... fied?"

She choked on her coconut drink. "Cute," she managed to utter. Once the spasm subsided, she answered, "No, I'm not petrified, but I am, ah, very, very curious. Again, what's going on here?"

It was time to lay the cards out on the table. She leveled her gaze at him. "You're running a bloody resort for aliens, aren't you? Extraterrestrial aliens."

The tick in his jaw expressed his struggle. His grey eyes darkened to midnight black. "Petra, if I tell you, then I'll have to--"

"Okay, I get it. It's one of those 'if I tell you, I have to kill you' scenarios." She snorted. "Sure."

"No." His slow smile sizzled her insides. "It's a 'if I tell you, you have to marry me' scenario."

"Whoa! What?" She blinked, and blinked again. "That's crazy. No, I don't think so."

He clapped his hand over his heart. "By the stars, you wound me, my dear.

"You'll recover." She finished her drink, and then set it down with a thud. "Look, Kelvin, this isn't something to joke about. I held up a gosh darn awful human skin. I saw a green, human shaped head sticking out of the water. I *saw* those things. I *felt* that rubbery mass. You can't charm your way out of this... mess."

"Petra." He reached over and took her hand, sandwiching it between his. "I'm not joking. And I'm not intending to charm you. Not intentionally, at any rate." He gave a brief smile, but then was serious again. "You're an intelligent woman. A very intelligent woman. As I've said, I was drawn to you when you were but a girl, and I'm even more drawn to you now. I..."

He raised her hand to his lips. A soft kiss burned through her skin. "I had an epiphany last night, my dear. Last night, lying next to you." His broad shoulders raised in a shrug. "I can't help it. I love you, Petra Jane Richardson. It's the honest truth."

Omigosh! Omigosh! I can't believe this. This can't be true. This can't be real.

But the way he was looking at her, tender and loving, made her heart nearly explode into a thousand pieces. Could Kelvin be the one for her? So much more than a brief affair? Life partners? The one who would love her forever?

Cold reality intruded on her bliss. She had to be practical. Her track record with men was lousy, to say the least. Bob had been the latest in her ever-growing list of bad choices. How could Kelvin fall in love with her? Why would he actually care for her?

She pulled her hand from his and folded her arms across her chest. "I don't believe you. You're just saying this to get my mind off of what I'd seen. Of what I'd said."

The server arrived with their food. Petra stared at her plate. She never felt less like eating.

Then again, neither did Kelvin. His brows drawn, his lips tensed, he looked more somber than she'd ever seen him.

When she lifted her fork to sample her pasta, he extended his hand to stop her.

"Petra, why do you doubt me? You're all I can think about, and believe me, right now I have a great deal on my mind. I love you, sweetheart. This is the truth. And so is this--the green head you saw in the waters of the bay belongs to Tarrnak, a native of Vela."

"Where is Vela?" She curled her upper lip. Was he going to say Venezuela again?

Kelvin circled his fingertips over the back of her hand. "Vela is a planet in the blue supergiant star system of Velorum. Velans are strongly psychic. That being the case, Tarrnak is aware of how I feel about you. He advised me to let you know."

She couldn't move; she could hardly breathe. It was as if she was frozen in her chair.

A lopsided grin lifted Kelvin's lips. "I'd be foolish not to follow

Tarrnak's advice. No one should ignore a Velan's recommendation."

"But..." Oh good gosh! Could she believe her ears? "So I'm right? This Taurus City Travel Agency really does cater to... extraterrestrials?"

"Human and alien, Petra." Kelvin sliced into his filet mignon. "However, you're not right about me. About my sentiments for you."

In that second, her world shifted. Instead of feeling shock at having validation that Humans weren't alone in the universe, she experienced shock at learning that maybe, she wasn't alone here on Earth. That maybe here was someone who loved her. That maybe Kelvin was the man for her.

She opened her mouth to speak, but all she could manage to say was "Oh!"

Obviously, that was enough.

Kelvin pushed his chair away from the table and stood. "Well said, my dear. I see you and I are of the same mind." Easing her chair out, he gently lifted her to her feet. "We should seal our understanding with a kiss."

Gazing into his bottomless eyes, she smoothed her hands up his back. "Yes, we should. Definitely."

Their joining was in slow motion. At first their heated breaths mingled, and then gradually, deliberately, their lips met. As their kiss deepened, she sighed, which then turned into a moan of surrender. Even the air around them crackled with desire. Kissing Kelvin was just as she'd imagined. A hunger she'd never experienced before shot through her core, branding her. His heart thudded against her with a savage beat that called to her primitive soul.

She was lost. Right then and there she knew she would do anything for this man. Anything at all.

He moved from her lips to feather tiny kisses up her cheek to then rest on her forehead. A moment passed, and he again sought her mouth. "Petra, my love," he murmured. "I propose we take care of our hungry stomachs, and then concentrate on our hungry hearts. Are we agreed?"

Dragging herself away, she drank in the sight of him. Oh how her heart did soar. "Agreed."

After he helped her back into her chair, she smiled up at him. "Kelvin, no matter what happens, I just want you to know that I'm very happy."

He lifted her hand to his lips again. "As am I, my love. Deliriously happy. And I'm certain my Velan friend can predict nothing but happiness for us in the future, so there's no need to worry."

Velan. Petra sat up ramrod straight. Kelvin's mention of the alien was like a splash of cold water on her heated emotions. Why did this new love have to be so bloody... convoluted? For goodness sake, why couldn't it just be her and him without thinking about space aliens?

In her experience, people in love only needed to focus on their own desires, not navigate the murky depths of extraterrestrial affairs.

Chapter Twelve

She was uneasy. Kelvin knew that for a fact. The reality of what he'd confirmed tonight was taking a severe toll on her. Delayed stress. Petra tried to hide her apprehension, but her tawny eyes had lightened to the frigid color of pure gold. And though temperate breezes warmed them as they'd sat beneath the stars, she shivered.

He couldn't blame her. If he'd just learned that everything he'd taken for granted in life was really one hundred and eighty degrees different, he'd be none too happy as well.

They returned to the house in silence, and now she walked up the stairs without animation. Each step seemed to steal more and more of her energy.

"You're cold, sweetheart." He curved his arm around her slender waist, pulling her slightly against him. "Let me warm you."

She blinked rapidly. Was there a hint of wetness in her eyes that she tried to hide? "I... I'm sorry, Kelvin. I'm just, oh I don't know, I'm scared."

"Quite understandable, my dear. How could you not be upset? And that's exactly why we, we here at Taurus City, have a strict rule to never reveal ourselves to the natives."

"Then why did you? Why did you tell me this?"

He paused with her at the top of the stairs and slid his fingers through her long hair. Her strands were soft and silky, just as he imagined the rest of her to be. "I'm aware that we haven't known each other long, and yet I do know you are as honest and trustworthy as they come. I want you to know the truth, Petra. You deserve the truth."

Her breathing came rapidly. She darted her gaze everywhere but at him. "I, ah, what about what you said? That doesn't mean you really have to marry me, does it?"

Cupping her face in his hands, he leaned in close, almost touching her lips. "*Have* to marry you? Yes, I do, but sweetheart, only if you say yes." He sobered his smile. "I *want* to marry you, Petra. But I'm not doing this right, am I? First I'm supposed to ask your father for your hand."

She pulled away. "My dad? Omigosh, you want to meet my parents?"

"Of course. Isn't that how it's done? Let them look over their prospective son-in-law? See what his prospects are? Find out if he can take care of their little girl?"

She nibbled on her lower lip. "That's not a good idea. My dad's default setting is anger. If things don't go as he wants, then it's World War III. No joke."

"Typical male." Kelvin grinned. "What about your mom?"

Petra shrugged. "Mom's like a scared mouse. She goes along with whatever Dad thinks."

"You see this as a problem?" He kissed the tip of her nose. "You don't think I can win over Papa Richardson?"

"Frankly, no, I don't. Dad'll call you the Rebound Guy, along with other more offensive words."

Kelvin felt her tremble, then she continued, "You see, I was going with someone. For a few months now. In fact, Bob and I had plans to vacation together this summer, so I was going to refuse this assignment. Then I found out he cancelled our plans. He went fishing with his buddies instead." She smiled grimly. "Naturally, that was the end of that, so I was free to come here."

"This Bob fellow must be an idiot, to which I'm eternally grateful." Kelvin lifted her hand to his lips, turned her hand over, and then gently kissed her palm. The warmth of her skin sent shivers of pleasure down his spine.

"Oh! I, ah, Dad hated Bob, so while he was glad that I terminated the relationship, he also hated that I traveled here. With my dad, the key word is hate."

Kelvin enclosed her in his arms. "Never fear. I can handle your father," he whispered in her ear.

Now *she* shivered. "But he'll ask you all kinds of questions, and he'll demand answers. He'll want to know what you do for a living. He'll want to know specifics. And how much money you make. Where you're from. What your family background is. What your political beliefs are."

She paused to take a deep breath. "I mean, you're from, y'know, outer space, for goodness sake. That's not going to go over well with my dad."

When she sucked in her lower lip, Kelvin was tempted to nibble on her as well.

"I just met you, Kelvin. We're attracted to each other, sure. But love? Commitment? Marriage? Marriage is, well, it's a forever step."

"Indeed it is, sweetheart." Starting with her forehead, he trailed his lips over her soft skin to find his way once more to her mouth. "And that's exactly what I want with you. A forever step. *The* forever step."

He pulled away and then enfolded her in his arms. "But you're right, of course. That kind of commitment is too soon for us. Right now, anyway. How about if we just see where this leads? Just you and me--"

"And Tray." Her voice held a hint of laughter.

"Tray, to be sure, but not right this particular minute, hmmn?" He found her lips again. She tasted like fruity wine, warm honey, and desire, all rolled into one.

"Mmm," she murmured as they kissed. "Yes, you're right. Not this particular minute." Then she shifted her weight and moved out of his embrace. "But let's just check up on him before we, ah, proceed. And also we'll make sure Ellen F. has gone home, okay?"

"But of course." He curved his arm around her as they walked toward Tray's bedroom. "I wouldn't have it any other way."

He loved this woman. No matter what she said, talk of marriage wasn't too soon for him. Historically, Lacertus family members took their time in finding their mates. And when they did, they married for life. Kelvin had waited thirty-one Terran years. Perhaps his young self had known, all those years ago, that Petra and he were meant to be together. Perhaps, for the last eleven years, he'd been waiting only for her.

Whatever the number, he was more than ready to take that most important step: marriage to Petra. By the stars, he couldn't wait to make her his.

* * * *

Petra cast a shy glance Kelvin's way as he opened his nephew's bedroom door. She couldn't believe this was happening. A dreamboat guy--the very one she'd crushed on way back in junior high--said he wanted to not only marry her but ask permission from her dad. How cool was that? How traditional in the extreme. And yet...

And yet how totally bizarre, since Kelvin was anything but traditional. How could an extraterrestrial be considered traditional?

Oh, her head ached just from thinking about it. Her heart, on the other hand, swelled with such deep emotions, she thought it would burst.

If this was the forever kind of love, then she was hooked--pure and simple.

Kelvin and Petra Lacert--

One step into Tray's darkened room and she knew something was wrong. Tray's uneven breathing filled the somber atmosphere. He slept, but it was a fitful sleep. Intermittent moans disturbed his sleep. Tossing his head, he suddenly snorted, reached for his poomba, and then resumed his heavy breathing.

Goosebumps rose on her arms. "Something's not right," she whispered to Kelvin. "Maybe we should wake him up?"

Kelvin moved to the side of the bed farthest away from the door. He held out his hand to prevent her from following. "No. Stay back. Get Georges and the guards."

But why? No matter what Kelvin said, she had to find out what was wrong. She had to look. Peering over his shoulder, she saw Ellen on the floor. Or rather Ellen's still body on the floor.

Omigosh! The woman's back was arched in an exaggerated manner, and her arms and legs were wildly flung out from her core. Her eyes were frozen wide open and the grimace on her face...

Petra shuddered. It was obvious that Ellen was no longer alive.

"I'll, ah, I'll go get them, and also call the doctor." Petra glanced at Tray as he slept. "Maybe you should move him into my bed."

Kelvin nodded. "Good thinking." He scooped the child up into his arms.

Tray's head lolled against his uncle's strong chest. "Tummyache," the boy mumbled. "Cookies."

Had he eaten too many cookies? Or... had one of the cookies contained something toxic?

In a flash, Kelvin met her gaze. That same thought must've occurred to him.

He gestured for her to leave. "Call Cornwell Young first. Have him look Tray over so he can run some tests."

Her heart in her mouth, Petra rushed to do as Kelvin asked, calling and briefing the doctor, and then alerting Georges and the guards.

Thankfully, it didn't take Cornwell Young long to arrive. As he entered the bedroom, Petra gently shook the boy awake. Tray gave her a sleepy smile, and then held her hand.

He didn't seem to be in much discomfort, so that eased her mind. Tray answered Cornwell's questions and didn't murmur a protest when the doctor took a blood sample.

His dark face grave, Cornwell nodded assurance at her. "The boy seems fine, Petra. I'm gonna examine the blood, and then we'll know for certain." He removed a small cube from his medical bag and then dropped it into a tall glass of water. It fizzed into a myriad of bubbles. "Here, boy, drink this."

"It tickles my nose." Tray sneezed, but then downed the entire fizzy medicine. Once done, he scooted back down under the covers and closed his eyes. "Tired." He yawned.

An eyeblink later, he was in dreamland.

Petra took Cornwell's arm and moved away from the bed. "What do you think? Was it too many cookies? Or..."

Or something sinister?

"Can't say. I'll run some diagnostic tests, but it could be a case of upset stomach." He reached into his medical bag again and then set down a box of those fizzy cubes. "Give him one of these every four hours. Just for today. This'll replace necessary electrolytes. Have him eat something bland for breakfast. Toast, banana, clear broths--y'know the drill."

"Okay, but what about...?" Words failed her. She gestured toward Tray's bedroom.

"Ellen F.'s body? C'mon, let's have a look. Sounds like cyanide poisoning to me."

Petra bit her lower lip, and then straightened her shoulders to brace herself to view what was next door.

They both walked through the bathroom into the now crowded bedroom. Bjorn and Raulf, along with three other security personnel, hovered around, busy with different tasks. Kelvin stood off to the side, conferring with Sergio Iguana.

Cornwell knelt beside Ellen's lifeless body. He leaned forward and sniffed something on the floor. "Chief, here's a partially chewed stick of gum. Must've fallen out of her mouth. Bag it. I want it analyzed."

Petra slid her gaze over the poor woman, and then looked away. She swallowed down hard.

While Sergio complied with the doctor's order, Kelvin moved to stand beside Petra in such a way that the horrific scene was no longer in her sight.

"You shouldn't be here, my dear. Why don't you go to bed? Slip in next to Tray. Try to get some sleep."

Sleep? How could she possibly sleep? No bloody way. She cleared her throat. "Do... do her sisters know?"

"I've told Valli, their travel director. She's breaking the news to the Ellens now." Kelvin massaged the bridge of his nose. "Needless to say, the cloned sisters were close."

Clones. Petra shivered. Well, that explained how six people could be identical, didn't it?

"I have no idea of how hard this will hit the Ellens," Kelvin shook his head. "Will they be able to manage? Their grief may be all consuming."

Cornwell left the body to join them. "Your nephew doesn't exhibit any signs of toxicity, Kelvin. As for this, naturally we don't have all the facts, but my preliminary report, based on the contortions of the body, is that the gum was laced with cyanide. So the blasted question is how did Ellen F. get a stick of poisoned gum?"

"Was this self-inflicted?" Kelvin asked.

"You're thinking of Conni True's suicide, but this isn't the same. Not in my opinion. Cyanide is a helluva way to go, y'know. Besides, why would this Ellen end it all here at your house? She wasn't under investigation."

Petra had had enough. One more word about Ellen's death and she was sure she'd turn green. She held up her hand. "I'm going to follow your suggestion, Kelvin. I-I'll be next door with Tray. See you in the morning."

After washing up, she closed the bathroom door and padded over to the bed. Tray remained sleeping on the left side so she slid under the covers on the right.

Her muscles, so tensed up, refused to relax. Taking a few deep breaths,

Petra concentrated on emptying her mind.

No matter what she did, she kept harping back to one question. How had a day, that had started out so right, end on such a grisly note?

Chapter Thirteen

In between wearing his "cordial host" hat at Sunday services for the conference attendees and scenic picnic lunches at various sites around the island, Kelvin squeezed in a suspicious death investigation. In the interim, all remaining Ellens had been interviewed, along with travel associate Maizie from Team Antarctica. Everyone that'd had contact with Ellen F. within the last twenty-four hours gave their story to the investigation team: Security Chief Sergio Iguana and Operations Director Owen Greenacre.

Kelvin sat behind his desk and reviewed his staff's report. Yes, the method of death was chewing gum thickly laced with cyanide. No, no one admitted to seeing Ellen F. with a pack of gum. No, suicide was not considered probable for Ellen F.'s demise. Yes, yesterday's serious demeanor was usual for her. The general consensus, even from her sisters, was that Ellen F. was in her normal state of mind.

The good news was that Tray hadn't suffered any type of poisoning. Overzealous cookie gobbling had been the cause for his discomfort.

Hell. Kelvin threw the report down on his desk, scattering the papers across its polished surface. No matter what security measures he put in place, the murderous viper was always one step ahead. How could he rid Taurus City of this dangerous and malignant infestation?

Unable to sit any longer, he jumped up to pace around his office.

"Kelvin." Jade Dunbar's clipped voice came through the intercom. "Do you wish to see--"

He slammed on the intercom button. "No interruptions! Hadn't I made myself clear?"

The silence at the other end rebuked him. Double hell. He had no right to take his frustrations out on his assistant. "Sorry, Jade. Just give my regrets to..."

"Petra Richardson."

Petra. He smiled. Perhaps she was what he needed right now. "Jade, send Petra in."

If he wasn't mistaken, he thought he heard a slight harrumph. A few seconds later, Petra opened the door and walked in.

He blinked at the sight of her long sleeved neon orange shirt. "My dear! You positively glow in the dark." He gestured for her to close the door. "And you're exactly what the doctor ordered."

Dark blue smudges under her eyes indicated the lack of sleep. "Yes, I do stand out in this shirt, don't I? I thought I should wear something vivid to help me stay awake."

As she gazed at him, her brow furrowed and her ruby lips parted. She rushed over. "Are you doing okay? You look awfully tired. Can I get you something?"

With all the turmoil she'd been put through, here she was, worrying about him. He took her hands and rubbed his thumbs over her soft skin.

"I'm better now, sweetness." He leaned down to steal a honeyed kiss. "Tell me, how's my nephew?"

"Tray's fine. He's watching Heckle and Jeckle cartoons with Georges. Every four hours he'll drink one of the fizzy cubes the doctor gave him." A smile briefly lit her face. "Once Tray gets his energy back, though, I predict he's going to be imitating those birds again, nonstop flying and swooping."

Still holding her hand, Kelvin led her over to the cushioned sofa. "And to what do I owe the pleasure of your visit?"

"Well, I wanted to know if there was any news about, you know, about what happened last night." She blinked her large amber eyes at him. "How are Ellen F.'s sisters handling her death?"

"Good question. I was concerned about their reaction and whether they would need replacements to take their places at work. To be blunt, overwhelming grief does tend to diminish one's abilities. But, they all, from A down to E, assured me that their jobs wouldn't suffer. That they wanted to work. That they would be fine."

He shrugged. "Valli insisted the Ellens wouldn't be affected. She felt there'd be no need for an alternate crew. That seems unnatural... In any event, I decided that the sisters needed to take today and tomorrow off. To compensate, we'll divvy up the workload just for these two days. Obviously, that will affect the remaining team associate, Maizie. And Valli herself. With the conference, however, the need for the Travel Department should be greatly reduced. I don't anticipate it to be a hardship."

"Hopefully not." Petra sighed. "Is there something I can do to help? With that or with something else?"

The more he thought about it, the better confiding in her sounded. "Perhaps you can. Perhaps, as an outsider to Taurus City, you just might have a different perspective on this... situation."

She gave his hand a squeeze. "Okay, I'm all ears."

Taking in her rounded curves, he grinned. "Hardly. But we'll discuss that later. Now, here's the short version. As I mentioned before with Conni True, there is a rebel group called the Continuers. Their goal is to take over the stewardship of Terra--of Earth. My family, the Lacertus line, has been in command since the beginning."

"Stewardship of Earth," Petra repeated. "That just sounds so wrong. Why is that necessary?"

"Why?" He lifted his eyebrow. "Greed, mostly. Terra--Earth--is considered a jewel, and has been much coveted for millennia upon millennia. Although you might find this hard to believe, wars have been fought to possess the planet. To prevent further destruction, Galactic leaders decreed this compromise, this stewardship. A group of Terran natives were selected and then transplanted to the third planet of Tau Ceti, a type G sun in Cetus Sector. There, the members of the Lacertus family were trained and tasked with the administration of this pleasure dome. Under the Lacertus administration, all aliens throughout the Milky Way Galaxy have the right to visit your world. What you see here..."

His arms stretched wide to encompass the office and beyond. "... is nothing more than a glorified travel agency."

"Wow." She rested back against the cushions. "That is so... so mind-boggling."

"Exactly. So these Continuers want to depose us. As you know my brother's wife was killed. It was an explosion in deep space. The Velan, Tarrnak, did I mention that the Velans are psychic? In any event, Tarrnak received information that the ship's explosion wasn't an accident. Evidently, all direct Lacertus family members are in danger. My brother Will and Tray. In the event of their deaths, I'm next in line.

The horror of what he'd just said was reflected in her widened eyes.

Kelvin rested his hand on her knee. "So that's the background. An infiltration of this magnitude has to involve a member or members of my key staff. That's not to say there aren't recruits in support personnel as well. Obviously Conni True was one of those. But in order to have gotten this far, the traitor must be a significant member of this organization."

"I agree. Why don't you tell me about each one? Your feelings about them. That kind of thing."

He nodded. "First off, just so you know, I have better relationships with the men. I do tend to trust the guys more than the women."

"That's interesting and understandable." She couldn't hide her smirk. "I'm honored you're trusting me with this."

"Right. Let's start with Todd Boiler, the Finance Director. He's been here the same amount of time as I have. He's an amiable man. Gets along with everyone. Easy to converse with. We often spend our downtime together. Sightseeing, having a few drinks. That sort of thing."

Petra caught her lower lip on her teeth. "I haven't talked with him too much. He does seem nice. Tends to use odd phases, though. Kind of like--"

"Sergio Iguana. Yes, they're both colonists from Capella 8--a planet in the super hot yellow-orange binary star system in the Auriga sector. Since the temperature is always scorching, natives tend to speak with descriptive hot phrases."

"Hmmn, I guess that explains it."

"Whatever it's worth, I trust Todd."

"Good to know."

"Then there's the Medical Director, Cornwell Young. As you know, he's brusque, but definitely has a heart of gold under his rough exterior. Loves being on Terra. He's re-upped four times, bringing his number of years here to fifteen. Tau Ceti native, as I am. I've known him the longest, and I also trust him."

"Okay. That's a good thing, especially since Cornwell treated Tray's symptoms last night."

"Precisely. This brings us to Josephus Hammer, the Human Relations Director. Also a Tau Ceti native. Sometimes I detect a slight friction between us. Like two alpha males butting heads. Perhaps he resents his secondary status."

"Secondary?"

"Joe is not number one."

"And you are?"

Kelvin grinned. "Of course."

"You have some doubts about Joe, then." Petra persisted.

"Yes, I do. On to Owen Greenacre, the Operations Director. He's got Wanda Cropper's and Niko Starling's departments under him. Tau Ceti native. He's our oldest member, so maybe there's a generation gap at work here. My assessment is that he's somewhat pompous and thinks of himself more than the team. Therefore, yes, I have some doubts about him."

Kelvin waited a moment for Petra to gesture for him to continue. "Sergio Iguana, our Chief of Security. This is a very demanding job. Especially now. I have to say things haven't been going smoothly for Sergio lately. Recently, there have been numerous breeches in security. Ambassador Hunt slipping out of the alien section to attend your welcoming party, just to give one example. So while I do trust him to a degree, I question his allegiance as well."

For a moment, they both sat in silence, lost in their own thoughts.

Kelvin took a deep breath, and then exhaled. "The last male on the key staff is Niko Starling, Head Chef. He's from the farming co-op Deneb 4, Cygnus Sector. Niko is a happy-go-lucky fellow. I honestly believe the only thing he's interested in food. Quite a jolly cook. I trust him."

"What about your butler Georges? Isn't he a key member of your staff?"

"Good point. I suppose he is. Since he handles household matters, I didn't include him. Apologies. Georges is a product of Bokar, the second planet in the Alpha Circini star system. It has an extremely harsh environment. Georges has been with the Lacertus family since Tray's birth. And to answer your unspoken question, yes, I do trust Georges."

"Thank goodness," she murmured.

"Now for the females. Jade Dunbar, my Executive Assistant has been with me two years. She's also a Bokar native. She's efficient and very good at her job." Kelvin ran his hand through his hair, debating on how to phrase this next tidbit. "She and I have indulged, from time to time, in casual sex."

How would Petra take that news? Would she over react? Pout? Make a fuss?

He glanced at her. Hell, he couldn't tell a thing. Her breathing remained even and no emotion showed on her beautiful face. He hurried to explain. "That's over now, of course. But I trust Jade."

Petra raised her thin eyebrow. "Ah, but is she a jealous type? I do get those vibes from her."

"Hmmn. I hadn't thought of that. It's true, Jade can exhibit jealous tendencies. Not overly jealous, but that's something I hadn't taken into consideration. Perhaps her loyalties can be called into question as well. We'll consider her an unknown quantity."

"Okay. Next?"

"Next is Valli Proximus, the Travel Director. She's a Tau Ceti native. The Proximus family is a prominent one on Tau Ceti. She's competent, intelligent, and well organized. Somewhat coldly impersonal. I'd say she's also a bit sharp in her dealings with her associates. Although she and I have never been together, in that way, I believe she has a, er, a fancy for me."

Petra grinned. "Who doesn't?"

He returned her grin. "I don't care about anyone's fancy except yours, my dear girl. So, back to Valli. She's a question as well."

"Who's next?"

Kelvin thought a moment. "Wanda Cropper, Manager of Reservations and Accommodations. She's a sturdy farmgirl from Deneb 4. Dependable, true, but too brassy, too rough and tumble for my taste." He rubbed his jaw. "Plus, I think she also has a fancy for me. I'll put her on the questionable list."

"Right. Anybody else?"

"That brings us to the Travel Teams. The rest of the Ellens, and then Maizie." He cleared his throat. "The Ellens, well, what can I say? They're from Shaula 9, Scorpio Sector. Planet Shaula 9 suffers a shortage of colonists. To remedy this dilemma, the planetary government has been a strong proponent of Human cloning. While these people are workhorses--busy bees would be an apt description--the lack of personality is one of the drawbacks to this program."

Petra rubbed her forehead. "Have I mentioned how bizarre all this is?"

Kelvin took another deep breath, then slowly released it. "Personally, I find it difficult to relate to clones. But the question here is, why would one of the Ellens, or all of them for that matter, cause the death of what is essentially, part of herself?"

"And I thought I had it rough teaching middle schoolers. Oh boy!"

"Again, all the Ellens are in question. As is Maizie, from Team Antarctica. I don't know her well. She's from Deneb 4, as is Wanda Cropper. I think my objection to her is the same as for Wanda. Not the fancying me part, though. I have no idea about that."

Kelvin stood and then stretched his back. He walked over to the large window to glance outside at windblown palm trees. "So that's it. Quite a cast of characters, right?"

"What about Felicia Alvarez? Not that I suspect her, or anything."

He turned back around. "The Human Relations Administrative Assistant? No, Felicia isn't part of my key staff. She's from Terra. A native Earther as you are. She has no idea about the scope of the Taurus City Travel Agency."

Petra joined him by the window. "By the way, not to bring your ego down a peg, but Felicia fancies someone else."

"Indeed? Who is this lucky soul?"

"Her boss, Joe."

"I wasn't aware of that. I wonder if Joe returns her regard?"

"Hard to say. But I'm glad to learn that Felicia isn't an extraterrestrial."

"What's wrong with extraterrestrials?" Kelvin pulled Petra to him and smoothed his hands down her back to cup her derriere. "Mmmm, delicious."

Trailing soft kisses over her forehead, and then down to the tip of her nose, he then stopped on her luscious lips. She tasted just like honey. "We're not all green bug-eyed monsters, you know."

She raised her arms to hug him around the neck as she returned his kiss. "Oh, I know that now, Mr. Lacertus. Such an education you've been giving me."

By the stars, she was magnificent. Fondling her curvaceous butt, he whispered in her ear, "How I yearn to complete your education!"

Her heartbeat pounded against his chest as he was certain his drummed against hers.

For all too few minutes they explored each other, lost in eager kisses, intimate caresses, and fevered moans. The sound of the intercom, however, caused them to jump apart.

"Sorry to interrupt, Kelvin," Jade's voice blared out into the office. Frankly, she didn't sound sorry at all. "Georges is on the line. He says Traynor is very impatient for Petra Richardson to return."

Kelvin met Petra's gaze. Her darkened eyes conveyed her thoughts, her desire, her lust. Hell. No, double hell. He didn't want her to leave. Ever.

Running the tip of his tongue over his lips, he retasted her. Then he returned to business by pressing the intercom button. "Tell Georges that Petra will be returning to the house shortly."

Kelvin remembered about Petra's comment on possible jealousy. He added, "Thank you, Jade."

Turning to Petra, he gathered her in his arms again for one more magic moment. Then he stepped away. "I'm missing you already. As does my nephew. It seems us Lacertus men can't get enough of you."

"The feeling is mutual, Kelvin." She gave him a wink. "I-I'd better go. But I'll think about this..." She touched her lips. "And what you told me about your key staff members. Maybe, fingers crossed, I can think of something--anything--that might be of help."

She glanced down at the floor, her dark lashes resting against the curve of her cheek. Then she looked back up at him. "Will I see you tonight?"

"God, I hope so." Kelvin's voice was ragged with emotion. He couldn't help how he felt. It was tearing him apart to be away from her.

"Good." Petra smiled and walked to the door. She turned back around, smiled, and then went on her way.

Kelvin groaned. How could he concentrate on serious matters now that he had tasted heaven?

* * * *

Wow. Oh, wow. After Petra closed the office door, she felt her knees start to buckle. Holding onto a desk with one hand, she patted at her heart with the other. He was so dreamy...

The scent of a sweet perfume recalled her to her surroundings. Thankfully, no one, especially Jade Dunbar, was around to catch Petra's besotted expression.

She continued through the outer office, down the stairs, and out into the crisp afternoon air. A thought niggled her. Jade had just been at her desk a moment before. Where had she disappeared to? Restroom? Or maybe she hadn't wanted to stick around to see Kelvin's latest love interest.

That unwelcome thought continued to niggle. Petra twisted her lips. Was what Kelvin felt for her long-lasting love? Or was it only lust? Who knew? How could she really know for sure? After all, he was an extraterrestrial, for goodness sake.

Sliding into the driver's seat in her small car, she slammed the door shut, also shutting out her ambivalent feelings. She didn't need to think about that. Instead, she needed to concentrate on what he'd said about his key personnel.

The drive to Kelvin's estate wouldn't take long so she traveled slowly over the narrow road. No other cars were in sight to interrupt her thinking. Everyone must've been busy with the conference. The alien conference.

She sighed. Would she ever get her mind wrapped around all this mind-boggling information?

Never mind. Focus, Petra.

Right. The main thing that she came away with from Kelvin's discourse was that he considered all the women on his staff to be on the questionable side. But, of course, he could've been mistaken in his assessment.

Using her intuition, she narrowed the male list down to only one: Owen Greenacre. He seemed too suave, too debonair, too smarmy. It was difficult to tell just what was going on behind his faded blue eyes. Yet, at his age, why would he be interested in overthrowing the Lacertus clan? After all, if he was determined to be a traitor, why wait until he was in his late sixties, early seventies?

As for the women, Wanda and Maizie seemed harmless. Down to earth. Good-natured. Trustworthy. Maybe Petra felt that way because both women were from the same environment.

And the Ellens couldn't possibly be conspirators. How could they kill or sanction the killing of Ellen F.? Everything Petra had read about identical twins indicated some type of psychic link. Wouldn't clones be even more connected? One thought occurring simultaneously between all six of them?

She suddenly shivered. When Ellen F. died, had the other five somehow experienced their sister's pain?

Don't think about that. No, there was no way the Ellens could be responsible for this atrocity.

So that left Jade Dunbar and Valli Proximus.

Petra drummed her fingers on the steering wheel. Knowing Jade had been Kelvin's bed partner certainly wasn't a point in her favor. But there wasn't anything concrete against her... except that she had a jealous streak. Then again, she'd said the sea lions on the beach were tame. How could wild animals be tame? With those sharp, pointed teeth? Wouldn't they attack if they felt threatened? Males especially could be aggressive. And the way Tray grabbed the sea lions around the neck...

Petra shook off the image.

Yep, Jade was definitely a possibility.

So that left Valli to consider. There also wasn't anything Petra could put her finger on with the Travel Director, except that she did seem cold. Detached. And what was it that Kelvin had said? That she came from a prominent family on that home world of Tau Ceti 3. He hadn't mentioned that info with any of the other staff members. Maybe somehow, that was important.

At the fork in the road, Petra veered toward the left, but then she spotted a stopped car to the right. The hood of the vehicle butted up against a spiny straight cactus that shot up to the sky. A collision? The driver's door stood open and on the dusty ground...

Omigosh! A woman lay stomach down in the dirt. Her arms were underneath her and her blue-jeanned legs were limp against the ground. She wasn't moving. Was she okay? Was she alive? Who was she?

Petra pulled over, and then dashed out of her car. A silent breeze fluttered the brim of a floppy straw hat on the woman's head.

She knelt beside the woman. "Oh! What happened? I'll go get help."

As she reached out to turn the woman over, she caught a flash of motion from above. And then, bam! Something heavy crashed against the side of her head.

A scream of pain died before she could open her mouth. Then she fell, mouth first into the dirt.

Chapter Fourteen

With most conference attendees now out on day trips to the various Galápagos Islands, Kelvin studied background information in the database concerning his key staff. He focused on his list of possible traitors. So immersed was he in the personnel records that he didn't hear the phone ring.

And ring. And ring.

Finally, the annoying sound registered. "Where the hell is Jade?" Picking up the receiver, he barked, "Lacertus."

"Apologies for the interruption, sir," came Georges' accented voice. "Has the *mademoiselle* departed? The young sir is getting restless."

"What?" Kelvin glanced at the time. "Georges, she left here fifteen minutes ago."

The drive would've taken no more than five of those minutes. Perhaps she walked? Kelvin leapt to his feet to glance out the window overlooking the parking area. Petra's bright yellow car was no longer there.

"Georges, alert security. Have Sergio send out a team. I'm on my way."

Normally Kelvin wouldn't have been in a panic. But this was his love, his Petra. When she left the office, she'd intended to get to Tray as soon as possible. Which meant she should've already been at the house. But she was not.

Cold fear iced his spine.

Reaching the door, he stopped when the phone rang again. His first instinct was to ignore it and hurry outside to join the search for Petra. Then again, it might be Georges with the welcome news that she had arrived.

He raced back to his desk. "Yes?"

"Most hallowed sir, 'tis with regret that I disturb you."

The caller was Tarrnak, the Velan. "Perhaps we can talk later, Tarrnak? I have important--"

"I have essential information for you, sir. The message comes from above."

Kelvan froze. "Does this have anything to do with the Terran Petra Richardson?"

"I believe so, sir. The message was garbled, however you may find benefit in it. A vision came to me. I saw the female's comely face, and then a line of faint stars in Xanadu's night skies. I could not identify the group, but then a name did reveal itself. Alpha Piscium." Tarrnak paused. "I do hope Ms. Richardson is safe."

"As do I, Tarrnak. Thank you for this information." Kelvin terminated the connection. Rubbing his forehead, he reflected on Alpha Piscium. It was a star, in fact a close double star, that was located about one hundred thirty nine light years from Terra. Unremarkable and obscure. What did Alpha Piscium have to do with Petra?

Don't think about it now. Perhaps the answer would come to him.

It didn't take him long to reach the fork in the road. As he approached, his stomach dropped. Petra's yellow car remained on the side, but Petra was nowhere in sight.

Three security officers gathered evidence. Sergio himself headed the team. Cornwell Young was also present. He leaned against the vehicle with his arms folded against his chest. It was obvious the services of a medical doctor weren't needed... just yet at any rate.

Kelvin strode over to the security chief. "What do you have for me?"

"Not much, sir. Petra left the engine running hot. Her purse lay discarded on the passenger seat. By the tire marks in the dirt next to this cactus, we know a car, one of our cars, was stopped here. The cactus shows distress. Some spiny protrusions have melted down." Sergio pointed at the damage. "Footsteps in the soil have been deliberately wiped, most likely to hide the number of persons involved."

"Your theory, Sergio?"

The security chief flared his nostrils. "To sum up, it would appear Petra voluntarily left her car in order to assist someone. Someone who had an agenda."

Kelvin swallowed hard. "And then the bastards abducted Petra."

He prayed to the Almighty that those vermin had done nothing worse.

The doctor walked over and pulled Kelvin aside. "I heard the call and came out just in case I was needed." He scanned Kelvin's face. "Are you all right?"

"Am I all right?" Kelvin snorted. "No! Hell no. Ever since she arrived on the island she's been exposed to danger. What kind of shoddy administrator am I? Assassins, murderers, kidnappers... I've allowed them to run rampant. I've shamed the Lacertus family name."

His heartfelt sigh drifted out to mingle with the temperate sea breeze. "None of that matters. The only thing that's important is Petra. I love her, you know. I've asked her to marry me... but now..."

He couldn't go on. He closed his eyes to shut out the pain. "As you know, it's standard procedure for all Taurus City personnel and visitors to be injected with a subcutaneous microchip so we can track their positions. I didn't feel it was necessary with Petra. If I had followed the rules, we would be able to locate her like that." He snapped his fingers.

"Your losing control isn't helping her, Kelvin. Think, man! Is there anything else that might be of assistance?"

Kelvin ran both hands through his hair. "The only thing I have is something nonsensical. Does the star Alpha Piscium mean anything to you?"

"It's part of one of those blasted constellations here. Y'know, the last one--Pisces."

What connection did Pisces have with Petra? Other than both starting with the letter P?

Cornwell scratched at his grizzled five o'clock shadow. "The fish, eh? Piscium is one of the forms for the Latin word for fish."

Fish? Kelvin was more confused than he was before. Except that fish were associated with... water! Water and ocean. Ocean and boats.

Boats. Perhaps that was what the message meant.

"Sergio!" Kelvin yelled out. "Get your operatives. Search every boat docked at the marina. Board every vessel in the nearby waters. Waste no time. We're dealing with those monstrous Continuers. They've already killed one of our own."

He gnashed his teeth. "Petra Richardson *must be* found alive and unharmed."

* * * *

Ouch. Is someone hammering inside my head, trying to get out?

Petra tried to ignore the pain, but sharp and piercing, it refused to subside to a dull ache.

Wincing as she opened her eyes, she focused on the fuzzy scene in front of her. Why was...? Oh. The fuzziness came from blurred vision.

She blinked rapidly, and lifted her hand to rub at her eyes. Two hands moved up instead of one. Her wrists were tethered together, cruelly and tightly bound by some type of plastic cord. She had a maneuvering length of about six inches to work with. Looking down, she saw her ankles, also bound, and had about the same length of cord between them.

Okay, recap. What had happened?

The last thing she remembered was kneeling next to an unmoving woman. Then there was a flash of motion from above, and then the pain.

She touched the side of her forehead and came away with a handful of blood.

Bloodied, hogtied, and helpless. That was the downside. The upside was that she was still alive.

Right. So where was she? She looked around the small confining cabin. In view was a single-sized bed that she sat on. The walls were wood-toned with several built-in drawers. There was a tiny window--a porthole, really. Something shuttered it though, so she couldn't see outside. Nevermind that. Darn it all, it was way too small to escape through.

By the slight rocking motion, it was obvious she was on a boat. Maybe in the marina. Maybe outside the harbor in the waters of the bay. The boat engines were off, so it was quiet.

She hobbled to the cabin door--which was an impressive feat considering her ankles were fettered--and then carefully tried the doorknob. Locked.

But wait. She heard voices. Placing her ear against the hardwood surface, she concentrated on listening.

"I still do not understand why you wanted her brought here. Finishing her off by the car made much more sense," a man's voice complained.

Petra withheld her gasp. She recognized his crisp formal voice. It was Joe Hammer. Joe was part of this horror? Joe wanted to kill her?

Oh wow. She just couldn't think about that now.

She remembered that he did have a boat. A new catamaran. When she had first arrived on the island, her friend Felicia had boasted about being taken out for a dive.

Or *was* Felicia her friend? Petra strained to hear the second person's reply.

Rats. All she could hear was a low mumble. Male or female... who could tell?

Joe spoke again. "I know you hate him. I know you need for him to suffer. Believe me, I feel the same way. Sanctimonious bastard. Our main objective though is not Kelvin. Now that security is concentrating on the woman, we must strike fast. We need to eliminate the boy now."

Tray! Without thinking, Petra bit her lower lip, drawing blood. Oh, these people were monsters. How could anyone want to harm such a darling boy? How could she warn Kelvin? What could she do?

"No! We stick with the plan."

It was the other person. A woman. Try as she might, Petra couldn't identify the voice. The woman's volume swung from low to high. Petra could only make out some of the words.

"You stay ... boat ... Sunday fishing ... good alibi ... dispose ... body. She'll make delectable chum."

The sound of their maniacal laughter chilled Petra's soul.

"I ... attend to the boy... at my leisure," the woman continued. "There will be one less Lacertus to concern ourselves with."

Joe again: "No one will suspect us, my beloved. And once we get rid of Kelvin, our contacts will take care of Wilhelm. As they did his lovely wife. We finally will be free from their hated rule, and we shall rule in their stead."

Silence, and then Petra heard noises coming from above deck. The sounds grew fainter until they were gone. The woman must've been leaving the boat. Which meant Petra and Tray were now one step closer to death.

Think! Think! What can I do?

The engines started up. The rocking motion increased, throwing her off balance. She had to do something before the boat moved too far away from the shore.

Using both fists, she pounded on the door. "I have to use the restroom! I'm seasick. I-I have to throw up!" Over and over she yelled.

Joe's catamaran was new. She was betting he'd do anything to save the boat from being defiled by vomit.

She heard a muffled oath, and then footsteps hammering down a few stairs. Bolts slid back from their locked position.

Joe's long face had furrowed lines she hadn't seen before. His forest green eyes glowed with a haunted light. Narrowing his gaze, he glared at her.

"I feel sick." She gave a fake heave, covering her mouth with her hand. "I can't... hold it."

"Of all the..." He grabbed her upper arm and yanked her out of the enclosed cabin. "Come on then."

She had little time left. Still heaving, she surreptitiously took stock of her surroundings. No bathroom--called the head--on this level. Good. In front of her were the stairs. With her ankles bound, there was no way she could climb them, unless she hopped. She wasn't about to let him know that. Once she reached the four steps, she turned around, facing him.

"St-Stairs," she stuttered through her spasms. For greater effect, she coughed.

"Bitch! Dammit, hold it. Hold it in." He roughly hauled her up by the waist, and then with a grunt, dropped her down on the top step.

Her heart pounded, readying for action. This was it. It was now or never.

Still facing him, she thrust both fists down toward him, striking him on the facial cheekbones. It wasn't such a heavy blow, but it was enough to cause him to totter backwards. She spun around and carefully walked as rapidly as she could for the open deck. The last thing she needed to do was to stumble and fall.

She didn't have much time. *Hurry! Hurry!*

Once outside, she staggered to the railing and grabbed a circular life preserver.

A clattering of noises and enraged swearing spilled out from below deck. Joe was coming.

Inhaling deeply, she took a quick glance at the seaport and spotted the red and white lighthouse. The catamaran wasn't far from the marina, but hampered as she was, swimming was a risk. Then again, she didn't have a choice.

Holding that breath... and the life preserver, she jumped into the water.

Brrr! It was cold!

But she was free, and it was up to her to remain free. Her two hands holding the buoyant preserver, she swam with a flutter kick stroke, as furiously as she could.

"Damn you!" Joe Hammer's voice carried over the distance between them and over the splash of waves against the boat's sides. "Just wait until I get you--"

Boom! A deafening roar interrupted his tirade. Startled, she nearly jumped a mile out of the water. Jerking her head around, she saw the catamaran explode into a million pieces. The force of the detonation then created a tidal wave that sucked her under the water.

For a second, all sounds vanished. She was entombed by the sea. The next second, survival kicked in. She fought her way back to the surface, taking care to avoid splinters of debris in the water and debris raining from above. Spitting out seawater, she glanced back at what remained of the boat.

Smoke, fire, ashes. She gulped down hard. There was no bloody way Joe Hammer survived that. And, without a doubt, his catamaran had been rigged to blow by his unknown female companion.

Petra continued her swim toward the shoreline. Because of the explosion, help would arrive soon.

The sooner, the better. She had to warn Kelvin about what she'd heard. About the planned attempt on Tray's life.

* * * *

By the time Kelvin arrived at the marina, several security officers were already boarding standing boats in the harbor. Good, the search was underway. But what about those active vessels?

He left his car and then ran out onto the dock, not stopping until he reached the end. Scanning the waters for boats on the horizon, he prayed. *Please be unharmed, Petra. Where are you? Where can I find you?*

No answer but for the lonely caws of seagulls hovering on the breeze.

Wait. He spotted a catamaran out past the lighthouse. Didn't that boat belong to Joe Hammer? Yes, there he was, leaning over the railing. Why was Joe--

A thunderous explosion tore through the air. Joe's boat disintegrated into flames right before Kelvin's eyes. Before everyone's eyes.

"Petra!" He yelled out. No. No! He didn't want to believe it. He couldn't believe it. But logic dictated that Petra had to have been on that boat. Petra... and of course, Joe.

Kelvin had to get out there. A patrol speed boat attached to one of the pilings at the end of the dock would provide transportation. He climbed down into the boat and started to untie the moorings.

"Hold up, Kelvin! Let me, eh?" Cornwell Young sprinted down the dock. Although almost fifty, he was as limber as a man half his age. He expertly jumped down into the boat, dropped his medical bag, and rushed over to the controls. "I've powered up this baby before. I'll get you out there. Besides, I might be needed."

Kelvin swallowed his worry. The services of a doctor would definitely be needed. "Good. Thanks."

He turned back to the troubled waters. As the boat sped off, he scrutinized the wreckage. He caught sight of something just surfacing a few feet away from the rubble. Something bright orange.

By the stars! It was Petra in her fluorescent shirt!

"It's Petra! Near the lighthouse." Kelvin pointed at her bobbing figure in the water. As he watched, she lifted her head to look back at the catamaran disaster.

She was conscious. Thank the stars!

"We're gonna get there in two tics." Cornwell zoomed toward the lighthouse, drenching the two of them as the boat rose and then thudded against the water.

Kelvin kept his gaze on her, willing her to be unharmed. Willing her to hold on just a little longer.

"Petra!" he shouted, but the noise from the boat drowned him out.

Just as Cornwell started slowing the engine, she noticed them. "Oh! Oh, Kelvin!" She tried to wave but her hands were tied together.

The very sight of her so constrained caused his heart to harden. Whoever was responsible for this outrage needed to suffer everlasting torment.

Was it Joe? Or was he a victim, too?

Waves slapped at the hull of the boat now stopped alongside Petra. She tried to grab hold of the edges.

"Sweetheart, just relax. I'll get you." Kelvin slipped into the water, and then grabbed her under the armpits. He lifted her up, and Cornwell helped her into the back of the boat. She struggled to sit up and speak.

"Shh, just stay put, young lady, eh? Let me get these ties off you, and then I'll have a look at you." Cornwell pulled his medical bag out.

"Th-Thank you. I... but... I must... I've got to tell you about--"

"Tell us nothing, sweetheart. Just take it easy." Kelvin climbed into the speed boat, in the back, where she was. Holding her tightly, he gave thanks. While Cornwell took care of the restraints, Kelvin murmured soothing words in her ear.

Additional speed boats zipped by, looking for survivors of the shipwreck.

As she panted heavily to catch her breath, she closed her eyes, but then quickly opened them. "But I have to... I mean, Tray is in... danger."

"Slow down, Petra. What's going on with Tray?" Kelvin signaled to Cornwell to get his phone. "Call Georges. Increase security on the house."

After Cornwell ended the call, Petra talked, and what a tale she told. Josephus Hammer was a hated Continuer! *Had been* a hated Continuer, for without a doubt, he was no longer among the living. He had been in league with a murderous woman with an unknown identity. Their plan had been to get rid of all Lacertus family members.

In all likelihood, this woman had rigged Joe's catamaran to blow. And now she was on her way to kill Tray.

The estate was, of course, heavily protected, and yet the woman had the distinct advantage of having anonymity. She could be planning to strike now. She might be planning to strike later. Time was on her side.

Who the hell was this deadly woman?

Kelvin kissed his darling's forehead. Hell, the skin by her temple was raw, bloody.

"Cornwell, switch places," he ordered. "You tend to Petra. She's got a head wound. I'll get us back to the dock."

Now that she'd alerted him to the danger, she closed her eyes again, her mission completed. By the rhythmic rise and fall of her bright orange chest, she must've passed out.

"Relax, my dear," he said in a low voice. "We'll get this killer."

After the doctor swapped positions, Kelvin headed for the marina.

Chapter Fifteen

The violent rocking from the speed boat stopped. Fluttering her eyes open, Petra saw Kelvin tenderly wrapping her in a blanket. She smiled at him and tried to sit, but goodness, her head hurt so.

"Don't move, Petra. You suffered a concussion." He lifted her up and passed her over to Sergio Iguana as he waited on the dock.

Kelvin got off the speed boat first, with Cornwell grumbling behind him.

"Foolhardy way to travel," the doctor complained. "I'm as achy as if I've been hurled 3g's up through the blasted stratosphere."

Now back in Kelvin's muscular arms, she relaxed against him. While she did feel comforted and safe, another sentiment--a negative one--niggled her.

Powerless. A useless lump. She should be up on her feet and hurrying over to protect Tray.

She struggled to get down, but couldn't. Either she was too weak or Kelvin was too strong.

Rats. Truth be told, she felt as helpless as a newborn. And just as cranky.

He walked down the dock with her. Cornwell and Sergio were by his sides.

"I want to help, Kelvin. I need to go to Tray. If I can just hold him--"

"Hush, sweetheart. There's nothing I want more than to have you both together, but let's allow Sergio to give us an update on the situation, hmmn?"

The security chief delayed speaking until they had reached the main walkway. Kelvin set her down on a covered bench and then folded his arms against his chest. "Spill."

Sergio nodded. "I've got all available team members crackling around the house and grounds, sir. They're spread out over the perimeter like lava. White-hot and ready to vulcanize any suspicious characters. Guarding the boy inside is Georges, along with Bjorn and Raulf. A few of the household staff are there, too. Have no fear. With the new tachyonic particle protection system, no unauthorized personnel can enter without Georges and the security guards' approval."

While Kelvin and Sergio talked, she smoothed her saltwater-drenched hair back off her forehead. She was missing something. Something to do with that unknown woman. She closed her eyes to concentrate.

Cornwell interrupted. "Your head hurt, Petra? C'mon, I'll give you--"

"No, thank you, but that's not it." She stood, albeit shakily, and held onto the back of the bench for support. "Kelvin, I just thought of something."

He placed his hand on her shoulder and firmly pressed down so she sat. Then, taking her hand, he sat next to her. "What did you think of?"

"I saw the woman. I mean, it must've been her by the cactus. She was lying in the dirt. A hat covered her hair so I don't know what color it was. She looked to be of about medium height and she was slender."

"That description fits Jade Dunbar, Valli Proximus, and the Ellens." He stroked his chin.

And Felicia as well. But Petra kept that observation to herself.

"Also," she added, "the woman had to have heard the explosion, but she doesn't know that I survived. That I eavesdropped on her conversation with Joe. So she must think she's in the clear. That everyone will assume that Joe was the sole traitor." The more Petra thought about it, the more she believed she was right. "Which means the woman might feel as if she doesn't need to make a move against Tray right now."

"Interesting hypothesis," Kelvin murmured.

"In fact, one of the phrases I overheard was her saying 'I ... attend to the boy... at my leisure'. So you see, she might be biding her time."

"I'm on your wavelength." Sergio pursed his lips together. "Sizzling suns! With the house as protected as it is, this woman would be torched in a second should she endeavor to breach security."

"Exactly." Petra released a heavy breath. Thank goodness he understood what she was saying.

Kelvin squeezed her hand. "You have an idea?"

"Yes, I do. I'm thinking you should go back to your office. Business as usual. Maybe reconnoiter. Watch and observe your everyone. Maybe if we're lucky, this woman, whoever she is, will be there. Maybe she'll incriminate herself."

Kelvin smiled. "By the stars, not only are you beautiful, my dear, but quite clever as well."

Petra didn't look or feel beautiful at the moment, but it was certainly sweet of him to say so.

He stood, and then conferred with Sergio and Cornwell. Once they left, he held out his hand to help her up. "It's time for you to get back to the house."

She got to her feet. "Oh no, that wouldn't be good. It might ruin everything. The woman could somehow be watching. So I should go with you. Hidden from view, of course. How about I stay in the security room with all the monitors so I can see and hear what's going on?"

He thought about it, but his piercing grey eyes turned stormy. "I need for you to be safe, Petra. By the stars, these last few hours have been... hell, they've been horrific. I can't take another chance on losing you."

His voice was raw with emotion.

For a moment they stared at each other. He said so many wondrous things with his gaze. Her heart flooded with love.

Love? Oh yes! She loved this delicious man. As strange as it sounded, she felt like she was floating a couple of inches above the concrete sidewalk.

If only...

The sound of a nearby car starting up recalled her back to earth. "But I'll be in the same building as you are, Kelvin. You can even stop in to see me."

She shivered. No matter how warm the blanket was covering her, she still had been completely soaked. "And you can make sure I have a change of clothes, too, okay?"

Kelvin reached down and hoisted her up in his arms. "My dear, you are determined to turn my hair grey, aren't you? Come on then, let's get back to the office."

Enjoying the solid feel of him--her new love--Petra settled back into the luxury of his arms.

* * * *

Kelvin's office suite had all the comforts of home--meaning he also had a washroom with a private shower off his office and connecting with the corridor. Petra locked the doors and took her time to rinse off the rigors of her ordeal. She cleaned her seawater-saltened hair and eased the pulsating shower jets onto her aching, weary muscles.

What a day. In fact, what a week. She'd only arrived on the island last Sunday... So much had happened since then. So many unbelievable things. One thing was for certain; she wasn't the same person as she had been last week.

Was that for the better or worse?

She smiled. With loving Kelvin, it definitely was for the better.

As she dried off, she gazed into the mirror. She now sported a beige bandage on her forehead near the hairline, courtesy of Joe Hammer for the gash and Cornwell Young for the dressing. The doctor had assured her the injury wouldn't leave a scar. She wasn't so sure. The wound had looked awfully choppy.

She dressed in the clothes Kelvin had gotten for her: a pair of comfy silk drawstring pants and an ultra warm fisherman sweater. And the laciest underwear she'd ever seen.

Mmmm! He was some considerate hunk, all right!

Twisting her still wet hair into a bun, she grabbed her purse that she'd left in the car, and smeared on a bit of lipstick. Time to get to the security room.

She unlocked the doors, then opened the one leading out into the corridor. She bumped into a massive chest.

"Please excuse me! I didn't see--" She looked up into the gigantic face of Ambassador Hunt.

For a moment, his immense body flickered. The next second, everything was steady.

Petra gasped. *Hunt must be an alien!*

"Lady," he growled. His golden gaze quickly swept over her. "An inorganic layer covers a portion of your forehead. Why is this so?"

She touched her bandage. "Oh, I, ah, I..." Darn it all. Tears sprung to her eyes. It was as if the dreadful impact of the last few hours had blasted right through her, leaving her defenseless. She turned her head away to hide her tears. "I had an accident."

"No." He shook his huge head, making his rusty hair fly about his shoulders. "You have been attacked. We know much about evil, Lady. One of your kind has injured you." Raising his bushy eyebrow, he thundered, "Was it Kelvin Lacertus?"

"Goodness, no!" Her surprise caused her to cough. "No, I..." She glanced around the empty corridor. "Let's go someplace private, okay?"

Hunt's golden eyes glowed brightly. He inclined his head. "We agree."

It was then that his deep, musky scent filled her nostrils. She shivered.

Leading him to the security room's antechamber, Petra opened the door. Good, the room was empty. "Here," she pointed to a group of chairs. "Let's have a seat and I'll tell you what happened."

He sat after she did. The chair underneath him groaned from his weight. The sound didn't bother him, though. He stared at her without blinking. She obviously had his full attention.

Her dilemma was that this story wasn't all of hers to tell. Not with the Continuers, not with the danger to Tray. So she stuck to what pertained to her.

"You see, for some reason, and I really don't know why, I was abducted. I--"

"When?"

"Early this afternoon. I was returning to Kelvin's estate when I saw what looked like a car accident and a woman lying face down in the dirt. I stopped to help--"

"Tender-hearted lady."

"Ah, well, as I bent over the woman, I was hit on the head." She touched the bandage. "When I came to, I was on a boat, locked in a cabin. I managed to escape, and as I swam back to shore, the boat exploded."

Hunt growled deep in his throat. "We heard the detonation. You are an extremely brave lady. We shall exact revenge. Against which of your kind, Lady?"

"Oh, no. Please, that really isn't necessary, Ambassador Hunt."

"We insist. Which beings committed this outrage?" He bared his strangely shaped teeth.

She toyed with the collar on her sweater. "It was Joe. Joe Hammer, the

Human Relations Director. But he... he was killed in the blast."

Hunt flared his nostrils. "That was too easy a death for pond scum such as he. What about the female?"

"I-I don't know. That's the truth. I didn't see her features."

He leapt to his feet. For a second, his body flickered again. For that second, she thought she was looking at a lion or a grizzly bear-- definitely ferocious.

Then his "normal" image returned. "The security chamber is through that door?"

After her nod, he lifted his head and roared. "Then we shall watch the screens. This female will make another attempt on your life, Lady. We cannot allow that. Come, the sooner we ferret out this noxious sub-creature, the better."

Petra followed Hunt into the security room. She couldn't help feeling a bit dazed. Whether she wanted it or not, she had another protector. An alien, bear-like protector. But no matter how he looked, he was on her side. That was all that was important.

✳ ✳ ✳ ✳

Kelvin took a sip of his vodka tonic and allowed the alcohol to burn a path down his throat. He stared at the disarray of papers that covered the top of his desk. Strange how things could be filed away, neat and tidy, and then the next moment, utter chaos.

He sighed. Last week, he mistakenly believed that everything was neat and tidy--everything going well during his three-year watch over the Agency. How wrong he'd been.

The Continuers had infiltrated Taurus City, to the detriment of the Agency, his nephew, and the woman he loved. He'd almost lost Petra. If she hadn't been so resourceful...

She would have died.

It was past time to take action.

Setting his tumbler down with a thud, he used the intercom. "Jade, would you have someone watch your desk? I need to talk with you."

His assistant had been back at her desk when he'd returned from the marina. Yet she'd been absent, noticeably absent, after Petra had left for his house earlier in the day. He didn't want to believe that Jade was a traitor. A murderous traitor. But if she was, their previous relationship would not prevent him from lowering the hammer on her... pun intended.

She entered his office and then closed the door. "Yes, Kelvin? Quentin from Reservations and Accommodations is taking the calls."

"Fine. Please have a seat." He studied her as she sat across from him. Her oval face seemed even paler than usual. Her freckles stood out against the chalkiness of her complexion. Her glorious mane of ginger hung limply, and her eyes were reddened around the rims.

As she smoothed a lock of hair behind her ear, her hand trembled. There could be no doubt of that. She then clasped her hands in her lap.

"As you are aware, your desk is required to be covered at all times. We have an adequate staff to assist you when your duties require you to be elsewhere." He paused for effect. "Jade, earlier this afternoon, you were gone from your desk for a lengthy period of time."

If possible, she whitened further. "I-I know. I am sorry, Kelvin."

"Sorry doesn't cut it, Jade. Where were you?"

She looked down and fiddled with her fingers. "I-I was indisposed."

He narrowed his gaze at her. "We had a dangerous situation here a few hours ago."

"What do you mean?"

"You didn't hear the explosion?"

"Well, yes, I did hear it. But I didn't think anything about it."

Double hell. He couldn't prevent his anger from showing. He slammed his fist down on his desk. "Jade, you *will* tell me. Or perhaps you'd rather have the chief of security use his interrogation methods on you?"

Kelvin reached over to touch the intercom.

"No, don't." Jade held out her shaking hand. "I'll tell you."

He sat back and waited.

"Kelvin, I--"

"You!"

The door to Kelvin's office slammed open with enough force to hit the adjoining wall. In burst the intimidating form of an enraged

AN ALIEN PARADISE by Susanne Marie Knight

Uortizk. Ambassador Hunt, obviously, since he was the only Uortizk on the planet. He wore his Human skin, however his violent emotion caused its image to flicker.

Hunt stalked into the office, pointing a finger--in reality a claw--at Kelvin's assistant.

"You have harmed the Lady!" Hunt roared.

Jade noticeably shivered in the chair. Who could blame her? No one in their right mind wanted to be on the receiving end of a Uortzk's fury.

Kelvin rushed to his feet to stand between the alien and his assistant. "Ambassador Hunt, what are you doing here?"

Before Hunt could answer, Petra's voice rang out, slightly out of breath. "Oh, here you are, Ambassador Hunt. Goodness, but you move so fast."

Quentin entered the office with an apologetic look. "I'm sorry, sir, about the interruptions."

"It's all right." Kelvin waved the man back to the front desk.

"Petra." He took a long moment to devour the precious sight of her. Then he remembered Jade. He stared down at his assistant to gage her expression.

The woman didn't seem surprised to see Petra. Which seemed odd, if Jade was the traitor. Perhaps she *wasn't* the one they sought.

By her crouched position, he could tell she was afraid, but there was something else. Something he couldn't put his finger on.

Petra discreetly managed to steer Hunt toward the couch. She sat, and then gestured for him to follow. "Ambassador Hunt and I were in the security room, watching the screens. The surveilence in your office has been activated, you know. Anyway, he, ah, noticed you and Jade talking, and thought that maybe... you know... maybe Jade had been on the catamaran."

Jade furrowed her brow. "Why would I be on a catamaran? Joe's the only one I know that has that type of boat."

Further evidence that Jade wasn't the murderer. She referred to Joe in the present tense.

Kelvin sat on the edge of his desk, just in case he had to referee any of the action. How Petra obtained Hunt as a guard dog must've been a fascinating story, but one he'd have to postpone hearing.

"Jade." His patience was at an end. "Why weren't you at your desk this afternoon?"

Her distress was painfully visible. She darted her gaze around the room before stopping to look down at her hands. "I was upset because I care for you, Kelvin. I cherished what we had, and, for me to see you covet someone else, I... I just became undone."

For an eternity, leaden silence hung heavy in the office, disturbed only by the rhythmic sound of harsh breathing. Hunt could claim responsibility for that.

Kelvin glanced at Petra. How was she taking Jade's announcement? She caught his gaze and held it. Empathy for the other woman shone deeply in her honey-colored eyes.

And as for Hunt, he sat in judgment with his arms folded against his massive chest. He glared at Kelvin, but didn't say a word.

Kelvin stood and paced to relieve some of his tension. "I am sorry for that, Jade. It wasn't as if we had an exclusive arrangement, though."

Jade nodded but didn't look at him.

He pursued a sudden thought. "What can you tell me about Joe?"

"Joe Hammer? He's a hard worker, of course. Personally, I don't know much about him. We did go out once, just for dinner. That was about six months ago. He's nice, but we didn't hit it off in that way."

Jade pushed back limp hair behind her ear. "Wait. Before, you mentioned a catamaran. Was it Joe's?"

"Yes," Kelvin replied. "That was what exploded." Another test. How would she react?

"No! Oh no, I had no idea. How did that happen? Was anyone on board? Is Joe okay?"

Hunt growled.

Jade blinked rapidly and stared at Hunt. "You came in here accusing me about a lady... Petra... on the catamaran." She switched to Petra. "Y-You were on the boat?"

"Yes, but I managed to jump overboard before... before the explosion."

Hearing those chilling words made Kelvin's heart beat in triple time. He gave a silent prayer of thanks.

Jade's face turned ashen. "What about Joe?"

"He's dead," Kelvin said flatly. "I just received word from Sergio that some of Joe's remains have been found."

Jade's eyelids fluttered, and not in a coquettish way. It was shock. She passed out against the back of the chair.

Hunt stood and then loomed over her. His nostrils widened as if inhaling her scent. "This one did not harm the Lady. We shall take her to your medical doctor for treatment."

The Uortsk must've excelled in lifting weights for he easily scooped her up, holding her under the knees and upper back. Her head however, lolled back without support.

Petra hurried over and elevated Jade's head to rest against Hunt's chest. "She'll be more comfortable like this."

"Tender-hearted lady." Hunt nodded at Kelvin and then lumbered out of the office.

Petra closed the door behind him.

Without conscious thinking, Kelvin strode over to her and took her in his arms. He leaned his forehead against her perfumed hair. "I love you, Petra."

She snuggled in next to him. "Oh Kelvin. This is all so overwhelming." As she sniffed, a lone tear slipped down her cheek.

"But we're closer, sweetness. I'm sure Jade isn't the traitor. Which leaves us with--"

"Valli and the Ellens." Petra shivered. "I don't think it's the Ellens."

Neither did he.

A beeping from the intercom broke the silence. Curving his arm around Petra, Kelvin took her with him. He answered the call. "Yes?"

"Quentin here, sir. Apologies for the interruption. Valli Proximus is here to see you. She wishes to confer in your office."

Petra and Kelvin exchanged looks. Valli was here. Now. As he'd thought earlier, it was past time to take action.

He gestured toward the connecting washroom. "Wait behind the door, sweetheart. Listen in if you can. I may need for you to pay us a surprise visit."

"But Kelvin, it's dangerous--"

He silenced her with a kiss. "You forget, we're under observation. Let's get this done, once and for all.

After she reluctantly went into the washroom, he pressed the intercom button. "Quentin, you may send Valli Proximus in."

Chapter Sixteen

Valli glided in as if she didn't have a care in the world. Her dark wavy hair attractively framed her elongated face. Her crisp white slacks were molded to her curvy figure and her scoop-necked blouse was low enough to provide a hint of the bounty of her breasts underneath.

Kelvin frowned. But she should have had a care in the world. At the very least, the blast of the explosion should've been the topic of every staff member's conversation.

Unless... Valli was the very person who had caused the explosion.

"Thank you for seeing me on such short notice, Kelvin. I know you must be very busy." She spoke like a queen, having the regal bearing that one expected, given her antecedents of the Proximus family line.

He stood and gestured toward the chair in front of his desk. "Always a pleasure, Valli. Please, have a seat. What can I do for you?"

He reseated himself, using the desk as a barrier to keep his distance.

She sat precisely, again as a queen might. "I've heard the most disturbing rumor. Something about a catamaran exploding?" She pursed her lips. "Was it Joe's? I tried to reach him but he's not answering his cell."

So that was the way she was playing this. Kelvin schooled his features. "Yes, I'm afraid it was his boat. I regret having to tell you--security is still searching for... parts of Joe's body."

Her slim hand flew to her lips. "Upon the star of Tau! Is it possible? Joe is dead?"

Acting certainly wasn't Valli's forte. "Yes, it comes to a shock to us all. Poor man."

She pulled a handkerchief from her small purse and dabbed at her eyes. "I am stunned."

Hardly. Kelvin suppressed his snort.

Turning her head toward the sideboard, she then stood. "I think I need a drink." She glanced at his nearly empty crystal tumbler. "Shall I refresh yours?"

Hell no! Ten to one she'd add a splash of poison. Although, if he did keel over, it wouldn't go unseen. The office was being monitored.

Besides, Petra kept an eye on him. She was peeking out from behind the washroom door. She hadn't closed it all the way. An open sliver remained.

Her audacity constantly astonished him.

He withheld his smile. "I'm fine, thanks. With this tragedy, I've got to keep a clear head."

Valli nodded, and then poured a generous amount of premium whisky. Twenty-five-year-old Chivas Regal, to be exact. Expensive tastes for a travel director.

Returning to her chair, she took a sip. A self-satisfied smile denoting the greatest of pleasure lifted her veal-colored lips. To use an old Terran expression, she looked like the cat that ate the canary.

She inclined her head. "How is your nephew taking the loss of his nanny?"

Kelvin's mouth tightened. "Are you talking about Conni True?"

Ah, a mistake! Valli's violet gaze traveled wildly about the office. Obviously she had meant Petra. But no mention had been made about Petra.

"Certainly, I meant Conni. Such a tragic case." Valli tut-tutted. "But what about Conni's replacement, that Terran, Petra Richardson?"

He saddened his voice. "Petra seems to be missing. We haven't been able to find her."

"Indeed? What could have happened to her? Was she..." Valli downed another sip. "Oh my. I know this is disturbing but what if she had been on Joe's boat? He mentioned to me that he found her attractive."

"Did he?" Kelvin drummed his fingers on the hardwood desk. "That is a possibility we hadn't thought of. I'll alert security. Give me a moment."

He used the intercom. "Quentin, call Sergio Iguana. He's with the marina detail. Tell him I'm with Valli Proximus here at my office. She thinks Petra Richardson might have been on the catamaran. The security team should be on the lookout for male... and female body parts."

After Quentin acknowledged, Kelvin turned his attention back to Valli. She had no idea Petra was right behind the washroom door. Valli still believed she was in the clear. And Sergio would understand the hidden message--that Valli was the woman they hunted.

"My thanks for that, Valli." Kelvin caught her gaze and held it.

The woman preened.

"Before I forget, Valli, did Joe harp on any particular topic? Something that might explain his actions today? Did he have any specific concerns?"

Here was an opportunity for her to talk. To reveal herself. Or hang herself, as it were.

And also to make Joe Hammer the fall guy.

With Valli here in his office, Tray remained safe. Without question she was concocting another plan to attack Tray in the future. Once the security level dropped, of course. As Petra had overheard the conversation on the boat, the woman had said, "I ... *attend to the boy... at my leisure.*"

Valli used her free hand to fluff out her wavy hair. "Joe did resent you, you know."

Kelvin lifted his brows in feigned surprise. "I wasn't aware of that."

She smiled. "Perhaps not you exactly, but the Lacertus family. The Hammer clan is an old and respected lineage. Joe told me that Tau Ceti was ripe for new leadership. He chafed at his second class status." A casual shrug briefly flashed her cleavage. "Although those were treasonous sentiments, I confess that at times I allowed him to rant."

"Why was that?"

"I felt it was safer that way for him to let off steam. Joe felt very strongly that Lacertus members needed to abdicate immediately."

Joe *and* Valli. Another phrase came to mind that Petra had heard: "*There will be one less Lacertus to concern ourselves with.*"

Kelvin steepled his fingers. "So you think Josephus Hammer was part of the Continuer contingent?"

"I guess he must have been." She tapped the cleft in her chin as if thinking. "It's possible that he lured Petra to the catamaran with the idea of hurting you. After all, you did seem to be rather fond of her, Kelvin."

Valli noticed. And past tense as well. Interesting.

He glanced at the wall clock. Where the devil was the security team?

AN ALIEN PARADISE by Susanne Marie Knight

"I'm always fond of women, Valli."

"Is that so?" She got to her feet, and then slowly undulated her way to his desk like a deadly cobra. She reached into her purse.

The washroom door burst open. "Did someone mention my name?" Petra came charging in like a fierce Scandinavian Valkyrie. Instead of wielding an avenging sword, she brandished a spray can of air sanitizer.

As he'd thought earlier, her audacity constantly astonished him. Did she think aerosol disinfectant would be able to vanquish Valli?

The horrified expression on Valli's face revealed everything. She was shocked that her intended victim was still alive; that he must have been stringing her along; and that she was now cornered like the rat that she was.

Kelvin leapt up, sending his chair crashing back against the wall. He grabbed Valli's purse, threw it out of reach, and fastened her hands behind her back, all before she knew what was happening.

"You bastard!" Valli screeched. "You Lacertus bastard! My people will revenge me. None of you are safe. Do you hear me? The Proximus clan will rule!"

She was a banshee bent on destruction--twisting, kicking, and jabbing at him.

He had his hands full, that much was certain, but he held firm.

Finally, Sergio barged in with three of his men. She was no match for one, let alone four additional men and they quickly subdued her.

After Valli was secured, Kelvin took Sergio aside. "Make sure there are no cyanide pills on her person, as it was with Conni True. We have a valuable prisoner here. This one carries much information that will aid in rounding up the Continuers back on Tau Ceti."

"Bastard! I hate you!" Valli glared at him. She ground her teeth with a crunching sound.

He had an anxious few moments, afraid she'd stashed a cyanide pill in her mouth. Seconds ticked by. Thankfully, she didn't collapse and start convulsing on the floor, although she probably wished she could take the easy way out.

If cyanide poisoning could be considered easy.

Sergio signaled for his men to move the prisoner. "Don't you fear, sir. I'll turn up the heat on her."

Once they were gone, Petra walked over to Kelvin. "Omigosh, that was so intense."

He knew without a doubt his wide smile reflected relief. Pointing at the spray can, he asked, "Does it stink that bad in here?"

"No, silly." She stepped closer. "This was all I could find in the washroom to use as a weapon."

He lowered his head to graze his lips against hers. "Well, you don't need it anymore."

She dropped the can on the floor and smiled. "Thank goodness for that." Petra threw her arms around his neck and enveloped him with her warmth.

Leaning down, he brushed his lips against hers again, then gently, tentatively, covered her mouth. Her taste ignited a fire down into his core. "Mmmm. I do like this."

She pulled away to whisper, "Yes, I know. You're always fond of women."

Chuckling, Kelvin guided her back to his embrace. "Come back here, you. You're the only woman I'm fond of... more than fond of."

Gazing into her eyes, he held her tighter. He deepened the kiss, losing himself in the wonder of her arms. "I love you, Petra. Don't ever leave me."

With all hell breaking loose beyond his office door, he was thankful the monitoring team allowed him these few minutes alone with her.

For once in his life, he didn't care about duties or responsibilities. About the Taurus City Travel Agency, about his position as a Lacertus, or about anything at all except this extraordinary woman.

"Tonight," he murmured into the shell of her ear. "Tonight, you will be mine."

* * * *

Petra couldn't wait any longer. It was ten o'clock and her eyes would not stay open. She slipped under the covers, grateful for the sensation of silk sheets sliding on her skin. Taking several deep breaths, she allowed every muscle in her body to relax.

It had been one helluva day.

After she had been escorted back to Kelvin's house, Georges had been solicitous and Tray very sweet, but nevertheless, she'd felt as wrung out as a dirty towel. If only Kelvin was here to cuddle with her, comfort her, and just make things better, but that wasn't to be. He was a very important man. With the conference still going on, he had duties. Responsibilities. Obligations.

Closing her eyes, she sighed. She'd waited for him long enough. All she needed right now was the blessed oblivion of sleep.

* * * *

She was drenched. Covered with water. If she didn't swim to the surface, she'd drown.

Thrashing about, Petra moaned at the same time. She couldn't free herself. Something held back her arms, preventing her from reaching the surface.

"Sweetheart! Sweetheart, it's okay. It's just a nightmare. You're safe."

It was Kelvin. Oh, thank goodness. She opened her eyes to find him next to her in bed, his handsome face hovering right above hers.

He kissed the tip of her nose, and then tenderly outlined the bandage on her forehead. "You gave me quite a scare, sweetness."

"Oh Kelvin!" She pulled him close, transferring her shudders of fear into his strong, muscular body. Three breaths later, she felt better-- completely over her fright. Now a thousand shivers pleasurably zipped through her.

She gazed up at him and smiled. "Hello! How long have you been here?"

"Not long enough." He cupped her face in his hands, cradling her, and leaned in for a delicious kiss. "How are you doing, sweetheart?"

"Much better." She ran the tip of her tongue over her lips, tasting him. "Mmmm, and you know what? I'm even better now."

His mouth met hers, melding together--a mixture of love and lust. Passion and desire. Infinite longing and intense hot-blooded sex.

"Petra." He nibbled his way over to her ear. "Petra, I almost lost you."

His breath stirred the hot flames within her. "Don't think about that. That's over. We... we're here. Now. And I need you... so bad."

Sliding his fingers into her loose hair, he kissed her deeply. Rocking her to her core. Ecstasy spiraled within her, and truth be told, she was about to explode.

When he gently and then not so gently kneaded her breasts through the encumbrance of her nightshirt, she almost cried out. She bit her lip to keep quiet. After all, Tray was just next door.

Arching up against Kelvin's hardness, she moaned. "Oh Kelvin. You're driving me wild."

"Darling Petra," his voice thickened as his hands explored her body. "You're so soft, so sweet, so tasty."

He pulled the nightshirt up, exposing her breasts. The cool air rushed in, causing goosebumps. Kelvin would warm her. She smiled as she got rid of the offending article.

"Now that's what I call service," he murmured as he suckled one nipple, and with one hand, massaged the other.

"Oh!" A coiled jolt of energy shot up through her spine. "Oh hurry, Kelvin!"

She practically hummed with need for him. Like a finely tuned instrument begs to be played and appreciated, so did she beg. *Play me. Make me sing.*

Breathing heavily, he removed his pajama bottoms and then settled on top of her. "Petra, my own one. I have waited so long for you..."

She sunk her teeth into his shoulder as he sunk his hardness into her. Throbbing, thrusting, swirling with passion, she spun out of control. Nothing else in the world mattered. Just Kelvin. Only Kelvin. They were here, together, and bound by love's embrace.

Love. Safe, secure, and loved.

Muting the cry of her release, Petra hugged him for all she was worth. It was his turn next. Stroking his hair, she savored the thrust of his climax.

Still kissing her, he relaxed on top of her. "Petra, you are divine. I love you, sweetheart."

Mmmm, so delicious!

"I love you too, Kelvin," she murmured into his ear. Yes, this was love, and she had it bad. Or rather good.

Grinning, she closed her eyes as she drifted to sleep on heavenly comfy clouds.

Chapter Seventeen

When Petra woke up, she was alone. Kelvin had already left. Sighing her regret, she threw back the covers. Then she spotted a piece of paper next to the pillow. It was an old-fashioned handwritten note.

Sweetheart, it read. *You are delectable! I'm sad we can't linger in bed and, well, you know! Conference sessions are starting early today. The good news is that it's almost over. Tomorrow is the last day. Take your time getting up, dear one. Tray's being looked after by Juanita and Inés until you're ready. See you tonight. All my love, K.*

Petra sighed again, but this time the sigh was due to lover-ly memories. Goodness, Kelvin was delectable, too. She couldn't wait to see him... and to have a "take two" session with their lovemaking.

It didn't take her long to shower and dress. After a bit of makeup, she applied a fresh bandage to her forehead. The wound actually looked well on the way to being healed. Maybe there was some kind of special curative properties to the covering.

These folks from Tau Ceti certainly had some advantages, didn't they?

She found Tray playing outside, flying his poomba around.

"My friend! My friend! Yay!" He nearly knocked her down with his enthusiasm.

"Easy, kiddo, easy." Patting his shoulder, she turned and thanked Juanita and Inés for watching him. Then she knelt down to his level. "Tray, how about if we went to your uncle's office today?"

"Will we see Uncle Kel?"

"Probably not, but I'd like to go to the Travel Agency office to see someone else. Felicia. I think she could use company today."

The boy wrinkled his nose. Obviously he needed something to make the trip worth his while.

"Tell you what. Let's get ice cream first, and we'll get a cone for Felicia, too."

"Cool beans! I'm gonna get Rocky Road!" He gave her a sideways glance. "Two scoops?"

She laughed. "You drive a hard bargain, kiddo. Two scoops, it is."

174

With Raulf and Bjorn following in a separate car, they took the short drive to the ice cream hut, and then, with three Rocky Road cones in a to-go container, they continued on to the Travel Agency building.

Felicia sat behind her uncluttered desk, but with her shoulders slumped, she faced out the window. She didn't turn around when Petra and Tray entered.

"Hi, Felicia. We thought you could use an ice cream."

"Golly!" The woman circled back around. Her dark eyes lit up. "I didn't hear you come in. Oh, thanks for the ice cream. I, well, it's so good to see you." She gestured toward the couch by another set of windows. "C'mon, let's sit over there, away from my desk."

Petra glanced at Tray. With him busy licking his two scoops, she and Felicia could have a chance to talk.

Petra handed out napkins. "How are you doing?"

"Girl, I'm, well, I just don't know what to say. What to think. I can't believe my boss is gone and his boat blown up. Yikes! I'm in shock." She dropped her gaze. "We were getting along so well. I thought that he might... y'know, might be liking me."

"Oh, I'm so sorry, Felicia."

The woman leaned closer. "Rumors are going around like crazy. Imagine, there's some kind of scandal concerning Joe and Valli Proximus. I don't know what it's about, but she's no longer the Travel Director. And she's being detained. So, golly, we're short-staffed. I just don't know what's going on."

Petra couldn't share what she knew. Kelvin had said that Felicia was from Earth. So naturally she wouldn't have been privy to Tau Ceti information.

"Anyway," Felicia continued as she took a bite out of the cone. "I'm pulling out my hair." She grabbed hanks of tightly curled hair out to the sides of her head.

Tray looked up at her and giggled.

She giggled back, but then sobered her voice. "I'm filling in for Joe. On most matters. I guess there are some things that only the higher-ups like to handle, so Todd Boiler, the Finance Director, is helping out when needed. As for Valli's spot, Wanda Cropper has stepped in temporarily. Her boss, Owen Greenacre, is taking care of her stuff. As for Australia, the Ellens are splitting Ellen F.'s area. And Maizie, too, so there shouldn't be an overload there."

Petra finished her cone. "That's a lot to handle, Felicia. I'm so sorry."

"Yeah, well, takes a lickin', keeps on tickin'. That's the way it goes sometimes." Felicia shrugged.

Tray crunched on his cone, giving Petra and Felicia a few more minutes to get caught up on the news. He'd been so good, Petra didn't want him to start to get antsy.

Just as she was about to say goodbye, Wanda Cropper burst into the office.

"Hey there." The frizzy blonde narrowed her gaze as she scanned the room. "I'm looking for Jade Dunbar. Have you guys seen her?"

Goodness, was Jade missing in action again?

While Petra shook her head "no", Felicia went back to her desk. "Wait a minute. I've got a conference schedule here someplace." She pulled out her portable tablet and scrolled down. "Yeah, here it is. Jade and Maizie are holding a Q and A session for attendees who want to travel to Antarctica."

"Okay, good." Wanda scratched behind her ear. "I'll leave a note on her desk then. A change or two just came in for Kelvin's trip. Lor, there's so much happening right now. This Travel Director job is keeping me hopping."

"Kelvin's trip?" Petra tried not to sound anxious, but where was he going?

"He's always dashing around, isn't he? Yep, the Chairman let us know he wants Kelvin to accompany..." She glanced at Tray, who was now looking out the window and licking his fingers. She lowered her voice. "Accompany the boy back to their... er, home country. Everything's all set up for this Wednesday morning, but instead of an eleven o'clock departure, as we scheduled, it's now nine a.m."

While the other two women talked, Petra sat back in a daze. Kelvin knew he was going on a trip, but didn't mention it to her? Why didn't he tell her last night?

Actually they had been a bit preoccupied, hadn't they? A brief smile lit her lips but then vanished.

Or, at the very least he could've written that news in his note. He wrote about the good news: the conference ending tomorrow, so why didn't he write the bad news: he was leaving Wednesday morning?

His brother was on Tau Ceti 3. How far away was that planet? How long would the trip take? When would he be back?

Why hadn't he told her?

She drummed her fingers on the couch's armrest. Since Kelvin was taking Tray back to his father, what was she supposed to do here at Taurus City? The reason for her employment would be gone. Was she supposed to pack her bags and go back home?

Was this going to be another failed attempt at love?

Petra blinked back tears. Her heart had just been recently healed. Was Kelvin finished with her, as he was finished with Jade?

* * * *

Things were good. Great, in fact. Finally going Kelvin's way. The diplomatic conference was all but over, except for the formalities tomorrow, Tuesday. All lifeforms had enjoyed their stay on Terra; even Hunt seemed to be in an agreeable mood. Most likely the reason was that the Uortzk had assisted his much admired lady.

Kelvin's lady as well. Petra.

He grinned. His Terran was a powerhouse of seduction, that was for certain.

Added to all the good news was the arrest and interrogation of the traitor, Valli Proximus. With Sergio's skillful examination techniques, she had already revealed the identity of the remaining Continuer conspirators on Tau Ceti 3.

Yes, it was a terrific night all around.

True, they were down a few key personnel positions, but his remaining staff efficiently handled the extra workload and, of course, replacements were on the way.

They'd be needed here very soon. After a conference such as this one, there usually was an increase in the requests to visit Terra. The reason for this was simple: the ambassadors always had favorable reviews, spurring the desire to visit the fabled pleasure dome of this alien paradise.

Kelvin glanced at his office clock. Hell. The hour was late. At three in the morning, there wasn't enough time to get a good night's sleep. Nonetheless, he took the stairs leading to the parking lot. Even if he just held Petra as she slept, that would be enough--for now.

He grinned again.

Getting into the driver's seat, he headed for the house. How unfortunate that his brother decided to have Tray brought home now. It would be a one-month journey at best.

Kelvin released a heavy sigh. He had hoped to spend many carefree days with his Petra, before the onslaught of visitors began once again. It would be good for Tray to be with his father, though. Will missed the boy terribly.

So would Kelvin, and Petra also would.

Shunting aside those melancholy thoughts, he passed through security and entered his house. He took a quick look at Tray, sound asleep in his bed, before going into Petra's room. A soft nightlight illuminated her outline under the bed's comforter. She lie on her side, her dark hair curved down around her shoulders and pooled under the chin.

As he slipped under the covers, he watched her thick eyelashes flutter. He kissed a sweet spot below her jaw before spooning next to her.

"Mmmm, Kelvin?" she murmured.

"Expecting someone else, my love?" He chuckled.

She flipped over to face him. "You're cold."

"You can warm me."

Unexpectedly, she sat up, taking some of the comforter with her. "You're going on a trip."

He joined her in a seated position. Sensing her tenseness, he smoothed his hand down her lightly covered back. "That sounded like an accusation. But yes, you're right. My brother Will is eager to see Tray again. He requested that I escort the boy back to Tau Ceti."

"Why didn't you tell me?"

"Just learned about it yesterday afternoon, sweetheart. There wasn't much time to tell you."

"But I had to learn about it from Wanda. You didn't mention it in your note. I... I don't know. It bothers me."

Kelvin kissed the frown line on her forehead. "There's no need to worry, my dear one. I'll be back as soon as I can. Probably four to six weeks--tops."

She was still quiet. "I can't stay here."

"What do you mean? You've got to stay here, Petra."

"No, since Tray will be gone, there'll be nothing for me to do. My job-_"

"Forget the job. Look at this interlude as a vacation in paradise, all right? I'll make sure you get shown the islands, wildlife, whatever you want. By the time I return you'll be tanned and relaxed."

She sucked in part of her lower lip, something he longed to do. Instead, he outlined her succulent lips with the tip of his index finger.

"I don't know if I can do that, Kelvin. I'll feel like such a sluggard."

"Sluggard?" He snorted. "You are anything but, sweetness. Listen, it's just for a little while."

She wasn't responding to his lovemaking. "I'll... miss Tray. He's such a sweet boy. I'll miss you both."

Kelvin took her in his arms and held her tightly. "I'll be back soon. As I said, as soon as I can. A thousand meteor showers couldn't keep me away. And as soon as I can arrange it, we'll both travel to Tau Ceti. See Tray and Will, see the sights. Introduce you around. I'll show you how the other half of Humanity lives!"

His joke fell flat. She wasn't convinced. Why was she so troubled about this?

"Promise me you won't leave, darling," he whispered into the shell of her ear. "My staff will take care of you, and I'll be back before you know it."

"But I--"

"Promise me, Petra." He would brook no further refusal. He butterflied kisses on her eyelids. "You will stay here and you will like it."

He felt her take a deep breath and then release it. Her shudder shook him to his very core. "There's no need to feel insecure, love. I'll be back for you. Now, promise me."

She exhaled again. "Okay."

"No, say it. Promise me you won't leave."

"I-I promise." Petra said it reluctantly, but it didn't matter. She'd pledged herself, the same as he.

But it was true, they would be apart for a long time. Kissing her more deeply, he leaned them back against the mattress to fully and completely love this woman for the remainder of the night.

Chapter Eighteen

Petra broke her promise. She'd had to. The day after Kelvin left, her mother had called with the news. Dad had been in an accident. A serious car accident. One that had sent him to a hospital for nearly two weeks, and now a nursing home to recover physical mobility.

Four compound fractures, three broken metacarpals, two cracked ribs... and a partridge in a pear tree.

She stared out the window on the air-conditioned New York City bus. No, there wasn't any humor attached to her father's accident. He'd broken his pelvis, too, along with suffering a concussion. The four awful fractures were on the tibia and fibula of both legs, and the broken bones were in his right hand. Naturally, his dominant hand. On the plus side, the cracked ribs weren't too painful.

If her father had been unpleasant to be around before, now he was simply impossible. Of course it went without saying he was an extremely difficult patient. His anger tore up everyone's equanimity. And his profanity and hurled insults...

She shuddered. His words would blast out of his room--a private room out of necessity because he was such a foul roommate. It was a sure bet every person within hearing distance eagerly anticipated his release to go home.

The bus stopped on its route and picked up a few passengers. At this time of day, there were plenty of empty seats. The doors closed and then the bus continued on its way. Her stop was the nursing home, about ten more minutes away. Since the family car had been totaled and she didn't own a vehicle, she accompanied her mother on the buses every day out to the facility. Two buses there and two back. *Every day,* for eight weeks now, they'd either been going to the hospital or the nursing home.

Exhaustion didn't even begin to cover how she felt. And seeing her father helpless but, of course, not docile was truly taking a huge toll on both of them.

The sway of the bus caused her mind to wander. Not surprisingly, it wandered to the beauty of the Galápagos Islands... and Kelvin. She missed him terribly. They'd had only a short time together and now...

Taurus City was so far away, as was Kelvin. Another world away, pun intended.

She'd written a letter before she'd left, telling him the reason that she had to go back home. Georges had promised to give Kelvin the letter once he returned.

She hadn't heard from him. Was he back? Did he still love her? Was he even interested in her? And how was Tray? She had no clue.

Darn it all, she was in limbo. As upsetting as the thought was, she felt like what she'd experienced back in July was akin to one of those summer fling type of situations. Or a Grade B teenaged movie. Should she pursue Kelvin? Should she wait and let him make the first move?

Petra propped her elbow on her thigh, and then rested her chin in her hand. Would she ever see him again? Oh, this pain of waiting was tearing her in two.

And yet the whole scenario was so bizarre. Extraterrestrials? Tau Ceti 3? A travel agency for aliens? Did she dream everything up? Did any of it even happen?

She shook her head. She'd never had much of an imagination. How could she have imagined all of this?

And Kelvin's kisses? No, they were real. He was real. She'd never experienced pure lovemaking like his before.

When the bus driver applied the brakes, she looked up to see her stop. She stood by the back door, waited, and then pushed open the folding doors. As she stepped off the bus, a humid breeze greeted her. The nursing home stood a few feet away.

Setting aside her daydreams, she braced herself, knowing she'd be in for another round of verbal abuse from her father. He'd badger her and wouldn't let up until he found out why Mom wasn't with her.

The plain truth was, her poor mother was weary--weary to the bone. Coming down with a cold, too. She'd wanted to come, but Petra had played the "you don't want to get Dad sick" card, until finally it had worked.

After walking into the building, she greeted the familiar receptionist behind her front desk, and then continued down one of the wide corridors. Soft sounds of instrumental music wafted over the loud speakers. Decorating the hall walls were hand-colored autumn leaves, even though it was still officially summer. Soon school would be back in session. In fact, it was only a week away.

Comforting aromas of cinnamon and freshly baked bread filled the air. The clanking of dishes, utensils, and the squeaky wheels from meal carts came from the residents' dining room as the clean up started. The lunch hour had already passed.

Petra nodded to residents that she had come to know, and the aides who worked hard to take care of them. Everything was the same as it was every day she visited.

She frowned. Except...

By the nurses' station, a tall black man leaned on the counter, talking with one of the staff. He wore a short white lab jacket and black slacks. His short Afro was peppered with distinguished grey.

She stopped mid-step. Oh good gosh! Cornwell Young? What was he doing here?

Rushing over to the station, she said a quick hello to the nurse, and then tapped the doctor on the shoulder. "Cornwell? Hello! I, ah, I'm so surprised to see you."

His wide smile dazzled her. "Petra! I knew you were gonna show up here soon, child. And you have a ton of questions, eh? C'mon, let's go have a talk."

She followed him in a haze. They went into one of the facilities' many sitting rooms; this one had a lovely view of the nearby Throg's Neck Bridge.

He sat across from her. "First, I'll apologize for not getting up here sooner. But it hasn't exactly been business as usual at Taurus City, y'know?"

"But... but why are you here?" That sounded wrong. She hurried to explain. "Oh, I'm so happy to see you, but why? And why the nursing home?"

"I heard about your father's accident, of course. And, y'know, medicine here is so twenty-first century." Cornwall made a boyish grin. "So I just administered a couple of dosages of our miracle concoction, *Fortis Ossa,* a treatment that initiates rapid regrowth of bone osteocytes. Your father's responding as he should. The fractures and broken bones will be completely mended in two days."

Her mouth dropped. "Two days?"

"Yeah. The hard part, although it's not too hard, is up to your father. He's gonna have to work out and strengthen his muscles. Y'know, physical therapy. Over the past two months of inactivity, there's been significant muscle loss. Not a big deal, though, and easily fixable. So your father should be ready to leave here soon."

Petra jumped to her feet and impulsively gave Cornwell a kiss. "This is fantastic! Thank you so much."

He brushed her away. "None of that now, child. Save it for Kelvin."

Kelvin. She tried to sound nonchalant. "Oh, yes, well, how is Kelvin?"

"He's with your father now." Cornwell winked.

For one split second, every cell in her body froze. "I-I'd better go..." The next second, she zoomed into gear, and hurried out the door.

If she wasn't mistaken, she heard Cornwell call after her, "Go get him, tiger!"

As she approached her father's room, she listened intently. Although the door was open, no foul words escaped out into the corridor. She heard the murmur of conversation, but nothing loud or unpleasant.

Inhaling deeply, she took a step into the room. Her heart almost stopped. Kelvin sat in a small chair beside the bed, focusing his attention on her father.

She lingered her gaze on Kelvin. Goodness, he looked like perfection itself. His dark brown hair was still in need of a comb, his wide shoulders were amazing in his tailored navy blazer, and the way his muscular thighs strained against his jeans... well, this man was the complete package. Her heart now bongo-drummed a primitive beat.

Maybe Kelvin heard. He got to his feet. "Petra." He took in her appearance, from head to toe.

She hoped he liked what he saw, but she could feel herself flush. "Kelvin, it's good to see you."

A muscle twitched at the corner of his mouth. "It gratifies me to hear you say that, my dear."

Her flush must've deepened, for she burned hot, as hot as fire.

"Well, grab a chair and sit down, Petra Jane." Her father waved his arm, the one with a cast on his hand. "Do I still have to tell you what to do, goddamn it?"

Kelvin quickly pulled a chair over for her. "Your father and I have been having a little chat."

"Goddamn straight. Do you have any idea what this man," Dad glanced at Kelvin. "Kelvin you say? That's a damn strange name." He looked back at Petra. "What he and that doctor say this new drug can do for me?"

She kept her gaze on Kelvin. "I saw Doctor Young by the nurses' station. He told me. I think it's wonderful, Dad."

Her father shifted position on the mattress. "*Fortis Ossa,* it's called. Bloody Latin. I feel better already. Where's your mother?"

While she explained about her mother not wanting to pass on her cold, Petra watched Kelvin out of the corner of her eye. He was so handsome. She wanted to eat him alive! But how embarrassing for him to be here with her father.

"Damn fool woman," Dad muttered. "Here I am, finally getting better and she can't handle a few sniffles."

Kelvin reached over and took Petra's hand. "Mr. Richardson, let's return to what we were talking about. Do I have your permission?"

"You're talking about Petra Jane, right? Only fool daughter I have. Only child that damn fool woman gave me."

Petra blinked. Was Kelvin asking Dad's permission to marry her? Or was she jumping the gun? "Oh, Kelvin, we haven't talked about--"

"You seem intelligent, young man," her father interrupted. "Why would you want to marry my Petra Jane? She's as foolish as they come."

Yes! Kelvin wanted to marry her! Petra took a deep breath, settled herself, and then wrinkled her nose. "Thanks for that ringing endorsement, Dad."

Kelvin stood, and lifted her to her feet. He curved his arm around her waist, and then leaned over to gently shake her father's broken hand. "Because I love her, sir. She means everything to me."

He brushed his lips against her ear. "I love you, Petra Jane. Say you'll marry me."

They had an audience. Her father's gimlet eyes watched every movement, and his big ears heard every word.

She nibbled on her lower lip. "Let's go someplace, ah, someplace else and talk about this, okay?"

"Okay, only if your answer is 'yes.'" Kelvin squeezed her waist, and then turned back around to her father. "We'll be back later, sir, to see how you're feeling."

Instead of an insult or a snide remark, her father nodded. "Go on with you then. But first, give me a minute with Petra Jane."

"Certainly, sir." Kelvin gave her another squeeze. "I'll be right outside."

As soon as he left the room, her father gestured for her to come closer. "You did good, girl. I like this one. Don't mess it up."

Whatever she'd expected, it certainly wasn't her father's approval. She felt herself beaming. Thanks, Dad. I... I'll try not to."

Giving her father a peck of a kiss, she hurried outside where Kelvin was waiting.

* * * *

The "someplace else" Petra picked to go was her neighborhood ice cream parlor. On the drive over--in Kelvin's rented Maserati coupe--she purposefully kept the conversation light and inconsequential. They had important topics to discuss. She wanted to make sure she had his complete concentration.

"This is where it all started," she explained as she led the way toward the back of the eatery where the booths were located. They both slid down the plastic upholstered benches on either side of the table.

"Where what started?" He reached out, taking her hands, and rubbing his thumbs over her knuckles.

Warm and wonderful vibrations wiggled up her arms. She gave him a shy smile. "Where Felicia first told me about the Taurus City Travel Agency. Where I first learned about Tray." Petra caught his gaze. "And where I found out who had recommended me for the job."

Kelvin raised his eyebrow. "I see. This is where you eventually agreed to my offer, then." He took a quick look around. "I do like this place, sweetheart."

Petra removed her hands from his to make room for the server to set down their two vanilla sundaes. "Here we are. This is one of my favorite desserts," she said as she spooned a bit of ice cream. "Delicious!"

He did the same. "Yes, it's good, but not as good as my favorite dessert."

"Really? What's your favorite?"

"You."

"Oh!" She felt heat creep up on her cheeks. "You're pretty suave and debonair, aren't you?" She took another spoonful. "So tell me. How was your trip? How's Tray doing? I bet his father was so relieved to see him. What about those Continuers? Is everything all taken care of?"

Kelvin smiled. "Avoiding the main issue, I see. No matter. I'll humor you. The trip was tedious, as usual. Being sucked through wormholes isn't the most comfortable way to travel. But we arrived safely."

Her eyes widened to the max. Wormholes! *Yikes*. She gulped down her unease.

"Tray's reunion with my brother was quite touching. Almost makes me eager to be a father."

"You don't want to be a father?" Oh good gosh. This was not good news.

His grey eyes twinkled at her. "Of course I do, Petra. But not just yet. I need to enjoy the company of my bride-to-be first, hmmn?"

Keeping quiet, she focused on her ice cream.

"As for the Continuers, several Proximus members were part of this outrage. Indeed, the entire family line has been disgraced. However, we no longer have to concern ourselves with them. Josephus Hammer, on the other hand, was acting alone. The patriarchal head of that line has been most apologetic."

"That's wonderful. I'm glad all that's over with."

"Quite so." Kelvin took his time in licking his spoon. "What about you, Petra? What have you been up to?"

Watching his talented tongue, she fanned herself with her hand. "Nothing as exciting as your trip, that's for sure. I, ah, I've been getting the lesson plans ready for the new school year. It starts next week."

"School, yes. About that..." He reached into his jacket pocket and pulled out a small powder-blue velvet box. Then he took her hand and placed the box in the middle of her palm. "Would you, perhaps, change your mind about school and marry me instead?"

Sure, she knew he'd mentioned marriage before, and yet for some reason, the reality of the proposal made her throat tighten. Tears sprung to her eyes. "Kelvin. I-I..."

"Open the box, dear one."

She slowly lifted the lid. A humongous diamond sparkled up at her. Cut in the princess style, it was large and square and large.

Her mouth flapped open but no words came out. She felt hot tears slide down her cheeks. Why was it that when a person felt the happiest, she cried the hardest?

He left his side of the booth and then got on one knee in front of her. "Petra, sweetheart, would you do me the greatest honor in the galaxy and consent to be my wife?"

While some might have considered his words to be exaggerations, Kelvin had every right to use "the galaxy" in his declaration.

Still no words could get past her lips. She stared at him and the diamond.

He lifted her hand and kissed it. "I'm going to take your silence as a 'yes.'" Removing the elegant engagement ring from the box, he then slowly placed it on her third finger.

The diamond winked at her. It twinkled and flashed and glittered. If she stared at it long enough, she was sure it would've hypnotized her. She just couldn't take her eyes off of it.

"Kelvin." She patted at her heart. "This is the most beautiful ring I've ever seen."

As he smiled, the left side of his mouth lifted a little higher. "Is it doing its job?"

"What?"

"Will you marry me?"

"Yes! Yes! I love you so much, Kelvin. But what about my teaching--"

"No buts, sweetheart. Hey, I know I'm not a run-of-the-mill type of guy, however do you think you can overlook my unusual... origins?"

Laughter bubbled inside her. She pulled him up to sit beside her. Then she raised her arms around him and pressed herself against him, tasting his vanilla flavored lips.

"Mmmm. Unusual origins don't begin to describe you, Mr. Lacertus!"

Thank heavens the back of the ice cream parlor was relatively private. Kissing Kelvin was the most pleasurable activity she could think of.

After their breathing became deeper, thoughts of a more carnal nature took over. She reluctantly moved away. "But truly, Kelvin. I'm due to start work next week. I don't want to leave the school in a lurch."

"Got it covered, sweetie. We've alerted an excellent teacher. Actually, she's worked for your school before so they have her records. She said she'll be thrilled to step into your shoes."

Goodness, he's thought of everything, hasn't he?

"Well, okay, but if I won't be teaching, what will I do? At Taurus City?"

He lifted his eyebrow. "Besides catering to my every decadent whim?"

She couldn't help it. She gave him a whack.

He laughed. "Right. I have thought this over. How about if we establish a school for both young aliens and visiting Human tykes alike? I envision it as a vacation school to occupy the little ones while their elders enjoy sightseeing. You'd have a staff and also would determine the curriculum."

Wow. She had to admit his idea did sound good.

Kelvin enfolded her back in his strong arms. "Have I won you over yet?"

"You haven't told me that you love me." She made a fake pout.

He shook his head. "You Earth women enjoy giving a fellow a hard time, don't you?" Taking her hand, he placed it over his heart. "I love you like crazy, Petra Jane. And I always will. Besides, you *make* me crazy."

As they kissed, she smiled with contentment. His kisses made *her* crazy!

This time Kelvin pulled away. "Let's make this truly official. Why don't you give your mother a call and tell her our news?"

Petra glanced at her diamond and sighed happily. "Let's do this instead. The apartment's just down the block. I'll introduce you and show her the ring."

"Should I be quaking in my shoes?"

"No, silly. No need to worry. You've already passed the test with flying colors. My father, who doesn't impress easily--obviously--really likes you."

Kelvin stood and then extended his hand for her to take. "Come on then. The sooner we get all the details out of the way and get hitched, the better I'll like it." He gave her a smoldering kiss. "The better I'll love it."

Petra took her new fiancé's arm and walked out into the humid afternoon air. Married--to an extraterrestrial. That did sound lovely, didn't it?

The End

Addendum A:

Lifeforms Mentioned in

AN ALIEN PARADISE

BRHITE: Planet Brhite, belongs to the yellow-white star Sargas, in the Scorpio Sector, Scorpio Constellation, Omega Quadrant.

This warrior race is strongly Humanoid. Savage. A native would kill you as soon as talk to you. They are heavily tattooed and muscular. Also, very flexible, and can bend over backwards. They have elongated ears that can extend out twelve inches.

The Brhite ambassador is Napa.

KYKANOPIAN: Planet Kykanop, belongs to the white star Alderamin, in Cepheus Sector, Cepheus Constellation, Beta Quadrant.

This race is strongly Humanoid. Natives have four suction cups at the end of each finger. They eat and drink with these suction cups. Natives have golden eyes and amber color skin. When natives are nervous, they heavily perspire.

The Kykanopian ambassador is Kamtos. Also mentioned is Citizen Korpos.

NEPHROSIAN: Planet Nephros 3, belongs to the red star Al Dhanab, in Grus Sector, Grus Constellation, Omega Quadrant.

This aquatic race is not Humanoid. Natives have a long, flexible tail that propels the body through water. Their round bodies have four legs with a type of claw/flipper that they use to maneuver.

PHI PAVONIAN: Planet Phi Pavonis 2, belongs to yellow-white dwarf star, in Pavo Sector, Pavo Constellation, Gamma Quadrant.

This arrogant race is strongly Humanoid. They are around seven feet tall, slender, and have peacock-like feathers that they spread while preening.

The Phi Pavonis ambassador is Sage.

SIRIUS: Planet Sirius 3, belongs to white star Sirius A, in Canis Major Sector, Canis Major Constellation, Alpha Quadrant.

The very peaceful race is strongly Humanoid. Natives have light blue skin, bushy white eyebrows that seem to have a life of their own, and brilliant white hair. When natives are stressed, they lose moisture and shrink. When this happens, they need to be immersed in water.

Mentioned is Citizen Dutto.

UORTZK: Planet Uortzk 4, belongs to yellow star Uortzk and blue-white companion star Rama, in Cygnus Sector, Theta Quadrant.

The antagonist warrior race is Humanoid. Natives are massive, have rusty colored fur, and fierce claws. They are an old, more advanced race than Humans. Indigenous to the Milky Way galaxy, their present planet is not the planet of origin. Rumor has it that the original Uortizk had been destroyed, possibly by the Uortizks themselves.

The Uortzk ambassador is Hunt.

VELAN: Planet Vela, belongs to blue supergiant star Velorum, in Vela Sector, Vela Constellation, Beta Quadrant.

The psychic race is strongly Humanoid. Natives are bald and have green skin and eyes. When upset, a phosphorescent shroud covers their head, emitting an unpleasant, earthy odor.

Mentioned is Citizen Tarrnak.

WN-GANITE: Planet Wn-Gan, belongs to yellow star Mebsuta, in Gemini Sector, Gemini Constellation, Alpha Quadrant.

This race is strong Humanoid. Natives have a glowing blue outline. When they are unwell or fatigued, their contour looks fuzzy. When they feel happy, their edges are purplish. When angry, the edges are green.

Mentioned is Citizen Oblan.

YEAMONL: Planet Yeamon, belongs to blue-white star Minkar, in Corvus Sector, Corvus Constelation, Gamma Quadrant.

The non-Humanoid race has telepathic abilities and persuasive ways. Due to a very dense atmosphere on Yeamon, natives are only about three feet high and move very slowly. When angered, they grow somewhat taller. When happy, they grow wider. They are incapable of sitting, and are always shuffling back and forth. They have four snake-like limbs.

Addendum B:

Human Worlds Mentioned in

AN ALIEN PARADISE

BOKAR: Second planet in the white star system of Alpha Circini, in Alpha Circini Sector, Circinus Constellation. Has a harsh environment for Humans.

CAPELLA 8: Belongs to yellow-orange star in the binary system of Capella, in the Auriga Sector, Auriga Constellation. Since the temperature is always scorching, Human colonists tend to speak with descriptive hot phrases.

DENEB 4: Belongs to blue-white supergiant star Deneb, in the Cygnus Sector, Cygnus Constellation. Human colonists till the soil on this co-op collective farm planet.

SHAULA 9: Belongs to blue star Shaula or Lambda Scorpii, in the Scorpio Sector, Scorpio Constellation. To remedy the shortage of Human colonists, Human cloning has been authorized on this planet.

TAU CETI 3: Belongs to yellow star Tau Ceti, in the Cetus Sector, Cetus Constellation. Countess millennia ago, Terran natives were transplanted to Tau Ceti 3 with the purpose of overseeing the sightseeing program to the stately pleasure dome of Terra: code name Xanadu. The Lacertus family line has been in charge of this mission from the very beginning.

Addendum C:

Aliens/Extraterrestrial Humans Mentioned in

AN ALIEN PARADISE

Bjorn. Home planet Deneb 4. Security guard.

Conni True. Home planet Tau Ceti 3. Nanny to Traynor Lacertus.

Cornwell Young, MD. Home planet Tau Ceti 3. Medical Director.

Dutto. Home planet Sirius 3. Tourist.

Ellen A. Home planet Shaula 9. Travel Team Africa.

Ellen B. Home planet Shaula 9. Travel Team North America.

Ellen C. Home planet Shaula 9. Travel Team Asia.

Ellen D. Home planet Shaula 9. Travel Team South America.

Ellen E. Home planet Shaula 9. Travel Team Europe.

Ellen F. Home planet Shaula 9. Travel Team Australia.

Georges. Home planet Bokar. Chief Executive Officer Kelvin Lacertus' butler.

Hunt. Home planet Uortzk. Uortzk ambassador.

Jade Dunbar. Home planet Bokar. Executive Assistant to the Chief Executive Officer Kelvin Lacertus.

Josephus Hammer. Home planet Tau Ceti 3. Human Relations Director.

Kamtos. Home planet Kykanop. Kykanopian ambassador.

Kelvin Lacertus, Home planet Tau Ceti 3. Chief Executive Officer.

Korpos. Home planet Kykanop. Tourist.

Maizie. Home planet Deneb 4. Travel Team Antarctica.

Moriah Lacertus. Home planet Tau Ceti 3. Deceased wife of Wilhelm Lacertus. Mother to Traynor Lacertus.

Napa. Home planet Brhite. Brhite ambassador.

Niko Starling. Home planet Deneb 4. Head Chef.

Oblan. Home planet Wn-Gan. Tourist.

Owen Greenacre. Home planet Tau Ceti 3. Operations Director.

Quentin. Home planet Bokar. Administrative staff.

Raulf. Home planet Tau Ceti 3. Security guard.

Sage. Home planet Phi Pavonis 2. Phi Pavonian ambassador.

Sergio Iguana. Home planet Capella 8. Chief of Security.

Tarrnak. Home planet Vela. Tourist.

Todd Boiler. Home planet Capella 8. Finance Director.

Traynor Lacertus. Home planet Tau Ceti 3. Chief Executive Officer Kelvin Lacertus' nephew.

Valli Proximus. Home planet Tau Ceti 3. Travel Director.

Wanda Cropper. Home planet Deneb 4. Manager, Reservations and Accommodations.

Wilhelm Lacertus. Home planet Tau Ceti 3. Chairman. Chief Executive Officer Kelvin Lacertus' brother and Traynor Lacertus' father.

If You Enjoyed This Book

If you enjoyed reading AN ALIEN PARADISE, I would be honored if you gave this novel a review. Your input is valuable to me! By leaving a review you help other readers come across new works, and that, in turn helps me. :)) Thanks again for reading!

Happy Reading!

Susanne Marie Knight

About The Author

Award-winning author Susanne Marie Knight specializes in Romance Writing with a Twist! She is multi-published with books, short stories, and articles in such diverse genres as science fiction, Regency, mystery, paranormal, suspense, time-travel, fantasy, and contemporary romance. Originally from New York, Susanne lives in the Pacific Northwest, by way of Okinawa, Montana, Alabama, and Florida. Along with her husband and the spirit of her feisty Siamese cat, she enjoys the area's beautiful ponderosa pine trees and wide, open spaces—a perfect environment for writing.

For more information about Susanne, please visit: her website at: http://www.susanneknight.com

Books By Susanne Marie Knight

Amazon.com: http://www.amazon.com/author/susanneknight

REGENCY ROMANCE

    CONTINENTAL MARRIAGE, A

    CONTRARY CONTESSA, THE

    MAGIC TOKEN, THE

    NOBLE DILEMMA, A

    PAGING MISS GALLOWAY

    RELUCTANT LANDLORD, THE

    "Very Special Christmas Present, A" -- short story

REGENCY TIME TRAVEL ROMANCE

    HAVE CHRISTMAS CARD... WILL TRAVEL

    "Lady Elizabeth's Excellent Adventure"--short story

    LORD DARVER'S MATCH

    THE QUESTING BOX

    REGENCY SOCIETY REVISITED

    SOJOURN THROUGH TIME

    TIMELESS DECEPTION

PARANORMAL ROMANCE

    COMPETITORS!

    COMING, THE

    "Family Secrets" -- short story

    GRAVE FUTURE

    KARMIC CONNECTION, A

    PAST INDISCRETIONS

    "Shades Of Old Glory" -- short story

"Special Delivery" -- short story

UNCOVERING CAMELOT

WAKEFIELD DISTURBANCE, THE

CONTEMPORARY ROMANCE

"Carla's One-Sided Crush" -- short story

"Grand-mère's Sainte Bleu" -- short story

"Happy Anniversary" -- short story

LOVE AT THE TOP

ONE WIFE TOO MANY

"True Love And Candy Corn" -- short story

"Zeus And The Single Teacher" -- short story

MYSTERY ROMANCE

BLOODSTAINED BISTRO, THE (Minx Tobin Murder Mystery, Case 1)

DUPLICITOUS DIVORCE, THE (Minx Tobin Murder Mystery, Case 3)

EMBEZZLED ENVELOPE, THE (Minx Tobin Murder Mystery, Case 6)

ILL-GOTTEN INSURANCE, THE (Minx Tobin Murder Mystery, Case 2)

TAINTED TEA FOR TWO

VIRTUAL VALENTINE, THE (Minx Tobin Murder Mystery, Case 4

YULETIDE YORKSHIRE, THE (Minx Tobin Murder Mystery, Case 5)

SCIENCE FICTION/SCIENCE FICTION ROMANCE

ALIEN HEAT

AN ALIEN PARADISE (formerly entitled XANADU FOR

ALIENS)

"Convert, The" -- short story

FOREVVER

"Homesick"-- short story

JANUS IS A TWO-FACED MOON

JANUS IS A TWO-HEADED GOD

"Special of the Week" -- short story

HORROR

"Cup O'Joe" -- short story

Printed in Great Britain
by Amazon

82778322R00120